"I AM A GENTLEMAN, DARLING.
I DO NOT SEDUCE. I WOO."

He leaned forwarand on her knee.

"Do you? And i   the middle of this lake

Alexander squashed the wicked grin that played for a moment upon his mouth. "No . . . had romance been my intention, I would greatly have preferred the hillside where I found you staring up into the clouds . . . Darling, I only wish you to reconsider your connection to Chillton. I know you are not yet betrothed."

Her cheeks reddened and Meredith leaped to her feet, sending the boat rocking uncontrollably. In the next moment, she toppled stiffly forward into Alex's waiting arms.

Her blinking wide eyes stared upward, and her gaze held his as her moist lips parted.

And at that moment, he knew, with all surety, that he would kiss her.

PRAISE FOR KATHRYN CASKIE'S NOVELS

LADY IN WAITING

"Four and a half stars! Top pick! Caskie's unique wit sparkles . . . and her clever plotting shines."
—*Romantic Times BOOKclub Magazine*

more...

A
Lady's
Guide to
Rakes

Also by Kathryn Caskie

Lady in Waiting
Rules of Engagement

A Lady's Guide to Rakes

Kathryn Caskie

NEW YORK   BOSTON

Cover design by Diane Luger
Cover photo illustration by Tony Russo
Book design by Giorgetta Bell McRee

Warner Books

Time Warner Book Group
1271 Avenue of the Americas
New York, NY 10020
Visit our Web site at www.twbookmark.com

Printed in the United States of America

First Paperback Printing: September 2005

10 9 8 7 6 5 4 3 2 1

For Brian,
who doesn't have a rakish bone in his body
(and who will be so relieved that I didn't include the
rest of this sentence)

Acknowledgments

There are several people I wish to thank for their above-and-beyond assistance with the creation of this story:

Shirley Vaughan of St. George's Church in Hanover Square, London, England, for assisting me with fact checking.

My dear sister-in-law Lynn Rowlett and author Sophia Nash for their great expertise and unending willingness to answer all of my questions about horses.

Nancy Mayer, whose knowledge of the Regency Era is surpassed only by her boundless generosity. Any historical errors are strictly my own.

Deborah Barnhart and Denise McInerney for taking time from their own busy writing schedules and lives to read and comment on this book before publication.

And finally, Karen Townsend, one of my wonderful readers, who supplied me with a list of amusing names for Mr. Chillton's cart horse.

Thank you all.

A Lady's Guide to Rakes

Imperative One

It is inadvisable to approach a rake without first observing him from a distance, where his seductive charms cannot overwhelm a lady's gentle sensibilities.

The maddening heat from the aged balloon's fire sent sweat trickling beneath Meredith Merriweather's corset. Still, she held the lens of her spyglass ever firm and focused squarely on the impeccably dressed gentleman strolling along the bank of the rippling Serpentine, some forty feet below.

"Oh, dash it all, can't you bring the basket any lower?" she shouted to her pilot as she momentarily lowered the spyglass. "Look there, he's getting away!"

"I'll see what I can do, Miss Merriweather, but I'll not be promisin' a thing," the Irishman droned, and Meredith was sure she saw him roll his eyes at her.

Movement caught her notice then and abruptly she lifted the glass to watch a sable-haired woman who approached from the north. "Go to it, Giselle," Meredith urged beneath her breath. "Work your charms."

Meredith held her breath and waited. Surely the man

would not be able to resist the French courtesan's dark beauty or the seductive sway of her hips. No man could. Giselle's allure was studied. Perfect.

A huge onion-shaped shadow fell over the gentleman as the balloon passed between him and the sun. He turned and, cupping the edge of his hand over his brow, peered upward, squinting at the balloon's massive silhouette.

Meredith's muscles tensed briefly, but then relaxed. Even if he saw her, she reasoned, there was nothing to fear. Balloon ascensions in Hyde Park were common-place these days, and seeing a great floating orb, while extraordinary, was certainly nothing to warrant suspicion.

She turned the glass on Giselle once more. "Oh *no*." Why was she beckoning him toward the trees? Meredith whipped the spyglass from her eye. Hadn't she bade Giselle to stay to the footpath—*in plain view*?

Meredith jerked her head around to be sure the balloon's pilot understood the urgency of the situation. "We're going to lose sight of them! Bring us lower, *please*."

The leather-faced pilot stared back at her with his queer, unblinking, insectlike eyes. Why wouldn't he do as she asked? She had paid him four times his normal fare, after all!

"Beggin' yer pardon, miss." He shot a nervous glance over the edge of the basket's frayed woven lip. "But another few feet and we'll be sittin' in the oak tops—or worse. How badly do you need to spy on that bloke? Is it worth crashin' through the bloomin' branches?"

Meredith gasped at his effrontery. "How dare you accuse me of spying! I am conducting a scientific experiment—one that you, sirrah, are about to ruin."

Tipping her gaze over the edge of the basket, she

peered at the unfurling leaves on the jutting branches just below, then turned and looked hard at the impertinent pilot. "We have at least six feet to spare. Drop her three, *please.*"

With a resigned shake of his capped head, the pilot waved to his tether handler, who stood squinting up at them from the ground below, and raised three stubby fingers.

The basket jerked and Meredith's hip struck the side hard. "Thank you," she admonished, leveling a narrowed eye at the pilot, who was working quite diligently to conceal the amused grin on his lips.

Spreading her feet wider for balance, Meredith rested her throbbing hip against the foremost corner of the basket. This was the closest she'd ever been to London's most notorious rake, and even though she floated above the treetops, it was still too close for her comfort. Already a lacy red rash was working its way across her chest, and as she nervously scratched at it, she noticed that her palms were damp too.

Having had her own heart and reputation shattered by one of his ilk just two years past, Meredith knew what sort of damage Alexander Lamont and his kind were capable of wreaking.

She rested her elbows on the lip of the basket rail and raised the glass to her eye, trailing her view down the gentleman's well-shaped form.

My word, even from this height, the rake's appeal was plain to her. His jaw was firm, angular and lightly gilded from the sun. He was taller than most men, certainly. His muscular shoulders were broad, his waist trim and—*oh dear.* Swallowing hard, Meredith hurried the spyglass downward so that only his thighs, his delightfully sculpted thighs, were in her sight. She had to admit, without question he was the perfect physical specimen of the human male.

Still, if tearoom chatter was to be believed—and when was it not?—he was also the perfect example of a rogue . . . and the absolute worst sort at that. His name had been linked with scores of ladies, from society misses to theater chorus girls. This, however, was not what elevated him to the veriest pinnacle of rakedom. Being caught in bed with the young wife of a highly respected minister in the House of Commons had given the rotter that distinction.

Not for a moment did Meredith believe, as others seemed to, that Alexander, the licentious Lord Lansing, had given up his rakish ways and truly reformed.

It wasn't possible. And Meredith would prove it by observing Giselle's progress in bringing out the rake's *true* nature.

Lud, now Giselle was leading him toward a bench beneath a massive oak!

"*Please,* just a little lower," Meredith implored the pilot.

He shook his head solemnly. "Not wise."

A growl pressed through Meredith's lips as she crouched down to the flooring and removed the last four gold coins from her reticule. Rising, she pressed back her shoulders and made her final plea. "Another guinea per foot you manage to lower this contraption."

The pilot hesitated for nearly a full minute, but it was clear by the tattered condition of the basket and the way he kept licking his weathered lips that he could already taste the money.

With her thumb, Meredith moved the coins around in her palm, making them clink together irresistibly.

"Oh, very well. Four feet," the pilot called out to the man below. "Not a finger more."

As if hearing the pilot's instructions, Alexander Lamont looked up at the great red balloon, which now hovered only thirty feet above ground.

Meredith quickly hid her spyglass inside the basket and gazed out over the Serpentine, as if studying the waterbirds on its glistening surface. Suddenly she felt a horrifying scraping sensation beneath her feet.

The basket was descending into the treetops! Her gaze shot upward in time to see a limb gouge the red bulb of fabric, tearing savagely into it. There was a deafening flatulent outpouring of air and the basket lurched and fell. Sharp protruding branches sprouted up around her.

With a frightened squeal, Meredith dropped low and cowered down deep inside the basket, protecting her face with her hands.

"The skin's been punctured. She's comin' down." The pilot's voice was thin with fear, heightening her own terror. "Hang on!"

"Hang on?" Meredith whipped her hands from her eyes and frantically searched the innards of the basket. There was nothing to grip. "To what, sir?"

"The rail, you twit. The rail!"

Crawling on her knees toward the pilot, Meredith slid her hands up the rough-hewn wicker side, scrabbled for the rail's lip and clung to it.

But the shift in weight was too abrupt. The basket, already deep inside the tree canopy, tipped to the side, pouring her out of its pot like a last drop of tea.

Her back struck a thick limb and pain sucked the

breath from her lungs. She gasped for air as she slipped from the branch and plummeted downward at a horrific speed, branches tearing at her gown and scraping her tender skin.

Meredith registered the wide-eyed shock in Alexander Lamont's eyes as she careened toward him. *Heaven help me!* She squeezed her eyes shut.

~

Bloody hell.

His ribs were cracked. Maybe his spine too.

At the very least his new blue cutaway coat was ruined. He was lying in the dirt, after all.

What in Hades had happened?

Alexander lifted his head from a clod of grass and focused his eyes on a most intriguing sight—a pair of bare female thighs traversing his middle.

Damn it all. No sooner had he vowed to remain celibate, to remain the veriest picture of decorum until marriage— or his father's passing—when women bloody well started dropping from the sky.

Lying flat on his back, Alexander shoved a heavy branch from his shoulder and blew at the dew-dampened leaves sticking to his cheek. Every muscle smarted.

Slowly he raised himself onto one elbow and marveled at the shapely woman who lay across his body in a crumpled mass of dark blue silk.

She wasn't moving, and for a clutch of seconds, Alexander was quite certain that she had gone and died right there atop him. But then he noticed the rapid rise and fall of her chest, and was able to breathe easier himself.

"Miss?" He gave his hip a bit of a buck. Still, she didn't budge. "You've cut off the flow of blood to my legs. I say, can you move?"

No answer. This was looking worse by the moment.

He raised his right hand and found it caught in a fine web of copper ringlets. Unable to disentangle himself, he finally wrenched his fingers through the hair, but his golden signet ring caught and snagged a long tendril.

He heard a groan, and suddenly he was looking into the bluest eyes he'd ever seen. Glaring blue eyes, the color and hardness of polished sapphires.

"Sir, do you intend to rip every strand from my head, or might you leave me a few?"

He didn't reply. He knew better, for there was no right answer. Women were shrewd that way.

Besides, her delicate hands, the color of sweet cream, were already working to free her hair. When finally liberated, she pushed up from his chest—with unnecessary force, Alexander decided, for at once unbelievable shards of pain knifed through his ribs.

Leaning back on her boot heels, she stared down at him, wincing ever so slightly as she bit into her pink full lower lip.

Framed by vibrant flaming hair, her oval face seemed unnaturally pale, save a scarlet scrape traversing her left cheek.

"Can you stand?" Her voice was soft with concern now and she lifted a hand to him. But there was anger in her eyes. Indeed, as well as something more palpable. Loathing?

How curious.

Planting his freed palm in the soft earth, Alexander

raised himself to a painful sitting position, willing himself not to grimace.

A look of relief eased across the young woman's delicate features. "I . . . I thank you for . . . cushioning my fall." As she spoke, she rested her thumbs at either side of her waist and from the tentative movement of her hands, he realized she was pressing her fingers to her spine. She sucked in a pained gasp. A twig snapped and she raised her eyes to a point behind Alexander's head. Then he heard his new French acquaintance's lilting voice: "You and your pilot are lucky to have been spared, *mademoiselle*. Look at the balloon."

Alexander glanced up into the guts of the oak, where he saw a large wicker basket skewered by a thick limb.

There was a sudden thrash of leaves and a weatherworn pilot dropped down from a wide branch and thudded down onto a patch of damp earth nearby.

A burly fellow with a coil of rope looped around his shoulder and armpit, whom Alexander took to be the man's tether handler, rushed forward through the trees, panting with exertion. "Is everyone w-well?"

"Aye, but we were just damned lucky." The pilot turned an angry gaze on the fiery-haired lass. "I told ye we were too low," he snarled, then shook a wild finger at the basket and the deflating balloon blanketing the tree's soaring canopy. "And look at my *Betsy* now! Ye owe me, miss, owe me quite a lot!"

The young lady turned her frantic blue eyes from the pilot to Alexander.

"I . . . I . . . *Oh dear.*" She brought a hand to her cheek, where three tiny beads of blood oozed up from the scarlet scrape; then her eyes turned back in her head and she crumpled back down atop him.

Forgetting his own pain, Alexander cradled her limp body in his arms. He looked from her wan features, rouged with that smear of blood upon one cheek, then gazed up to the pilot. "Do you know her name? Where she lives?"

"'Er name's Miss Merriweather," the pilot offered. "Hails from Hanover Square or somewhere thereabouts."

"*Mon Dieu,* is she going to die?"

Alexander looked up at the Frenchwoman as she collected, then handed over, what he took to be the miss's belongings. "No, my dear. But I fear she requires assistance without delay." Digging into his coat pocket, he fingered a cool coin and flipped it to his lovely new acquaintance. "This should see you home. I am sorry that I cannot help you with the stone in your boot, as you requested."

"*Merci, monsieur.*" The dark-eyed mademoiselle caught the coin and, with a grin, stuffed it into her bounteous cleavage. "And do not worry yourself about my boot. The stone will dislodge itself." She flashed a coquettish smile his way. "But then, perhaps it won't. Maybe you will be so kind as to come to ten Portman Square later this eve and check for me, *oui?*"

Alexander grinned, but kept to his task and lifted the pale young lady into his arms. Stepping over the clutter of broken limbs and leaf-sprigged branches, he started down the footpath.

"*Monsieur,* where are you taking her?" the Frenchwoman called out, a tinge of worry licking her thickly accented words.

"Home," Alexander shouted back over his shoulder. "I'm taking her home."

Home, he'd said.

Sweet heavens, Meredith only hoped he meant *her home*—and not his own beastly lair. Lud, what a pickle she'd be in then.

As he strode quickly forward, his muscled arm excruciatingly tight around her sore back, Meredith held her eyes tightly closed and continued feigning unconsciousness.

Yes, it was deceitful, but there was no help for it. Only, she wished she had been brave enough to fling herself onto her bruised back, instead of straight onto Lord Lansing's middle again.

But the balloon pilot was about to expose her experiment, wasn't he? She had to do *something* to stop him, and, well, fainting was the first method that came to her mind. Viola, her great-aunt, a kindred spirit if ever there was one, used this method whenever necessary and with great success. So why shouldn't she?

Of course, Meredith hadn't taken the time to think what events her fainting episode might set into motion. And now here she was in the arms of the most dangerous man in London, being . . . *Oh no.* She sniffed the air and cringed inwardly. *Anything but that.*

Horses. She smelled horses. She heard the grunts and scuffles of the beasts. Her heart began to pound a terrified tattoo inside her chest.

He'd taken her to a *stable,* of all places! Well, this little folly of hers had gone on long enough. She must end it this very instant!

In a most calculated manner, she allowed her head to loll lazily forward, until it struck a heavy button.

Time for a murmur.

Add a little sigh. Lovely, lovely.

Eyelids flicker and . . . open.

Oh hellfire.

As she lifted her lids, Meredith found herself staring into dark mossy green eyes, ringed with a tea-hued band. The combination was not unique. Meredith was sure that she had seen it before. But somehow the welcoming warmth of these particular eyes made her want to plunge into their depths and wade there a while longer.

"I see you've come back to me." Lord Lansing's lips lifted and he leveled her with a smile that made her blood fizz and her body go all jellylike.

A jolt of nervous realization skated through her limbs. Heavens! It was happening. She was being taken in by a rake—*again!*

Well, this time she wasn't about to give herself over so easily. The humiliation and heartache had nearly killed her before. *But it shan't again!*

Meredith glared up at him through narrowed eyes. "Sir, I implore you. Return me to my feet at once." She snapped her fingers twice, as she'd seen her great-aunt do when the servants were dawdling, but this only earned her an amused grin.

"'Ere ye are, my lord. Brushed him down for ye, just how ye like."

Meredith turned her head to see a stable hand leading forth the most gargantuan horse she'd ever seen. Its black hide gleamed almost blue, and even Meredith, who possessed an unnatural wariness—in truth, a horrible *fear*—of the beasts, had to admit this one was . . . well, rather spectacular.

In the next instant, Lord Lansing raised her up, as if she were no more than a feather (which, with her heavy thighs and plump bottom, Meredith knew was far from reality) and settled her upon the great equine's back.

"N-no!" Her hands shot outward and her fingers frantically clawed Lord Lansing's sleeves. Her lips were quivering now.

"There, there, miss. You shan't ride alone." With that, he cuffed his foot in the stirrup, swung a well-shaped leg over the horse's back and came down on the saddle behind her. Then the rake scooted close and pulled her tightly against him.

Against *him*. Yes, that part of him. Why, against her thigh she could feel every heated . . . *curve* through those tight deerskin breeches men favored these days.

Heat washed across Meredith's face, and given the milky whiteness of her countenance, she knew her cheeks probably glowed like hot embers in a hearth.

As he nudged the horse into a trot, Meredith reluctantly leaned her shoulder against his broad chest, and, resting one hand on his thigh for balance, she clutched his coat with the other.

He smiled down at her and sat up straighter in the saddle. It was at this moment that Meredith noticed his hair. Judging from the bit she could see beneath his hat, it was every bit as black as the horse's swishing tail.

"Hanover Square, is that correct?"

The deep tone of his voice rumbled inside Meredith's chest, sending a vibration clear through to her . . . Well, never mind.

"I am quite capable of walking, sir. So if you'll just let me—"

"Wouldn't think of it, Miss Merriweather. I've made it a practice. Whenever a woman tumbles out of the sky into my lap, I always see her home to the safety of her family."

He turned his mesmerizing gaze upon her. "And the name is Lord Lansing."

"I know who you are." Meredith cocked her head and met his gaze. "All of London—those of the gentler sex, anyway, know you. You, Lord Lansing, are London's most notorious rogue."

He laughed at that. "I fear you have me confused with another."

"I daresay, I do not."

"Ah, but you do. The Lord Lansing you refer to no longer exists. For you see, Miss Merriweather, I have reformed."

Meredith snickered at his gall. "Well, nevertheless, given your *former* reputation, and my gentle status as an unmarried woman, it would be imprudent of me to remain in your company. So if you will just stop and let me down—"

"I do apologize, Miss Merriweather, but I *will* see you to your home. Remember, women falling from the sky?" He poked a single finger into the air. "It is a rule with me. I cannot divert."

There was laughter in his voice, and in any other circumstance—and were he any other man—she might have smiled. But here she was, intimately pressed against London's worst rake, riding toward Mayfair. And there was nothing she could do about it!

"When you were in the balloon, I could hear you urging the pilot into the trees. What were you doing up there?"

"W-what?" As Meredith searched her mind for a plausible excuse, the rake reached beneath his coat and withdrew something brass. The minute the sun glinted on the lens, the blood inside her veins stopped flowing and, for an instant, she was sure she really would faint.

"This telescope was beside you. Were you perhaps *spying*?"

"C-certainly not!" As the horse trotted along, the pain in Meredith's back intensified, along with her anxiety. "I was . . . bird-watching. Yes, and I thought I saw a very rare species in the trees."

His lip twitched upward. "Really? I have done a bit of *bird*-watching in my day. What species do you mean?"

Heat pulsed in Meredith's earlobes. "The . . . um . . . the scarlet rogue . . . finch." Hesitantly she glanced up at him and caught the last remnants of a grin.

"I can't say that I am familiar with the *rogue finch*."

"Well, as I said, it is quite rare." Meredith turned her gaze and began to study, with utmost fascination, the narrow row house they were passing.

Heavens! Did she just see Lady Ashton peering through her parlor window at them? The last thing she needed was to be seen with the rake. Her reputation was already in the dustbin from her last encounter with such a beast. It was only her aunts' lofty standing in society that had prevented every drawing-room door from being closed in her face—even though the event that had led to her downfall was not even the least bit her own fault.

Lord Lansing passed a handkerchief to Meredith. "For your cheek."

Meredith nodded and silently pressed the linen to her face, dabbing away the blood.

"There, now I can see your pretty face." His smoldering gaze made Meredith feel rather warm. "Looks like the bleeding has stopped."

"I am not surprised. The scratches are quite minor." Meredith raised her finger. "Turn here."

Lord Lansing tugged gently at the right rein and his massive horse trotted into Hanover Square. Meredith at last felt a modicum of relief, which heightened the moment the rake stopped before number 17 and leaped from the horse.

That is, until she realized she'd been left atop the great beast, *alone*. Horrible memories of her five-year-old self, lying in bed for months, her broken leg painfully bound, filled her mind.

Her fingers scrabbled for the saddle's pommel and there she sat, trembling even as Lord Lansing raised his broad hands to help her down.

"Allow me to assist, Miss Merriweather. Just let go of the saddle."

Her eyes went wide in her head. "I—I . . . cannot," she stammered. The horse was going to bolt, she just knew it.

Suddenly she felt his warm hands encircle her waist.

"I've got you now. Just relax your fingers."

But Meredith could not reply. She was shaking so badly that her teeth were chattering inside her head.

Just then, the front door opened and her two great-aunts, the ladies Letitia and Viola Featherton, stepped outside.

"Gracious, gel," Letitia, her turnip-shaped aunt, quipped. "What are you doing atop that huge horse, Meredith? Come down at once!"

Still, Meredith could not manage a single word in reply. Instead, she stared mutely back at her aunts and clacked her teeth at them.

"Sister, look at her fingers. They're as white as frost. The poor child is frozen with fear."

"I can see that, Viola. Which is why I wish for her to dismount." Then her Aunt Letitia caught the rake in her sights. "You, sir. You're a big fellow. Will you pull her from the saddle? Just give her a good hard yank. We've seen her like this before. I fear there will be no talking her down."

Lord Lansing gave her aunt a curt nod, then looked at Meredith. "Are you prepared?"

Meredith's teeth played castanets in response. *Lud, how mortifying!*

"Very well then, off you go." His fingers tightened around her waist and, with one clean jerk, Meredith's grip on the saddle broke.

An instant later, she was standing on her own two feet on the flagstone way before her aunts' fashionable Mayfair town house.

In perfect rakish form, Lord Lansing offered Meredith his arm, which she had no desire, but little choice, to take. Then, as if he were the most well-mannered of gentlemen, he escorted her up the few steps to her aunts.

Not wishing her aunts to fret, Meredith turned her face toward Lord Lansing, hoping to hide her injured cheek from the old ladies.

"Though I reside not far from here," the rake spoke to Letitia and Viola as they reached the top of the steps, "I daresay, we have not traveled in the same circles. My ladies, allow me please to introduce myself. I am Alexander Lamont . . . Lord Lansing." He bowed before the two old ladies, and they each bobbed a quick curtsy in response. "I believe you are acquainted with my father, the Earl of Harford."

"But of course. I vow, it's been several years since our paths have crossed, since he moved to the country." Aunt

Letitia turned to her sister. "Viola, of course you remember young Lord Lansing here."

"I do indeed. And I own, you are the mirror image of your father in his youth. Quite remarkable, really." Viola smiled brightly, even as Meredith noticed the briefest look of horror on Lansing's handsome face and surmised that her aunt's well-meant compliment had not been taken as such. "How do you do, Lord Lansing?"

"Quite well, actually. Though I fear that my visit this day is not a pleasant one. Your—" He nodded toward Meredith then.

"Our *grandniece*," the snowy-haired pair replied together.

"Your *grandniece* suffered a tremendous fall less than thirty minutes past, and I am not convinced she did not sustain some degree of injury." With great boldness, he reached out a hand and laid it, comfortingly, upon Viola's bony arm. "You see, she fell from a hot-air balloon, through an oak tree."

Both aunts snapped their heads around to Meredith.

"Are you injured, dear?" Aunt Viola asked, reaching out and drawing Meredith away from Lord Lansing and to her side.

Meredith opened her lips and, to her great relief, her teeth were no longer marching. "No, Auntie. I merely scraped my cheek a bit, and my back is a little sore. Otherwise, I am perfectly well, I assure you."

Aunt Viola studied Meredith for a moment, clearly trying to decide whether she was being completely honest.

There was no hiding the scrape on her cheek, but Meredith was not about to let her aunt know that her throbbing back burned like a branding iron. Viola, who always worried overmuch, would see her abed for a week or more. And she had too much to do.

"Do not fret about me, Auntie. It is true, I might have been gravely injured when I fell from the balloon . . . had this brave gentleman not cushioned my landing with his own body." She turned her gaze to Lord Lansing and forced a smile.

"Oh, how gallant you are, Lord Lansing!" her Aunt Letitia exclaimed, moving forward to squeeze his forearm. But then, she took note of the man's earth-marred coat beneath her fingers and grimaced. "I do hope young Meredith did not cause *you* any distress, my lord. I daresay, she is a spirited gel and is always getting up to some mischief or another."

Meredith softly groaned her displeasure, quieting when her Aunt Viola gave her a hard, covert pinch.

"Why, after all you've been through, my lord," her twig-thin Aunt Viola began, "you must come inside and join us for a restorative."

"As much as I would enjoy that, madam, I am afraid I have another pressing matter that requires my attention."

No doubt, Meredith mused, *pressing a certain French courtesan to a mattress.* Oh, she knew his sort all too well. No matter, Giselle would tell her all about it the next morn.

Lord Lansing pulled a visiting card from a concealed pocket in his dirt-encrusted coat and slipped it into Meredith's hand.

"Should you have further need of my services, Miss Merriweather, please do not hesitate to send for me." He flashed her a brilliant, knee-weakening smile.

With a slow nod to her, and a quick one to each of her aunts, Lord Lansing, the rake, bid them all farewell, leaped upon his massive horse and galloped from the square.

Her elderly aunts released pleased sighs.

Aunt Letitia caught Meredith's shoulder and hobbled along beside her toward the door. "My, he is a handsome devil, isn't he?"

"Indeed he is," Meredith murmured. "But then, they always are."

"Still, I feel I must caution you against forming a connection with the gentleman—for *any* reason—as I have heard rumors that in truth he is *no* gentleman at all."

Aunt Viola wrapped her thin fingers around Meredith's upper arm, but as they entered the house and turned into the parlor, it was her sister she addressed. "What a thing to say, Letitia. You must have heard, Lord Lansing has reformed. And you know what the ladies say. . . . A reformed rake makes the very best husband."

"Nonsense!" Meredith exhaled her breath. "I, for one, do not believe it for a moment."

Aunt Letitia widened her faded blue eyes, then shook her head at her sister, who winced when she took her meaning.

"Of course, a good, sensible gentleman, like your Mr. Chillton, dear, should always be a lady's first choice." A wisp of a giggle slipped through Viola's lips then. "I only meant that a reformed rake might know how . . . well . . . to *please* his wife."

Aunt Letitia chuckled heartily at that, until she toppled back against the settee beside her sister and gasped for breath.

Finally, as the two elderly ladies quieted, Meredith crossed her arms over her chest and raised her chin proudly.

"That may be, Auntie, but I am afraid no woman will ever know for certain—because there is no such thing as a reformed rake."

Aunt Letitia lifted her thick white brows. "You seem quite sure of that, my dear."

"I am." Meredith gave herself a secret little smile. She crossed the room, withdrew a red leather book of notes from the desk and laid it on the table before her aunts.

Aunt Viola wrinkled her nose. "Dear, I thought when you met Mr. Chillton, you gave up all notions of your guidebook."

"Yes, Chillton is truly a good and responsible gentleman, and I—I was lucky to make his acquaintance," Meredith began with a sputter, absolutely shocked that her aunts had so underestimated her dedication to her cause. "But my recent good fortune doesn't lessen the need to warn other young ladies about the dangers London's rakes and rogues may present. You cannot have forgotten what Lord Pomeroy did to me." A tremor vibrated through Meredith the moment she spoke his name, making her feel vulnerable, making her feel weak. How she hated that man and that one horrible moment from her past could hold such dominion over her.

"No, dear, we have not forgotten. Viola and I know that focusing on your guidebook helped you through some very painful, desperate times."

Then her aunts exchanged "the glance." Meredith hated "the glance" even more than she hated feeling weak. For it was the same look of pity Society gave her whenever she had the courage to leave the house. This was all the more reason for her to finish the guidebook. Why, if she could spare even one woman the pain of being pitied, of being shunned, then all of her scandalous research would be well worth it.

Aunt Letitia rose and lifted the book of notes from the table. "But you are happy now, dear. You have caught the eye of a most respectable man of business." Aunt Letitia opened Meredith's notebook and read the heavily inked title page. "And yet still you are continuing to research *A Lady's Guide to Rakes.*"

"I am." Meredith pinned her aunt with the most serious of gazes. "Don't you understand? I *must* continue my investigations. Indeed, I must amplify them. For after more than two years of hard work, my guidebook is nearly complete. And with Lord Lansing—the most notorious rake of them all—as my final subject, I intend to finish before the season ends."

Imperative Two

*Despite appearing quite attentive, a rake always
puts himself and his needs first.*

"Jupiter, Lansing, what in blazes happened to you?"

Alexander blinked and focused his eyes on the lanky
intruder who stood in the shadows of the foyer of Alexander's Grosvenor Square town house, sipping brandy.

Ah, Georgie Chambers . . . or rather, Lord Riddle
since his uncle passed last Michaelmas and made him a
viscount. Bloody hard to remember his elevation. Everything was changing too fast these days.

"Georgie, you good-for-nothing nob, what are you
doing here drinking my brandy? Duns collectors blocking
your door again?" No matter his social standing, he'd always be Georgie to Alexander, bosom friend since their
days at Eton, and, until recently, his cohort in sampling
the finer things to be had in Town, whether it be brandy,
women or a high stakes game of faro.

Georgie laughed. "Hardly. Thought I might try to convince you to stir up a little mayhem this eve, but from the look of things, I see you've started without me. You look bloody awful. What in God's name happened?"

"You wouldn't believe me if I told you." Alexander grinned. "So I shan't."

Shrugging his dusty blue coat into the awaiting arms of his attentive valet, Alexander followed Georgie into the library and accepted the brandy his friend offered him . . . from his own tantalus.

"Damn well ruined your cutaway, my man." Georgie raised his glass and drained every last drop with an audible gulp. "Take a tumble from the great black beast of yours? Or did some lucky lady's rotter of a husband come home unexpectedly and force you to dive out her bedchamber window?"

Alexander would have laughed if he didn't ache so. Balancing the balloon brandy glass in one hand, he gently probed his ribs with the other.

Who would have believed a plummeting woman could inflict such damage upon a body? The Merriweather miss wasn't large. When he lifted her atop his horse, his hands nearly ringed her tiny waist, though she had been a tad heavier than he'd expected.

Then he recalled the sight of those luscious thighs protruding from her bunched skirts as she lay atop him in Hyde Park, and a knowing smile lifted the right edge of his lips.

He wouldn't have minded feeling *those* legs wrapped around him. Not one bit.

As the wicked thought broached his mind, Alexander glanced up at the ridiculous portrait of his father hanging above the mantel, then huffed a frustrated sigh. His carefree days were over now, weren't they?

Damn it all. Damn his father and his highbrow expectations.

As he touched the rim of the glass to his lips, something tickled his finger and he glanced down to see a single strand of flaming hair twisted about his signet ring. He smiled as he pulled it from the gold circlet, remembering those glaring blue eyes peering down at him through tumbling copper locks.

"Ah-ha!" Georgie snatched the hair from his fingers. "I knew it! It *was* a woman." He dangled the strand before his gray eyes for closer scrutiny. "And a redhead too by the look of this."

Georgie turned to face Alexander again, his thick ruddy brows migrating toward the bridge of his hawkish nose. "Thought you preferred pale-haired chits, my man."

"Doesn't really matter now, does it?" Alexander dropped down into the cushioned wingbacked chair near the hearth, planted his heel in the carpet and studied the dusty toe of his boot. "Have to obey the old man's dictates these days."

Georgie exhaled a thin laugh. "Surely he didn't rule out women. I mean, a man has needs, after all."

"He might as well have." Alexander leaned back and swirled the dark amber liquid in his crystal glass. "I am permitted to court a woman of quality for the purpose of marriage."

"So no more evenings with actresses?"

Alexander shook his head.

Georgie winced. "No more afternoons with neglected wives?"

"And no more mornings with merry widows. It seems I am to be the very portrait of a perfect gentleman." Alexander lifted his hand resignedly and flicked his fingers in one direction, then another. "Or I lose all of this.

Cut off. I cannot have that, I simply cannot. As it is, he's already reduced my monthly portion to . . . Well, 'tis barely enough to keep me clothed."

"Damn me." Georgie exhaled his breath. "That's a bit harsh."

"Damned article in the *Times*. Who I bed is no one's business but my own."

Georgie lifted an eyebrow. "She was the wife of a prominent member of the House of Commons. Caused quite the stir, my man. Even *I* was shocked to read of the incident."

"Well, so was my father. Then he got it into his head that controlling my funds would control my behavior." Alexander blew out a long sigh. "And sadly, it seems he was right. I have no alternative but to bend to his wishes, until the old man finally succumbs to one of his dozen or so imaginary ailments and falls over Death's threshold. Until then"—Alexander cleared his throat, then mockingly raised his glass to the painting of his rotund father atop a great sable warhorse—"Alexander Lamont, noted rake and man-about-town, shall henceforth be known as Lord Lansing, stodgy gentleman."

"But a well-dressed, stodgy gentleman, me lord," added a gravelly voice from the passage.

He looked up as his valet, Mr. Herbert, entered the library with a fresh coat.

"Please stand, me lord."

Alexander eyed the bottle-green coat speculatively. "'Tis not the coat with brass buttons, is it 'One'?"

"One"—so called because this particular Mr. Herbert was the first of three Herbert brothers to join Alexander's household staff—peered down his thin white and red mottled nose. "No, me lord. 'Tis a new coat to replace the article ye left behind at the home of a . . . *friend* early last month."

"Indeed. Left it with Lady Fawcett, to be precise." Alexander rose, a bit slowly due to his aching ribs, and shrugged the dark green coat over his broad shoulders.

"Hooked over her bedpost, no doubt. Husband came home unexpectedly, did he?" Georgie's amused grin appeared above the curve of glass he held to his lips. "I daresay, Lansing, I think I fancy this new coat above all of your others. Just look at it. Must have cost your left stone. I thought you said you were short on funds."

Alexander straightened his sleeves and admired the elegant simple cut of the fine kerseymere coat. It *was* a fine coat. The lines perfectly set off the trimness of his waist.

"So perhaps the household manages without meat and sugar this month." He glanced up at Georgie. "A gentleman does have needs, after all."

The sun was already high in the sky, beating down upon Meredith's straw bonnet and heating her covered head like water in a kettle. She grimaced as she circled Hyde Park's new bronze statue of Achilles for the tenth time in as many minutes.

Perhaps eleven in the morn was a mite early to ask a courtesan to rouse herself for a meeting, especially if the lamentable Lord Lansing had indeed made his way into her bed. But Meredith had not been able to wait any longer to learn if her test of the rake's base character had been successful. And so, this morning, when the clock struck nine, she'd sent a missive to Portman Square asking Giselle to meet her at this very spot.

When the courtesan finally arrived, Meredith glanced up at the position of the sun. Only an hour late—*noon.*

The women had known each other for three months, but they were not friends. They were business associates of the oddest sort. Their first meeting had not been accidental. Meredith had had the occasion, at one of her aunts' musicales, to overhear two gentlemen conversing about a French courtesan, new to London, whose charm and grace were irresistible to those of the opposite sex.

Meredith knew at once that an alliance between them could elevate her rake research to an entirely new level. No longer would she need to simply observe a rake at routs or balls. With Giselle as her bait, she could conduct social experiments—put the rake into predetermined situations, then watch his reactions. The idea was brilliant, really.

And so, Meredith quietly learned as much as she could about the courtesan, and called upon Giselle at her home one day with a proposition (and money, of which the courtesan always seemed to be in need) in exchange for her expertise in seducing gentlemen—specifically rogues.

The idea of Meredith's guidebook, and her money, had greatly intrigued Giselle and a deal was quickly struck.

During the past weeks, with Meredith watching from the wings while Giselle took center stage, the two had conducted a good dozen experiments on both rakish bachelors and their more disreputable counterpart— the married lechers. Thanks to Giselle's expertise, Mr. Lawrence Longbottom and Mr. Finneas Douselight, both respectable society gents, provided excellent kindling for an entire chapter on married men. These two subjects, the "groping lechers" as Meredith preferred to think of them, preyed upon the powerless and were likely to seize upon any opportunity to slake their carnal desire. But thankfully, unlike the more dangerous bachelor, who had little need to conceal his unsavory activities from anyone, the lecher knew his bounds.

Yes, Giselle was the ideal person to enact Meredith's experiments. No one could play a man like the stunningly beautiful courtesan. Which is why Meredith was convinced Giselle would report that yesterday's scheme in Hyde Park resulted in success.

All of London was simply abuzz over Lord Lansing's overnight transformation from notorious rake to gentleman true. But Meredith knew better than to believe Society gossip, and she would prove them wrong, with Giselle's help.

Her night with Lord Lansing would constitute the premier chapter of *A Lady's Guide to Rakes.*

"Come, let us take the bench beneath the trees. 'Twill be cooler there." Heart thrumming with anticipation, Meredith took hold of the Frenchwoman's wrist, intending to lead her forward, but Giselle did not move. And indeed, she appeared almost distraught.

"*Mademoiselle,* I am sad to tell you that this rendezvous is quite unnecessary."

"W-what do you mean? Did not Lord Lansing call on you last eve?" Meredith bent her long legs a bit so that she might peer beneath the brim of Giselle's bonnet and search her dark eyes for the answer.

"No, he did not."

"He didn't?" Disappointment, then the oddest feeling of relief, flooded through Meredith. Confused at both her reaction and the fact that Lord Lansing had not done as she'd expected, she bit her lower lip and exhaled over the bunched pink flesh.

The courtesan laid a gloved hand softly atop Meredith's. "I know you are displeased, and I must admit, I am quite surprised myself. I've never misread a man's desire. *Never*."

Meredith's outlook brightened at this bit of news. "You are sure of his attraction then?" *So perhaps all is not a loss.*

"Oh, *oui*. He even gave me . . . Oh, how do I say it? The . . . um . . . *staircase* look. Is that correct?"

"The what?"

"You know it, *mademoiselle*. The *look*—up and down, up and down." Giselle waved a pointed finger vertically about her torso.

Meredith laughed. "Yes, I do know it." But then the amusement dissolved from her lips as she considered what this meant. "But if he was attracted, as you say, why didn't the rogue act? It makes no sense to me."

"Well, if I may, perhaps it is as I have heard whispered over tea. He has *reformed*."

Waving her hand in the air, Meredith dismissed the idea completely. "Impossible. A leopard cannot change its spots. No, there has to be more to it."

Giselle suddenly clutched Meredith's arms and stared up at her. "You do not suppose he is injured . . . from your fall, *mademoiselle*?"

Meredith curled her lip. "Preposterous. I am not so petite as you, yet he lifted me onto his horse quite easily. He is as strong as a bull."

"That may be, but his face was pale with pain after you landed atop him. I saw this myself. Why, you might have cracked his ribs—or worse."

"Oh dear. I had not considered . . ." The disturbing thought sent the blood draining from Meredith's head and she felt just the slightest bit dizzy. Beads of perspiration burst about her temples and the horrid corset that her aunts always insisted she wear suddenly felt overtight, making it difficult to breathe.

Concern cinched Giselle's brows. "Are you well, *mademoiselle*? Shall we move into the shade of the trees now?"

"No, no, I will be fine. I just need to know why Lansing did not call." Meredith opened her reticule and began to fumble inside for the vinaigrette she oft carried for her ever-wilting aunt Viola, but instead her fingers snared a visiting card. She lifted it to her eyes and blinked as her gaze focused on the extravagant flourishes, which clearly indicated a grand ego in whomever had designed it.

A broad grin pulled at Meredith's lips. "And now I have entrée to do just that." She waved the cream-hued card in the air.

Giselle's eyes centered on the name engraved upon it: *Lord Lansing, 23 Grosvenor Square, Mayfair.*

"Indeed. The beastly rogue himself. When he gave this card, he said I should contact him if I needed further assistance." She bounced on her heels. "And so I shall."

"But for assistance with what, *Mademoiselle* Merriweather?"

Meredith's brows drew tight. "Oh botheration. I don't know." She waved farewell to Giselle and started forward down the pathway, feeling instantly revived. "But I will think of something."

~

The thin cane chair his father sat upon creaked in protest, and Alexander trained his eyes on its delicate legs and stretchers, worried that they would bow under the esteemed Earl of Harford's considerable heft.

Could have picked something more appropriate to his size. Something *less* expensive. Didn't he see it was a bloody slipper chair? And from Marie Antoinette's own bedchamber, no less . . . or so the dealer at Christie's had claimed when he sold it to him.

"Sir, would you not be more comfortable beside the window?" Alexander urged hopefully. "I daresay, it's a scorcher this day."

His father shook his head and leaned back until the chair tilted and balanced his weight on its two rear legs. Alexander winced.

Striding over to the tantalus, Alexander filled a glass with brandy and held it out to his father, hoping to coax the old man, whose penchant for fine drink far exceeded his own, to remove his ample hindquarters from the slipper chair.

"Bring it here, boy." Salivating already, the earl smacked his lips together, blotting away the wetness. "I've exerted myself quite enough already making my way into Town to see you."

Bound in a brocaded satin coat—clearly fitted without proper regard to his girth—his father raised his arm and, with palm upward, beckoned Alex forward with a curt inward wave of four sausage-like fingers.

"Yes, Father, and I appreciate your visit . . . though I am unsure as to your purpose." Alexander hesitated a moment. Did he really want to hear the answer? His father never left his country house without a damn good reason. "Have you heard something of concern? I own, if you have, it's a load of bunk, for I have been the perfect gentleman on every count since our . . . discussion." Alexander hoped his father would laugh at that, or smile. Hell, *something* to ease Alex's conscience.

The earl frowned. "Actually, yes. The moment I arrived in Town, I received a report from my man of affairs that you were observed in Hyde Park carrying a woman from beneath a canopy of trees. Her hair had fallen and her clothing was in disarray. It would appear you are back to your old behavior and have had a romp in the woods." A scowl appeared on the earl's face. "I thought you learned your lesson after the last . . . incident, but I see now that I must tighten the reins further."

When Alexander realized his father's mistake, he opened his mouth to respond, but was cut off. His father would have his say and it was useless for Alexander to interrupt with the truth of the event until the earl had finished his rant.

"I've always said you were far too like your grandfather. Mad old Highlander, still running the crags and valleys of Loch Awe with plaited white hair and a hunting kilt. He doesn't give a lick about propriety either. But you are a Lamont, my heir. I will not tolerate his sort of wild behavior in my son. I will not!"

Resigning himself to the fact that the truth would have to wait, Alexander poured the last of the brandy into his glass, then stared disappointedly at the empty cut-crystal decanter, barely listening as his father continued talking. *Bloody hell.* He needed another bottle, and what with its cost, one would think it was liquid gold. Better to buy a case while he still had *some* funds, for who knew how long he could maintain this mask of decorum.

Alexander glanced up at the earl, knowing from experience that it was important to give the appearance of undivided attention.

"Which brings me to the reason for my visit this day."

Well, it is about damn time he got around to it. Alexander replaced the decanter in the tantalus, straightened it so it aligned perfectly with the table's edge, then raised his eyebrows in expectation of his father's revelation. "Yes, sir?"

"Becoming a respectable gentleman is not enough. I've decided that you must marry before I die."

The roots of Alexander's hair rose up from his scalp. "I apologize, sir. I could not have heard you correctly."

"No, no, boy, you heard me right. I want you to take a wife—quickly too. Get her with child. I want to know the Lamont line will carry on after I am gone. Do this, and your entire portion will be yours again to squander as you please."

Alexander took pause at this, then downed his brandy in a long, continuous gulp. *Marriage* now. These sudden dictates were rapidly evolving from bad to worse. "But, sir, surely there is no rush to the altar. Why, you are as robust and healthy as I."

Here it came.

"I fear that is not the case. Why, my heart was thudding against my chest not two eves past. Felt like a bloody swallow was trapped in my rib cage. Lord Rushley succumbed to the very same condition only a fortnight ago. Died upon his own horse." The old man shook his head decisively. "No, mustn't waste any time, my boy. Why, I might expire this very night, for all the hope my doctor gives me."

Alexander turned away and settled his empty glass upon the table. Nonsense. His father was always dying from something or other—while holding Alexander's portion just out of reach. This was just another high-handed ploy to bend his son to his stubborn will.

"Don't shudder so, boy. Marriage will benefit you immensely. Nothing like a woman of quality to settle down a young buck and instill in him some responsibility."

Alexander opened his mouth to speak, but his father raised his hand to silence him.

"Don't interrupt. I know you don't believe it now, but I tell you 'tis the truth. Why, your mother made me the very man I am today. Without her, I'd likely still be carousing with the ladies and spending my eves with the gentlemen at White's."

Alex could feel his countenance growing paler with each passing second. He lifted the bellpull and was about to ring for a bottle of Scottish whiskey or even wine, when his butler, his valet's identical brother, Mr. Herbert, entered the room with a silver salver upon which lay a letter.

The second Mr. Herbert, known as "Two," paused before Alexander. "Do forgive this transgression, me lord, but I was bade to deliver this at once."

Cinching his brow, Alexander took the letter from the tray and dismissed the butler, then broke the scarlet wax wafer and opened it. Immediately the sender's name leaped out at him: *Miss Merriweather.* Very quickly he read the short letter, then refolded it and slipped it into the pocket cleverly stitched inside the breast of his coat. "Now, Father, you were saying—"

"You cannot conceal that pleased look in your eyes, so don't even try. The letter is from a woman."

"I beg your pardon, sir?" Alexander took the chair beside the window and nonchalantly tried to glance out for any sign of the Featherton carriage.

Foolhardy reaction, he knew, for certainly Miss Merriweather would not venture to a bachelor's lodgings—no matter how daring her two great-aunts claimed her to be.

"Do not attempt to deny it. Who is the letter from? And it had better not be from that dark-haired actress—Rose, was it? Oh, don't look so surprised, I know all about your exploits. Hell, all of London does."

"My *past* exploits, Father. Those days, thanks to your intercedence, are long behind me." Alexander removed the letter from his coat, eager to prove to the earl that he had changed. "If you must know, the letter is from Miss Meredith Merriweather—grandniece of the Featherton ladies of your acquaintance. She fell from a balloon in Hyde Park and I rescued her. It was my rescue of Miss Merriweather that your spies observed. Not a romp. I tell you, Father, I have reformed *entirely*."

"Is this so? Your story certainly paints a different picture." The earl sat quietly, pondering this new information. "But what of this letter? Was she observed in your arms? Has her reputation been damaged?"

"No, sir. Miss Merriweather simply wished to express her appreciation for my assistance in escorting her home after the fall, and has requested the favor of my counsel in the purchasing of a horse."

This request, of course, made no sense to Alex, for the gel was utterly petrified of bloodstock, was she not?

"Ah, well . . . the Featherton ladies are well-known in the upper reaches of society. Though I am not acquainted with young Meredith, her name is not altogether unfamiliar to me. . . . I can't say why, though."

The earl twisted the overlong hairs of his eyebrow pensively, making Alex wonder if revealing Miss Merriweather's name had been prudent. But then, as if coming to some decision, his father's eyes suddenly brightened and excitement animated his entire face.

"But if she is kin to the Featherton sisters, I cannot allow this to pass. Whether your intervention in Hyde Park was for the noblest of reasons, the fact remains that you were observed—and rumor travels quickly in Town."

Alexander squinted back at the earl. "Precisely what are you saying, sir?"

"Whether or not it is yet evident, I fear Miss Merriweather has been compromised by this event. You must make amends. She is of the Quality, and just the sort of woman you require. So I say, go to it, boy. I should be happy to make her my daughter."

Alexander leaped to his feet. "Sir?"

"I daresay I shall be hard-pressed to make myself any clearer."

"But I am afraid you must, for I am quite certain I have misunderstood your words."

"Damn it all, boy, is something amiss with your hearing? My time is short and I have made my decision."

"But, sir—"

"There will be no discussion . . . if you know what is good for you." The earl glanced around the ornate room, then laid upon Alexander a gaze more forbidding than he'd ever seen. "Correct this situation and please your father. That's all it requires for your bank to be restored to your control. I vow, I shall not meddle again in your private affairs."

Though the air in the room was thick and stifling, a chill iced Alexander's skin. "As long as I marry the Merriweather girl before the conclusion of the season."

"That's my boy."

Imperative Three

A rake will find innumerable reasons to touch a woman. This serves to put her at ease and make her more receptive to later touches of increasing intimacy.

～

The next morning, just after Meredith sat down in the dining room to break her fast, she received a written summons. It was immediately clear that this was no ordinary beckoning from her aunts, who normally relied on their butler, Mr. Edgar, to track her down when she was needed.

This time there was a peculiar urgency infused in the inked words that so roused Meredith's curiosity that she was compelled to abandon her cup of chocolate, her favorite treat in all the world, and race into the parlor.

"Yes, Aunties?" Meredith waved the short missive in the air as she studied her two elderly great-aunts. They were sitting side by side on the parlor settee, dressed in identical lavender frocks, as was their habit, and were grinning madly up at her. Meredith lowered the slip of paper. "You wished an interview? Your note indicated some urgency."

"No, dear gel. I fear you are confused. *We* do not

require an interview." Laughter began to leak from Aunt Letitia's mouth in tiny saliva-laced puffs.

"What Sister means, Meredith," Aunt Viola began, "is that we just received notice that a gentleman is about to call upon you. We only wished for you to be prepared."

"I am to have a caller?" Meredith glanced from one aunt to the other, waiting patiently for an answer.

Aunt Letitia slid a cream-hued card from its hiding place inside her sleeve. Meredith reached for it, but her aunt snapped it back. "Ah, ah, ah. You will learn who it is soon enough." Now both of her aunts were chuckling.

Lovely. They were making a game of prolonging her suspense.

"Aunties, will you not tell me who is coming to call?"

Heavens, she only hoped it was not Lord Lansing. It was only ten in the morn, after all, and Meredith was sure the note she'd sent the rake yesterday, requesting a meeting at the stables in Hyde Park, suggested a four o'clock appointment.

True, Meredith had thought about changing their appointed meeting time. She had been thinking of little else since the break of dawn—and she was growing most impatient watching the clock in the passage make its minute-by-minute journey to four. But unless Lord Lansing was such an expert on women that he could intuit her wish for a morning meeting—it simply could *not* be the rake.

Having come to this logical conclusion, Meredith inhaled a deep, cleansing breath. For some reason, this realization disappointed her a little. Hardly enough to notice, though, and certainly not enough to cause her worry.

Just then, the door from the passage opened, giving a high kittenish mewl of a sound and drawing Meredith's attention. There, entering the parlor behind Mr. Edgar, her aunts' dutiful butler, was her dear Mr. Chillton.

They'd met through Mrs. Albert Trevor, who was not only a dear friend of the Featherton sisters, but coincidentally resided in the town house abutting Mr. Chillton's in Russell Square. Noting that Mr. Chillton was a successful and respected importer of spices and goods from India, Mrs. Trevor quickly contrived to see Meredith paired with him, hoping for a match that would save the Feathertons' grandniece from the disgrace of being left at the altar by Lord Pomeroy.

The Featherton sisters thought Mrs. Trevor's plan a grand one indeed, and an "accidental" meeting was arranged. To Meredith's great relief, she found Mr. Chillton to be handsome, gentle and kind. Mr. Chillton evidently found Meredith quite suitable as well, for he commented to Mrs. Trevor that with such good society connections and obvious breeding, Miss Merriweather would make him an ideal wife. And so Meredith and Mr. Chillton's courtship began.

For Meredith, "Mr. Chillton" it was, never Arthur, for the gentleman was nothing if not a stickler for propriety and that was how he preferred Meredith always to address him. Never mind that he had courted her for well over one year and had claimed on more than one occasion to be quite fond of her.

Inwardly this pricked Meredith like the thorny spines of her pet garden hedgehog. But it was only a name, a small thing, was it not? A tiny quirk in his character that she knew she would find utterly endearing in time.

Mr. Chillton bowed his long, lean body before both her aunts, then tipped his golden-haired head to her. "Miss Meredith, you look quite lovely today. . . ." His eyes widened suddenly. "Good heavens, what has happened to your cheek?"

Without thinking, Meredith slapped a hand to her face to cover the scratches stretching from her cheekbone to the edge of her mouth. Was it so noticeable? Truly, it was only a couple of marks, hardly red at all anymore. "Tree branch" was all she said. She was not about to mention her balloon ride or its purpose, and she was certainly not going to mention her fall. To do so would only invite unwanted questions, the answers to which Mr. Chillton would never understand.

"Need to be more careful. Watch where you are going." Though he was smiling, his gaze drifted lower to the deep square neckline of her newest sapphire frock. Now his pale blue eyes were communicating an altogether different message.

Oh no. Meredith had hoped he'd admire her dress as much as she did. And why shouldn't he? It was certainly the most voguish one she owned, with its sprinkling of iridescent seed pearls gleaming at the edge of the scalloped lace sleeves and adding dramatic allure to the bodice.

"I had hoped I might convince you to accompany me for a ride through Town." He paused, then raised a blond brow. "I have brought the phaeton . . . the one I told you about. You remember, the one I recently purchased from my neighbor."

"Oh yes, indeed, I do remember." Meredith nodded her head, though, in truth, she didn't recall the subject having ever been mentioned.

Chillton turned his head and shot her aunts a satisfied smile. "Of course, Miss Merriweather would have told you all about it. Cost a tenth of what a new wheelie would." His chest seemed to puff with pride. "Why waste a pretty penny on a new conveyance, when a perfectly serviceable older phaeton is available, eh?"

When neither aunt replied, likely having not a clue what to say to such a comment, Mr. Chillton shifted his gaze to Meredith. She realized, though somewhat belatedly, that he was waiting for her to speak.

Taking her cue, Meredith hurriedly crossed the room, drew back the curtain and peered through the wavy glass. There sat a rickety phaeton, with no less than three hand-width gouges in the varnish down its side.

Chillton's frugal nature never failed to perplex Meredith. He was a truly wealthy merchant, to be sure, yet he lived a step above a pauper. For instance, he insisted on using tea leaves four times before discarding them. And though his London town home was the grandest on Russell Square, a bequeath from his late grandmother, he never entertained. But perhaps most shocking was what she'd overheard a visiting chimney sweep tell their footman: Mr. Chillton barely owned a stick of furniture. Didn't see the need.

None of this made sense to Meredith. Why did the man, rich as a nabob, consistently deny himself the comforts his bank could afford him? But it didn't really matter, she always reminded herself. In time, this too would become just another dear peculiarity she'd become quite fond of.

After all, even she had to admit that the phaeton was a great improvement over his grandmother's ancient town carriage. She offered her young man a beguiling smile. "As always, your thriftiness is to be commended, Mr. Chillton."

Aunt Viola joined Meredith at the window, barely

concealing a full-body flinch when her gaze fell upon the phaeton. Still, her aunt turned to the gentleman and sighed pleasedly. "Yes, you certainly know how to manage your funds, sir."

Though Viola's gaze had remained on Mr. Chillton the entire time she was speaking, Meredith had the oddest notion that her aunt's words were somehow meant for her to consider.

Chillton tipped his head to her aunt in proud thanks before retraining his attention on her. "So what say you, Miss Meredith, care to make a morning of it?"

Meredith took one more glance at the phaeton's peeling paint and split leather squabs, then gave her beau a brilliant smile. "Nothing would give me more pleasure, kind sir."

Why did she get the feeling she was just another of his bargains, ruined but still serviceable?

Chillton's gaze snagged upon her deep neckline once more, and if Meredith wasn't mistaken, she glimpsed a grimace. "Is something amiss, Mr. Chillton?"

"No, of course not. Though on my way to Hanover Square, I did note a distinct breeze. Might I suggest a fichu, Miss Merriweather? I would not wish a ride in my phaeton to cause a cold upon your . . ." He slapped a hand to his chest, but then blood rose into the tips of his ears, making them glow crimson. He allowed his hand to fall away. "I beg your pardon, Miss Meredith. I did not wish to offend."

"Offend? Oh heavens, sir, you, in no way, offended me." Meredith almost laughed aloud. "However, had you said—"

Both aunts were upon Meredith in an instant, and she thought that they were trying to stifle her reply, which, in hindsight, would surely have taken the conservative Mr. Chillton aback.

Aunt Viola leaned back and stared at Meredith, her watery blue eyes suddenly brimming with tears. She kissed both of Meredith's cheeks. "Oh, my gel, my gel."

"Auntie? What is wrong?"

Viola shook her head and took two steps back, waving her emotional reaction away with a dismissive hand.

Then aunt Letitia flung her arms around Meredith and embraced her so enthusiastically that she actually expected her ribs might be crushed against her backbone.

What in heaven's name were they all about?

"Auntie," she covertly whispered into Letitia's ear as they hugged. "The phaeton is old, but I am sure it is still quite safe. You needn't fear for my life."

Aunt Letitia pulled back, grinning at Meredith. "Oh, you are such a silly goose. Don't you realize that Mr. Chillton is going to—"

Aunt Viola edged past her sister, intentionally cutting off her next words as she tossed her own fichu around Meredith's shoulders. "Dear child, though we may seem like a pair of mother hens at times, we shall not fret one bit today—for you will be with Mr. Chillton, the most responsible and levelheaded man in all of England."

Yes, she would be. And her aunts were right not to worry. For nothing exciting or the least bit dangerous happened around Mr. Chillton. *Ever.*

And, well, that was one of the things she liked best about him.

Due to One's insistence, Alexander began dressing at two o'clock in the afternoon, even though an hour and a half didn't seem quite adequate time to dress for such a vital occasion. After all, his entire financial future might well depend on this meeting in Hyde Park, but his valet knew his business, and so Alex would have to trust him.

"I must look dashing, One, but not as if I put any effort into it."

"Carelessly handsome, milord?" Mr. Herbert said from behind the open wardrobe door.

"Exactly." Alexander removed his dressing robe and cast it to the bed. In the reflection of the cheval mirror, he caught a glimpse of the interlocked chain of dark ink ringing his muscled bicep. He clapped a hand over the Celtic tattoo and grimaced. "And a tightly woven lawn shirt."

Mr. Herbert glanced around the wardrobe door and, realizing his employer's concern, slapped a hand to the Celtic ring permanently inked into his own arm. The slapping of the ring was akin to a secret handshake, a promise of unity within the Lamont clan. His Scottish grandfather had had the ring inked into Alexander's arm, a Lamont rite of passage, when he was but a lad of fourteen summers. Nothing had ever made him feel so wed to his wild Scottish roots—nothing had made him feel so proud. Today, however it was not the proud Scottish warrior he wished for Miss Merriweather to see, but the refined London gentleman.

"Right, my lord. I know just the thing."

And indeed he did. For an hour later, Alexander was dressed, his neckcloth wrapped expertly in the most fashionable—yet wickedly starched—*Trone d'amour* tie and every hair combed into place.

Mr. Herbert stood before Alexander with the tortoise-shell comb poised in the air. "Shall I, sir?"

Alexander thought on it for a brief moment. "Why not?"

"Well, me lord, ye did promise the earl. . . ."

Yes, he had agreed to maintain the look and manner of a gentleman. But was not his mission this day the seduction of Miss Merriweather?

"Do it, One."

Mr. Herbert deftly snared a bit of ebony hair in the comb and, with a flick of his frail wrist, let it fall. "There, me lord. 'Tis done."

As the thick lock of hair swept his brow, Alexander sighed with pleasure. Damned odd how something so seemingly insignificant could revive a man.

He looked at his dangerously handsome reflection in the mirror and sighed with approval.

Didn't matter a lick if it was only for the day.

Lansing, London's most notorious rake, was back.

~

Meredith squinted her eyes at the small gold timepiece; then, huffing a frustrated breath, she dropped the watch back inside her reticule. She looked behind her, then turned and looked up the length of Rotten Row for the tenth time in as many minutes.

Where in blazes was the widow? This whole meeting with Lord Lansing would all be for naught if the widow did not arrive before he did.

Meredith had met the woman one year past, when she had joined her aunts in paying their condolences after the untimely death of Mrs. Heywood's third husband. Given the circumstances, Meredith had been quite surprised to find the widow in such high spirits, and with a gentleman at her elbow. That is, until later she learned from her aunts that the bawdy widow married as often as the season changed. In truth, it was common knowledge among the ton that she'd *pleased* at least three wealthy husbands into early graves, earning her the title "the merry widow."

Still, despite her late husbands' bulging coffers, the widow enjoyed her cards almost as much as bedchamber liaisons, and it was no secret that she was always in want of a guinea, a romp beneath the coverlets . . . or a man who could supply both.

For this very reason, Meredith had recently secured the widow's assistance with her social experiments. With both the widow and Giselle in her employ, the variety of Meredith's experiments increased, and because the widow's lusty reputation preceded her, never once had she failed Meredith in drawing out the desired results in a rogue. And this time would be no different. As expected, the widow had not so much as blinked an eye when Meredith offered her a fistful of guineas if she simply seduced the handsome Lord Lansing.

Just then, as if she'd conjured forth the Devil by thinking of him, a shiny black carriage emblazoned with the distinctive Lamont coat of arms drew up before the stable posts.

Oh no. Meredith flung herself behind an ancient chestnut tree. Why couldn't he have arrived late, as was the usual way of rogues?

Resting her cheek against the trunk's bark, she leaned forward just barely enough to witness Lord Lansing descend the carriage steps, and with a grand smile upon his all-too-handsome face, he disappeared through the open stable door—in search of *her.*

Nothing about this day had gone at all as she'd expected. Why, given the way her aunts were acting this morn, she was sure Arthur . . . *blast* . . . Mr. Chillton was going to offer for her during their ride in his phaeton.

But he didn't.

Of course, he would someday. Soon too, she expected, for at least twice this month he'd commented on her suitability as a wife in the presence of others.

Even her own sisters and her great-aunts voiced their expectation of an eventual union. As did Chillton's younger sister, Hannah. Why, to hear her speak, one would think that Meredith had already strolled down the aisle with Arthur . . . um . . . Mr. Chillton.

Oh yes, an offer of marriage was inevitable. It just hadn't come today—though she'd have been willing to bet a guinea it would have. She glanced down through her aunt's blond-lace fichu, at the deep neckline of her new sapphire gown. Probably the cut of the frock. It was clear Mr. Chillton didn't find it attractive.

Meredith pulled a tiny leather book from her reticule and muttered the words that she scribbled inside. "French-cut, bosom-revealing gowns only appeal to—"

"Me," came a deep, satiny smooth voice beside her ear, making the downy hairs at the back of her neck rise as her shoulders lurched up with surprise.

Meredith snapped the leather book closed and swung her head around. "Oh, L-Lord Lansing. I . . . um . . . wasn't aware you'd arrived."

"Of that, my dear, I am quite sure." His lips pulled away from his teeth and the beast flashed her the most dashing of roguish smiles, making her feel all wilty and weak.

Curse him. Without removing her gaze, she widened the cinch of her reticule and crammed the book and pencil inside. "I was just writing myself a reminder of sorts."

"So I see." The rake raised a perfectly curved, dubious brow. "I do apologize for interrupting."

"No harm d-done," she stammered as she turned to face him fully. "Just something I remembered reading in *La Belle Assemblée*."

A light, warm breeze fluttered through the trees around them, rustling the thick ebony lock at Lansing's brow and calling Meredith's full attention to his flashing green eyes, ringed with a fringe of dark lashes that any woman would envy.

Meredith could not seem to look away from his eyes. It was almost as if she'd been baited into a trap from which she could not extricate herself.

From the edges of her vision, she saw his hand raise up and then felt the warmth of it on her cheek.

"Why, the scratches are nearly gone. How can that be?"

Startled by his boldness, Meredith did not even attempt to brush his hand away. "My Aunt Viola applied some cream to them. My former lady's maid concocted the balm—it heals scrapes and burns like nothing I have ever known."

"You fell quite a distance. Are you truly well?"

"Indeed I am." Meredith didn't wish to discuss the condition of her body with anyone, and especially not with a rake.

"I am pleased to hear it, Miss Merriweather."

She had just about summoned the courage to push his

hand away from her face when his fingers moved. She felt the warmth of his touch as his fingers dipped into the depression just above her collarbone. Her mouth opened, and she knew she must object to his all-too-familiar touch—for she was practically promised to another—when suddenly her aunt's fichu was whisked from her shoulders.

He chuckled softly, breaking the gaze that held her. "If you follow *La Belle Assemblée,* Miss Merriweather, surely you are aware that such a beautiful gown requires no additional adornment, especially on such a blistering day."

Meredith felt her cheeks going pink with embarrassment and she snatched the fichu from his hand. "Sir, I did not ask you here to discuss current fashion." She swallowed, and nearly cringed when she heard an audible gulp. "Am I correct in understanding that you are an expert in bloodstock?"

"You are." Lord Lansing lifted his arm to her. "You wish my counsel, Miss Merriweather?"

Meredith cleared her throat and stood there staring at his elevated elbow . . . just hovering there . . . waiting for her. She must look quite the ninny. Finally realizing she must move forward with her experiment without the assistance of the more skilled widow, she relented and took his arm. "I do, my lord. As you are well aware, women are not permitted within Tattersalls, so I must entrust an agent to do my bidding."

"There are agents for hire."

"Perhaps, but none so knowledgeable as you—or so I have heard about Town." As they walked toward the stables, Meredith glanced up at the rake and saw a pleased grin slip across his lips.

When they reached the stable doors, Meredith halted and searched for the widow once more, but the amorous mistress was nowhere to be seen. She turned her gaze to the stable's black cavernous opening. The scent of horses and straw was thick, and her heart began to pound.

What was she to do now?

"Miss Merriweather, if we are to discuss horseflesh, we must go inside." Lord Lansing drew her forward a step, but she dug her heels into the earth.

"D-do we?" Her breath was catching in her throat. This was not part of her plan!

Where is that widow? Does payment for services mean nothing to her?

"I say, darling, shall we?" Lord Lansing tugged gently at her arm again.

"My lord, the day is stifling indeed. Would it not be preferable to view the horses out here . . . in the f-fresh air?"

He gazed at her in that subtly amused way of his, then released her arm and plunged into the darkness of the stable innards alone.

There was a loud clop of hooves on packed earth, and a moment later, Lord Lansing emerged from the darkness, leading forth a startlingly large bay. Meredith's eyes widened as he took her right hand and pressed the lead into it.

"My l-lord, I cannot—" But no other words would come.

"I am here to protect you. No harm will come to you as long as I am here."

He ran his bare hand over hers and patted it soothingly. And somewhere inside her, she believed him. She did feel safe in his company. Though she knew she should not—

for in truth, no woman was truly safe from a rogue of his caliber, were they?

"Just hold tight," his deep voice instructed, "whilst I review with you the features of utmost importance when considering bloodstock."

She nodded dumbly, unable to do anything else. Her teeth were already lining up for their clattering march.

"For me, legs are all important. 'No legs, no horse,' a wise man once said." He bent and ran his hand down the equine's front leg. "They should be straight, clean and blemish free."

Then something extraordinary happened. His gaze slipped from the horse's quarters and affixed to her own legs, which, due to the prevailing wind, were now perfectly visible through her thin dress.

"Long legs are a most admirable trait. Yes, indeed." He smiled to himself as his eyes trailed upward from her ankles, over her thighs and to her hips.

Lud, the man had a way of making her feel perfectly naked!

Raising his gaze, he noticed her narrowing eyes and snapped his attention to the horse once more. "Long legs produce a longer ground-covering stride . . . most desirable for racing."

"I see." Meredith managed to sound thoughtful, for she did not wish for the rake to know he was having a . . . *visceral* effect on her. Even if it was ever so minor, and certainly not enough to warrant concern on her part.

His hand slid slowly up the horse until it rested on the chest area behind its front legs. "A deep heart girth is also one of my preferences, for a larger heart and lungs. . . ." His gaze flitted most deviously to the deep cut of her frock, before returning to the beast. "Well, I've found a deep heart girth a good indicator of . . . *stamina*."

Straightening, he ran his hand along the slope of the bay's back. "Her overall confirmation should be balanced." He approached Meredith then and stepped behind her. "May I?"

She had no idea what he was about. But if it would assist in moving along this course in horseflesh and get her out of Hyde Park sooner, she'd agree to almost anything. She nodded.

He laid his hand against her spine and eased it achingly slowly down to the small of her back. "An easy slope of the back is what you want. Nothing all ramrod straight and stiff."

All of Meredith's blood seemed to follow his hand's downward motion, and pooled hotly . . . well, somewhat lower. How dreadfully mortifying! She should leave this very instant. In fact, she would. Meredith opened the hand grasping the lead, intending to let it fall, but the rake bent her fingers back over it. "No, no. Don't let go. Too dangerous with the horse so near," he warned.

A shudder rattled through her and she obeyed and tightened her grip, though she was not sure if the man should be believed or not. Still, best not to risk injury . . . just in case.

All of the rake's attention was fixed on her face now, and not on the horse at all. "Some claim that clear, intelligent eyes and a long, graceful neck are unimportant, but for me, it hints at superior breeding." His hand moved to her jawline and he gently ran the back of three fingers along its curve.

"A pretty head, while not essential, is always a delightful bonus." He smiled and released a pleased sigh.

That's it. She'd had quite enough of his so-called lesson. Seizing his hand in hers, she shoved the lead into it.

"Thank you, my lord," she very nearly snarled. "I shall consider what you have said and get back with you about my bloodstock needs."

"But, Miss Merriweather, there is still so much more I have to teach you."

No doubt. "I—I fear my sensibilities are presently quite overwhelmed by my proximity to the horse."

Lord Lansing peered at her quizzically. "Why, pray, if your fear is so great, do you seek to purchase a horse?"

Why indeed? Meredith searched through her mind for a logical response. She couldn't tell him that engaging him as her horse agent was simply a ruse to prove what a beast he truly was.

"The horse is to be a gift." Well, now, that sounded reasonable, did it not?

"For whom?" That challenging brow of his flicked up.

"Um . . . for my betrothed."

Lord Lansing's eyes widened to the size of halfpennies. "I—I beg your pardon, Miss Merriweather, did you say—"

"I did, my lord." A great thick lump rose up in her throat as she repeated her lie.

"My *betrothed.*"

Imperative Four

A rake allows women to initiate conversation topics in which he will appear interested. This gives the woman the impression that she has much more in common with him than is true.

❦

Mr. Edgar, who held three bonnets in his arms, dutifully followed Aunt Letitia into the parlor, where Meredith and Aunt Viola were finishing their morning chocolate.

"Oh dear, just as I'd thought. Put your cups down, ladies. Put them down at once. Have you forgotten?" Aunt Letitia seized Meredith's wrist and guided her cup quickly to the table. "'Tis already ten o'clock. Mustn't be late for the birth breakfast!"

No, wouldn't want to miss a single moment of Beth Augustine's inane celebration.

Never mind that Beth Augustine—that would be *Mrs.* Chauncey Augustine for all of one year now—was Meredith's least favorite person in all of Mayfair. Possibly in all the world.

For the former Miss Beth Dooly, Meredith's fellow classmate at Miss Belbury's School for Girls, had not only mercilessly ridiculed Meredith for years, but also urged the other young ladies to do the same.

At the time, what most frustrated Meredith was that she could not put her finger on a single instance when she might have done anything to earn such hatred. Nothing could explain Beth's many cruel games. One morn, Meredith had awakened to find her red braids severed and lying on the floor. Another time, she'd dipped a spoon into her porridge only to discover hearth ash mixed into it. But what hurt her most was when Beth convinced the other girls to pretend they could not see or hear Meredith. Having recently lost her parents, Meredith keenly felt the imposed loneliness and began to play her own clever pranks on her teachers and the school staff—simply to be noticed.

When Meredith learned that she was to come to live with her aunts in Mayfair, a stone's throw from Beth's family home on Berkeley Square, she'd convinced herself that things would be different outside the confines of Miss Belbury's. At first, she actually thought Beth had grown a heart in her adulthood, for she was kind and generous . . . once she learned Meredith was blood kin to the grand Featherton ladies, anyway.

That is, until the day Meredith fell from Society's grace after being left at the altar. Beth's behavior when Meredith was at her lowest proved just how beastly the woman could be: she supplied the *on-dit* columnist of the *London Times* with a detailed account of Meredith's humiliation on her wedding day. It took a full month, and a palmful of guineas, but Meredith eventually confirmed to her satisfaction that Beth was the columnist's anonymous source. Mrs. Beth Augustine was soulless, and as far as

Meredith could gather, to this day, the wench hadn't changed at all.

Meredith rose and took her straw bonnet from Mr. Edgar. "I am ready, Auntie." Truth to tell, she would rather empty all the chamber pots on Hanover Square than go to this horrid breakfast. But her aunts wished for her to attend the event with them, and as her sister Grace oft reminded her in her frequent letters, Meredith owed much to the two old women.

Meredith knew this was true. For without their aunts, she and her two older sisters would have been cast out on the streets after the death of their parents.

Still, Grace, thinking Meredith was as much of a hoyden as their older sister, Eliza, would not leave her behavior to chance. When Grace had last visited, she shoved her wailing golden-haired son into Meredith's arms, and forced from her a promise always to do as their aunts asked. Why, the child's screams made her ears throb and his nappy reeked so powerfully that Meredith would have agreed to anything at that moment just so Grace would take the child away. So promise she did.

An hour later, because of that very promise, Meredith found herself standing in the Augustine parlor, surrounded by a dozen other unfortunates who'd been pressed into oohing and aahing over Beth's black-eyed, moonfaced babe.

"What is this?" Beth asked loudly, drawing the attention of everyone in attendance. She snatched Meredith's left hand and held it close to her dark brown eyes. "What is this?" She turned her gaze and met Meredith's eyes. "No ring? Can it be that Miss Merriweather is not yet married?"

Meredith's chest tightened. "I daresay, you would

have heard had I wed, *Beth*." She twisted her hand from their hostess's firm grasp.

"Oh, that's right. Do forgive me, dear." Beth let out a long, sad sigh and pushed her lower lip outward. "I own, it completely slipped my mind that you were left at the altar at St. George's Church."

Anger suffused every fiber of Meredith's being. Her fingers folded inward into a fist, and had her aunts not leaped before Meredith, the new mother would have soon been sporting a swollen purple lip.

"Of course, you could not have heard, Mrs. Augustine, being confined as you have been, unable to attend upper-society events," Aunt Letitia said.

Aunt Viola slipped her arm around Meredith's waist. "You see, Meredith is all but affianced to Mr. Chillton, of Russell Square."

"R-really?" Beth stammered.

Ha! It *was* lovely watching Mrs. Augustine claw the air for words.

"In fact," Aunt Letitia added smugly, "I do not doubt that we shall all be together again at a wedding breakfast before the year is out."

"Is this true, Miss Merriweather?" Suspicion sharpened Beth's gaze.

"'Tis." Meredith cringed inwardly as the single word burst from her lips.

"Well, I shall be counting the days to the happy event," Beth said, turning to nod to the ladies encircling them. "We all shall. Shan't we, ladies?"

As the entire assembly of women bobbed their heads in agreement, Meredith's cheeks burned as surely as though they'd been pressed with a branding iron.

For if Chillton did not offer for her soon, in Society's eyes, she, in addition to all else, would be branded a liar.

~⁀ゝ

"Damn me, man, I just don't know how much more of your gentlemanly behavior I can take." Georgie nudged his gelding up the small slope near the center of Hyde Park and drew his mount alongside Alex's to better make himself heard. "You're just . . . oh, I dunno . . . no bloody *fun* anymore."

Alexander snickered at that. But it was true, wasn't it? The old man's dictates were crippling, and damnation, they were making him old beyond his years. Why, just last eve Alex had plucked out a wiry gray hair he'd found jutting from his right sideburn. Had to have One check the rest of his head to be sure there wasn't another lurking beneath his sleek black locks.

"And now he wishes you to marry the Merriweather chit." Georgie glanced sidelong at Alexander as their horses turned off the grass and trotted down the soft earth of Rotten Row. "You know"—Georgie paused for a long moment—"word is, she was left at the altar by that rotter Pomeroy."

"So I heard. Concerned me at first, but then I charged One with checking into the details."

"Good story?"

"Hardly. Miss Merriweather's aunts, the Feathertons, are well-positioned within Society. Pomeroy evidently saw the benefit of a connection and relentlessly wooed Miss Merriweather, though she was little more than a gel just out."

"Oh, I see where this story is headed."

"And you'd not be wrong. Once the man had her rapt, he apparently obtained a special license and rushed her to St. George's, hoping to ring her finger before her aunts became the wiser."

Georgie's ruddy eyebrows drew close. "Good plan. But why did he leave her waiting at the altar?"

"Because Pomeroy's a fool. He assumed that Miss Merriweather shared her aunts' financial affluence." Alexander tugged at the reins and his mount slowed. "When the dolt realized his error, he was off to Cornwall on the trail of some no-name heiress, leaving Miss Merriweather to face her ruin alone."

"Tarnished."

Alexander halted his horse. "While she might have been left standing at St. George's, believe me, there is *nothing* tarnished about that gem."

"Oh, so she's at least tolerable?"

"Lord, yes. *Gorgeous,* but in a . . . nonconventional sort of way. Flaming hair, jewel blue eyes and skin like porcelain."

Georgie laughed. "So she was the owner of the red strand of hair you found the other day. Already taken her for a romp, have you? Why, Lansing, what would your dear father say about that?"

"He can't say a bloody thing, for I've been naught but the veriest gentleman with the woman—not that I wouldn't have liked to have enjoyed her charms. But she wasn't the least interested."

"Well, blow me down. Losing your touch already?"

Alexander stiffened. "Hardly. Seems the Merriweather miss is already betrothed."

Georgie snorted back a laugh. "Since when has that stopped you?"

"Hasn't . . . and mightn't yet." Alexander exhaled slowly. "Still, I'll have to think on it a bit."

"What bloody for, man?"

"My father wishes me to marry her. If I tell him the woman is already affianced, he will simply mandate another eligible female. And this time, perhaps one not half as comely as Miss Merriweather."

"Well, then, there's only one solution."

Alexander pulled his reins back, and when his great ebony mount halted, he looked pointedly at Georgie and awaited the blessed solution.

"Why do I have to inform *you* this? After all, you're the master when it comes to deception." Georgie reined in his gelding. "Neglect to tell the earl anything. He's still burrowed into the countryside, is he not?"

"For the last ten years."

"You see, he won't be any the wiser."

"You didn't observe him when he last visited. He's serious this time. He has persuaded himself that I have somehow compromised Miss Merriweather, though I know 'tis only his excuse to see me snared in the parson's mousetrap before the season is through. No, if the Merriweather woman is betrothed, as she claims, he will learn of it soon enough."

"You say that as if you have some doubt, Lansing."

Alexander squinted up at the hot sun, then lifted his hat from his head and ran his fingers through his damp hair. "Let us just say that I am less than convinced of her betrothal. Had Two check the *on-dit* columns in the *London Times* for me, but there was no mention of her engagement. Still, I intend to know for certain before the week is through."

"And if, contrary to what she claims, she's not yet matched?" Georgie asked.

"Then Miss Merriweather will be mine for the plucking."

A grin sprang to Georgie's lips. "And your inheritance will be—"

"Mine again. All *mine*." Alexander allowed himself a momentary self-satisfied grin; then his thoughts progressed. "Got a few guineas to spare, Georgie?"

Georgie patted his coat until he appeared to feel the weight of his purse. "I do indeed. Have a mind to stop by White's?"

"Close." Alexander pinched the brim of his hat. "Lock's. If I am to truly win over Miss Merriweather, I could do with a new beaver topper."

~

"Quite respectable." Meredith stood staring at her reflection in the cheval glass. "What do you think, Hannah? Perhaps the white linen frock might be more appropriate for the occasion."

"Honestly, I don't think which gown you wear will matter to my brother."

Meredith chewed her lip. She was running out of time. In less than an hour, her Mr. Chillton—oh, and some other dreary guests Meredith didn't care a fig about—would arrive for her aunts' monthly musicale and she still hadn't settled on a gown.

"It does matter, Hannah. I was certain Arth . . . Mr. Chillton was going to offer for me on Tuesday. But he didn't, and I am sure it was the fault of my French-cut sapphire gown. I must have looked like a strumpet or the like . . . though I daresay I thought it quite lovely."

Distractedly Meredith remembered Lord Lansing's appreciative gaze when he saw her in the dress. She shook her head, hoping to whisk the man's image from her mind. It didn't matter what he thought, after all. *He's a rake,* she reminded herself. *A selfish, untrustworthy rake.*

In the mirror's reflection, she saw Hannah sitting atop the tester bed, kicking up one foot, then the other, in her utter boredom. "I seriously doubt it was the gown. My brother doesn't concern himself with such things. Probably just coughed up a hen's feather."

Meredith turned and faced her. "You really think that's all?"

"I do." Hannah slid forward until her feet met the floor. "La, a gentleman doesn't offer for a woman from such an esteemed family every day. I do not doubt some small amount of fear and worry plagued him . . . not knowing whether you would accept his troth—"

Meredith clutched Hannah's upper arms. "But I would have accepted. Truly, I would have. You will make sure he knows this, won't you? He has nothing to fear from me."

Hannah laughed as she brushed a lock of hair from Meredith's face. "Do not worry yourself over this. I will make sure he knows of your feelings—though I own, I may be wasting my breath. For maybe he plans to offer for you this very eve."

Presenting a weak smile, for it was all she could muster, Meredith sent a silent plea to the heavens: *please, please let her be right.*

She couldn't face the humiliation of being brushed aside . . . again.

The moment Chillton's eyes met Meredith's own, she knew that the virginal white embroidered gown was indeed the right choice. Why, it trimmed at least three years from her age.

Even Hannah, who was in the first bloom of youth, claimed they would be taken for twins this night—though not the identical sort, owing to differences in their hair. Meredith's coif being so vivid and Hannah's as black as the depths of a well.

And who was Meredith to argue? The dress not only made her look as though she'd just left school, but she felt actually far younger than her one and twenty—*practically a spinster*—years.

Oh, she didn't miss the derisive look Mrs. Beth Augustine gave the girlishly prim white gown, but honestly, Meredith wasn't going to let it concern her this night. Let everyone think what they would. It was Chillton's impression that mattered, and judging by his supreme attentiveness this eve, she knew the new *demure* Meredith garnered his complete approval.

As she took his proffered arm and allowed herself to be guided to her seat, Meredith caught notice of more than one lady's interested gaze.

Ha! She'd show them all. Despite her ruin, she would marry respectably. And soon too.

Meredith adjusted her fichu to cover her bosom more fully, and did not miss Chillton's endorsement of her behavior. This was the Meredith he wanted—and the one he would have.

All he needed to do was ask, and she would be forever his. She could get used to wearing less stylish clothing.

She always preferred comfort, anyway. And, well, Chillton was absolutely right. She would succumb to far fewer colds upon her chest with a fichu providing extra protection, now wouldn't she?

Hannah seated herself before the pianoforte and had just lifted her rich voice in song, when Meredith heard the door to the music room open, then close once more. Hoping to see who had had the audacity to arrive so late, she turned her head ever so slightly—for she did not wish to appear less than rapt by Chillton's sister's song—when her gaze met that of the rude latecomer.

Heat shot into her cheeks, and she yanked her head forward. It was none other than Lord Lansing.

Oh . . . my . . . word.

Meredith worked to swallow the massive lump that had risen into her throat. She could feel the rake's gaze boring into the back of her head, making her own eyes widen until she feared they might pop out and roll right down under the pianoforte.

What in heaven's name could her aunts have been thinking, inviting the rogue here? This was a gathering of genteel society, after all, and Lansing had the veriest worst possible reputation. Oil and water did not mix. How mad were her aunts to have even attempted such a feat!

From the corner of her eye, she could see Chillton notice Lansing's poorly timed entrance as well. His golden brows rose before he politely returned his attention to his sister's song. But now the muscles beneath his high cheekbones were repeatedly tensing and releasing, making the pale skin of his handsome face ripple like a pond on a windy day.

Oh perdition! Everything had been going so splendidly this eve, too. Meredith turned and narrowed her eyes at Lansing, making sure he saw her. The rogue had absolutely destroyed Chillton's earlier buoyant mood. Anyone could see that he'd ruined everything!

Worse still, she was going to have to spend the entire musicale attached to the rogue's side. There was no help for it. If she did not keep Chillton and Lansing on opposite sides of the room, her lie—that she was already affianced to Chillton—might slip out. What a twist she would be in then.

So she had no other choice. Once Hannah finished her set, Meredith knew she simply would have to excuse herself from Mr. Chillton and greet the rake.

Blast Lord Lansing.

Blast, blast . . . blast him!

Imperative Five

A rake knows it is easier to steal another's lady than to keep his own.

Bloody hell. What kind of look is that?

Alexander blinked his eyes and refocused his gaze on the pert Miss Merriweather, who, quite inexplicably, was dressed as a simpering young miss just out. She had even gone so far as to top her frothy white confection of a gown with a staid lace fichu, making her look a bit like a frosted tea cake.

Not her usual dress. At least he didn't think so. On the last two occasions of their meeting, she had worn vibrant jewel tones, which were entirely more complementary, given her flaming hair and flashing blue eyes. Alexander raised his gaze from her ridiculous gown to her lovely face. *Damn me, her* daggered *blue eyes. Why in bloody hell is she looking at me that way?*

He'd only arrived, what, maybe thirty minutes later than the invitation had suggested? And half an hour was not nearly so tardy as to warrant a glare like that. Why, her icy stare was enough to chase a lesser man's jewels up inside his body for protection.

Alexander hadn't missed the perturbed glance from the gentleman beside her either.

As he reluctantly studied him, to Alexander's surprise, the man reached out his hand and set it atop Miss Merriweather's. Alexander straightened his back and stretched out his neck for a better view over the annoying sway of feathered heads between him and the gentleman.

There, he had them in his sights again. *Damn it all.* He was still doing it—*touching her,* in plain view of her aunts, no less. Alexander bristled as he watched the man's thumb gently caress the side of her gloved hand.

Well, he'd been a bit too hasty in labeling the man a gentleman, hadn't he? For, indeed, it was clear the man was not.

And just where had he found that coat, anyway—in a dustbin?

As the tinkling of piano ivories ended and the songstress rose to acknowledge her audience, Alexander studied the coat's too wide lapel and coarsely woven wool.

No, not a gentleman at all, or at least not of the level that belonged in the upper reaches of Society, that was for certain.

Oh, how dull of me. Must be some poor relation the Feathertons were compelled to invite to their musicale.

Yes, that had to be it, Alexander decided, for this particular man surely could not be Miss Merriweather's supposed . . . *betrothed.*

There was a shuffle of feet, and Alexander fought to regain his view through the tight crowd of shifting frocks and cutaways. Then, much to his frustration, someone blocked his view entirely. "I say, madam, would you please step to the left, I cannot see—"

The woman before him cleared her throat.

Damnation. "How can I assist you, madam?" Alexander turned his gaze to her face and belatedly realized that it was none other than the sapphire-eyed Miss Merriweather standing directly before him.

How delightfully perfect. She had come to *him*. Well, that made his task this eve all the easier, didn't it?

A pleased smile started to pull at the corners of his mouth, but then it skidded and faltered.

For though Miss Merriweather was smiling warmly at him, the look in her eyes was still as frosty as icicles.

Suddenly a high-pitched cry erupted from somewhere behind him. He turned his head slowly to see a past-her-prime miss, who looked damned familiar too, standing shoulder to shoulder with an older woman with gray-streaked hair piled high atop her box-shaped head.

"Mama, 'tis *him*." The dark-haired chit raised a finger and pointed, in the most rude fashion, directly at him. "Oh, take me home, take me home at once. I cannot bear seeing him."

The milling throng seemed to take notice exactly then and pivoted, almost as if they were one, to look at Alexander in anticipation of a scandal.

Instead of hustling the young lady from the house, as Alexander truly had hoped the older woman might do—given the worried look in her eyes—she plowed forward through the crowd. Alexander turned his body to face her, ready for an attack.

The older woman poked him hard in the chest and spoke in low, fierce tones. "You, sir, are no gentleman, breaking my gel's heart the way you did. Did you ever care for her?"

Alexander looked over the crone's shoulder at the dark-haired woman standing several feet behind her. He had to admit, something about her face looked vaguely familiar.

"Ah! I thought not. Well, it doesn't matter, anyway. She is married now. Always deserved better than the likes of a London gallant, anyway." At the conclusion of her words, she poked his chest one more time for good measure, then spun around and quit the house with her daughter.

"Wait! You need not leave, Lady Delphine." Lady Letitia, followed closely by her sister, forced her way through the crowd in pursuit of the distraught pair of guests.

Alexander exhaled; then, belatedly remembering that Miss Merriweather stood behind him, he whirled around.

"Dreadfully sorry about that." He shook his head. "Obviously had me confused with some other chap."

"Obviously." Miss Merriweather flashed him a wry smile, but her voice sounded strangely high and strangled, almost as though an invisible hand had wrapped around her throat and squeezed. "Lord Lansing, my aunts had not mentioned that you, sir, would be our guest this eve."

"Didn't they?" Alexander looked over Miss Merriweather's shoulder at the two old ladies who had just reentered the parlor and were now peering at them over matched lavender fans.

Well, that was certainly interesting. Had a couple of allies, did he?

He glanced at the blond gentleman who'd been sitting

beside Miss Merriweather earlier, and saw him chatting with the songstress.

Yes, this eve was suddenly becoming most intriguing indeed.

⁓

Heavens, the rake was staring right at Chillton—*right at him!*

Most unwisely, Meredith ventured a glance at Chillton too. He returned a bright smile, and then—*oh no*—he started for her. She had to get the rake out of here, even if only for a few moments, so she could redirect Chillton.

"Lord Lansing, I do not see a footman anywhere. Would you be ever so kind and bring me a glass of sherry?" She batted her lashes, in fair approximation—at least so she hoped—of Giselle, the French courtesan. "I confess, the room has grown rather stuffy and I have become unsteady on my feet."

The rake peered down at her.

Gracious me, he's tall.

"As you wish, Miss Merriweather." He tipped his head, excusing himself, then set out in search of refreshments.

And it was none too soon, for the instant Meredith turned around, Chillton was upon her.

"Who was that you were speaking with?" he asked. Suspicion was keen in his eyes. "I don't believe I've made his acquaintance."

"What, that gentleman who was just here a moment ago?" Meredith scrabbled for more time to come up with an answer that would please Chillton—rather than cause him to doubt her intentions toward him. Though it couldn't hurt to share his name now, could it? "That was Lord Lansing."

"Lansing?" A deep scowl etched all sorts of lines, ones she'd never seen before, in Chillton's otherwise handsome face. "Why he's a . . . Well, I shall just come out and say it—a scoundrel. Your aunts surely were completely unaware of his dark reputation when they made their invitation to him. For otherwise, I daresay, they would not have extended their hospitality to such a man."

Oh, this is not going well at all. "Dear Mr. Chillton, then you have not heard."

"Heard? Heard what?"

Meredith surveyed the music room quickly, to be absolutely sure Lord Lansing was not yet about. "He has *reformed*. Yes, it is the talk of Society. Lord Lansing has *completely* reformed."

Clearly dubious—as well he should be—Chillton opened his mouth . . . no doubt to argue Meredith's claim. She raised her hand. "Now, now, I was not inclined to believe it either, yet from all tearoom reports, he has not set foot inside White's, frequented a racetrack or dined with an . . . actress for nigh on three months. It's true, I tell you."

The tenseness in Chillton's face seemed to break, for the smocked lines at the corners of his eyes became suddenly smooth again. "Why the sudden change? There has to be a reason."

"Oh, there is, there is." She leaned closer and lowered her voice to a whisper. "Word is that his father is ailing, and Lord Lansing is due to inherit the earldom very, very soon. This, I believe, is the reason for his sudden change in behavior."

Chillton nodded his head as he listened. "Makes sense. If he isn't just having everyone on."

"I am certain his change is true. In fact, it has been rumored that he is looking for a wife." Why, that sounded jolly good. So good that she almost believed her own words.

"A wife? And he's got plenty of money, you say?"

Meredith nodded as Chillton's gaze drifted to his sister, and a slow smile turned his lips.

"Miss Merriweather, do you think Lansing might fancy my dear sister, Hannah? I own, it would be a weight from my shoulders to see her wed, what with her always getting up to some mischief or another. And though the man does sport a bit of a reputation, he is quite well-off, if I have heard correctly." He tapped the tip of his tongue to his upper lip as he pinned Meredith with his questioning gaze.

"I . . . believe he does stand to inherit a goodly f-fortune," Meredith stammered.

"A man of fortune, and obvious breeding . . . Why, I am convinced all he needs is the influence of a good woman, like my Hannah, for instance, to prevent him from any possible moral lapse."

Dear Lord. If Chillton thought he stood even a chance of matching his sister with the worldly Lord Lansing, he was utterly mad. From the corner of Meredith's eye, she saw Lord Lansing step over the threshold into the music room, carrying a brandy and a sherry in his hands. Her chest constricted.

Still, she had to separate the two men and this oddball scheme of Chillton's provided just the means.

"Dear Mr. Chillton," Meredith said brightly, "I shall make it my mission to learn just that this eve." She turned her gaze toward the door. Perdition, the rake was nearly upon them! "Best leave me alone with him, though, for I do not believe he will share any information with me if you are at my side."

"You are good, Miss Merriweather. Very, very *good*." He licked his lips as he seemed to study her just a moment overlong. "I thank you for your assistance in this matter, and shan't forget your willingness to do my bidding."

"You are very welcome, sir, but you must go. Hurry along now."

Meredith spun around just as the rake reached her side.

"Why, thank you, my lord. You are too kind."

"Please, Miss Merriweather, do call me Alexander. All my lady friends do."

Did he just say—no, surely not. Oh Lord, he did! He actually likened her to one of his *actress* friends! Meredith struggled to prevent the shock from contorting her features.

"I shall not, Lord Lansing. I . . . I mean *my betrothed* would find such familiarity inappropriate."

The rake glanced about the room until he spotted Chillton. "So is that the man?"

"My lord?" Of course, she knew he was asking if Chillton was her betrothed, though it made her head twirl just to think about answering.

"That gentleman over there. The one conversing with our delightful songstress."

She had no choice now but to follow his gaze to where Chillton stood. "Oh yes. I see who you mean now."

The rake lifted a single brow. "And?"

Meredith swallowed deeply. Lud, he'd forced her into a corner. "Y-yes. That is he—Mr. Chillton."

At her reply, the strangest look of disappointment came over his face—*Alexander's face*.

Oh, she'd never speak his Christian name, though it could not hurt to *think* of him that way, could it? After all, he *looked* much more like an Alexander than a Lansing, anyway.

His gaze studied Chillton for several long moments before he spoke again. "My dear, I fear he is not the one for you."

"Whatever can you mean? We are perfectly suited. Everyone agrees."

"That I seriously doubt. Just look at the man." He inclined his chin, compelling her to redirect her gaze to Chillton. "He's become old beyond his years. Stodgy even."

"My lord, you forget yourself. And more than that, you are completely wrong."

"I daresay I am not. Just look at him. Hardly the gallant. And were you to ask my advice, I would counsel you to choose a mate as handsome and vibrant as yourself." He snared her gaze with his own, then took up her hand and drew it before his lips as if . . . as if he were about to kiss it. Her insides turned a little flip in anticipation. "Someone like *me*, for instance."

A whoosh of warmth swirled around her body like a great woolen cloak. Meredith's breath snagged in her throat, making her exhale a barely concealed cough. "Well, thankfully, my lord, I did *not* seek your counsel." Meredith yanked her hand from his grip. "And . . . and furthermore, I do wish you would keep such horrid thoughts to yourself."

A low chuckle bubbled up from deep inside Alexander. "I pay him no disrespect, Miss Merriweather, I assure you. I am merely stating fact. A woman who has the pluck to float through Hyde Park in a tattered balloon will never be content living in her husband's shadow. You need adventure, excitement." Lord Lansing shook his head. "He is not even of Society. You do not live in the same world."

"I will be perfectly happy and we *do* travel within the same circles. Chillton is a great gentleman of commerce." Meredith raised her chin smugly.

The rake settled his gaze upon Chillton once again, seeming to focus on his . . . his coat. "You did say *great* gentleman of commerce, did you not?"

"I did."

Amusement lit his eyes. "Very well, though do remember my next words—you may have earned his promise of marriage, but you will never marry that man. *Ever.*"

Meredith's mouth fell open and there it remained for several seconds. "And may *you* come to recall my reply . . . as you swallow a rather large bite of humble pie—I *will* marry Mr. Chillton."

"Meredith," came a soft, feminine voice.

A faint scent of orange blossom beckoned her attention to Chillton's sister, who had suddenly appeared at her side.

"I do apologize for the intrusion. Your aunts bade me to send you to them." Hannah turned to the rake and smiled coyly at him. "I apologize to you as well, sir, for removing dear Meredith from your conversation. Perhaps I might provide adequate company until she is able to return?"

Alexander Lamont drew up to his full height and bequeathed Hannah with the most charming of bows, never once removing his all-too-seductive gaze from the young woman's batting eyes. "I shall be honored to share your company, Miss—" He looked to Meredith to bridge the gap.

A moment later, after providing the requisite introductions, Meredith crossed the room to her aunts, who were waving their fans excitedly as they conversed with Mr. Chillton.

Her aunt Letitia caught her wrist and drew her forward the instant she breached their circle of conversation. "There you are, dear. Mr. Chillton was just telling us that you were orchestrating a possible match between Lord Lansing and young Hannah. How wonderful!"

"Oh, um . . ." Meredith felt the heat shooting into her cheeks. "Actually, I was only seeking to learn if the earl's son might have interest in Hannah."

Her aunt Viola's eyes sparkled like fireworks over Vauxhall Gardens. "And? What do you think? I vow, Mr. Chillton and I are ever so anxious to know." She abruptly clasped Meredith's other wrist, sending her crystal of sherry splattering on the floorboards.

"Oh, heavens!" Aunt Letitia sputtered. "Viola, you've spilled our gel's refreshment." She turned to Chillton and fashioned a girlish pout for him. "Do be a dear, kind sir, and fetch Meredith another, will you?"

"Why, of course, Lady Featherton." Chillton clicked his heels together and bowed, then headed for the refreshment table set up in the dining room.

Aunt Letitia's eyes were twinkling now too. "Quickly, dear, have you been successful?"

Meredith cinched her brows. "Successful? At what may I ask?"

Aunt Viola shook her head. "Why, in your quest to lure the rake from his pressed and starched hiding place. We invited Lord Lansing here especially for you—for your research, you know."

"I didn't know." Meredith's heart double-thudded in her chest and her head grew impossibly light, making her feel rather unstable. Heavens, what she would not do for an empty chair! "I wished you had warned me, Aunties. For I was caught completely ill-prepared and I fear his attendance this night is a complete waste."

"Is it now?" Aunt Letitia waggled her thick white brows and inclined her head toward Hannah, who appeared to be giggling madly at something the rake had said. "Lord Lansing seems to be quite taken with Hannah. Perhaps her innocence will be bait enough to draw out his supposed rakish tendencies."

"Perhaps." Meredith studied Hannah and Alexander from her place by the pianoforte. "I own, I had not thought to try *innocence* . . . but 'tis a brilliant idea, Auntie. How clever of you."

Aunt Letitia swished her fan through the air, allowing the momentum to close the silken folds in her waiting palm. "I thought of nothing. 'Twas Chillton's idea to send his sister to fetch you."

"Chillton's?" As if suddenly hoisted by winches, Meredith's brows shot to her hairline. That was certainly a surprise. Her own Mr. Chillton had done something impulsive.

Adventurous even.

This proved that Alexander was completely wrong about him. The urge to tell the rake so was near overwhelming.

She glanced up at the couple once more. *Just one moment, please. That isn't Hannah with Alexander—well, not unless she's aged twenty summers in the span of a single minute.*

"Do excuse me for a moment, Aunties." Meredith quickly skirted the pianoforte for a better view. And then she recognized the woman, and relief flooded over her.

It was the merry widow! Her aunts must have unwittingly invited her.

Just then, the widow turned her head toward Meredith and gave her a secret wink. Marvelous!

Meredith marched triumphantly back to her aunts, who were busily extricating any information to be had from Hannah, who had joined them during Meredith's brief absence.

"No, I tell you," Hannah was saying, in little more than a whimper. "He wasn't interested in me at all. It's Meredith he fancies. She's all we discussed."

"Me?" Meredith couldn't believe what she was hearing.

Aunt Viola rose up on her toes and whispered into Meredith's ear, "Perhaps you, Meredith, should be the rake's wriggling bait . . . instead of Widow Heywood. Oh yes, do not appear so surprised. You did not think her attendance here was an accident, did you?"

"Sister is right," added Aunt Letitia into Meredith's ear. "Who else would be better able to conduct your experiments, hmm?"

When her aunts quieted, Meredith probed Hannah a little more.

"Why, pray, would he wish to know more about me? I am already affianced . . . er . . . I mean . . . my heart is already spoken for."

Everyone just stared back at her, making her small gaffe seem as wide as the Thames.

Why will they not stop staring? Say something. Some-one. Anyone. Just one word will do.

Please.

Meredith glanced at the door and searched her mind for any viable excuse to walk through it. "Just where is Chillton with my sherry? Perhaps I shall go and look for him, hmm?" She patted Aunt Viola's shoulder. "Think I will."

"Don't be nonsensical, dear, he knows where you are and the house is not so very large that he will become lost." Aunt Viola's attention pricked suddenly. "Oh look, Widow Heywood comes this way." She glanced at the widow, then at Hannah, who knew nothing of Meredith's experiments. "You remember her, Meredith. We paid her condolences after Mr. Heywood passed. The crowd is ever so large though, and I fear she may not see us. Would you greet her, dear? I do not wish her to feel forgotten this eve."

"Yes, of course. It shall be lovely to see her again—under more pleasing circumstances."

Dear me. Meredith lifted the hem of her skirt from the floor and charged forward, meeting the widow before she could reach her aunts and Hannah. Chillton would be back at any moment, and there was absolutely no way she'd be able to explain away her less than honorable "se-duction for guineas" arrangement with the widow.

When she reached the merry widow, Meredith wrapped her gloved hand around the widow's and drew her close, as if she meant to kiss her cheek. "Thank you for coming, Mrs. Heywood."

"Oh, Miss Merriweather, I am dreadfully sorry that I missed my appointment at the stables. I had a caller, and . . . was detained. Couldn't be helped."

Meredith gave a quick glance back at her aunts, who were doing their best to distract Hannah. "Never mind that. I handled everything. We haven't much time. Were you successful with Lansing just now?"

The widow leaned back and reached out for both of Meredith's upper arms. "No" was all she said as she sadly shook her head from side to side. "Would have liked that one in my bed too. And yet, his interest seems only to lie with one woman."

Meredith widened her eyes. "Who? Tell me who and I shall hire her on at once. That is, if she does not ask too much."

"She will not cost you a farthing, I am certain of it."

"Really?" Meredith asked excitedly. "Who is she?"

"*You,* child."

Meredith touched her own collarbone. "*Me?* Impossible." Though it wasn't really so impossible, was it? The widow was echoing Hannah's words of only moments past.

"'Tis true, I swear it." With that, the widow kissed Meredith's cheeks.

All of the warmth seemed to run out of her head as Meredith watched the widow continue on toward the Featherton sisters to make her good-byes and quit the musicale.

Meredith blindly felt her way to the pianoforte bench and sank down upon its glossy surface.

Could her aunt Viola be right, after all? Was *she* the best bait to draw out the rake? As much as she tried to deny it, she could not dismiss the logic of it. If she used herself as bait, there would be no chance of error. And, of course, she would not have to rely on spying for second-hand reports of the results.

And he had shown his interest at the stables the other day, had he not? Besides, she'd already tested every other sort of woman of allure she could think of: the courtesan, the widow, the innocent. And not one was able to elicit the desired response in the man—the response that would offer undeniable proof of the rake he truly was.

There was no other way, was there?

Meredith came to her feet and fixed her gaze on Lansing, then started across the music room for him.

Lord—oh, and Mr. Chillton too—please forgive me for what I am about to do.

For now that her course was clear, she would stop at nothing to prove her hypothesis.

Once a rake, always a rake.

Imperative Six

After a time, a rake may say the following to the object of his desire: "You are probably the best friend I have." This simple phrase serves to double a woman's emotional investment. Be on your guard.

❧

Two days later, Meredith sat primly beside Mr. Chillton in her aunts' parlor, waiting for him to tell her why he had come to call without so much as a card to announce his intentions. It was quite unlike him, which intrigued Meredith quite a bit.

"For you, my dear Miss Merriweather." Mr. Chillton spread his thin lips into a handsome smile as he handed Meredith a small box wrapped in a scarlet ribbon.

Meredith blinked at the case. "For me?" She turned her face up to him briefly, then excitedly tugged at the ribbon, letting it fall first to her lap, then to the parlor carpet. "Why, this is so . . . so unexpected."

Unexpected was putting it mildly. This was the first present Mr. Chillton had given her. *Ever.*

And the fact that she was now sitting with a small jewel box in her hand, placed there by Chillton himself, greatly confused her. This was totally out of character for her frugal beau.

Why, hadn't he once told her—when she had spotted a pair of pearl earbobs that were the perfect gift for her sister Grace—that purchasing baubles and trifles was a complete waste of money? One could not eat them. They did not provide warmth or shelter from the weather, and they did not serve any useful function. They simply glittered.

In the end, his logic had prevailed.

She'd never forget the horrified look on Grace's face when she opened her birthday gift: a wedge of salted pork.

Yes, Meredith had almost convinced herself as she lifted the box's lid and peered inside that she would find a brass button . . . or something useful like that.

She blinked.

Meredith lifted the brooch she found inside to the light. "No, this can't be a . . . Clearly, these stones are not . . . and yet they look so much like—" She held the brooch up to the last rays of sunlight squeezing through the gap between the curtain panels.

"I hope you are pleased, Miss Merriweather," Chillton said tentatively. "'Tis a diamond brooch, as you have guessed."

The back of Meredith's eyes began to sting, not because of the great value of the gift, but rather because she'd judged Arth . . . Mr. Chillton so unfairly. For though he seemed somewhat frugal at times, he was also a very generous man.

This proved it. Completely.

A radiant burst of happiness showered over Meredith.

"Mother sent it round for you," Chillton added in the next breath.

"Your m-mother?" Meredith could hardly pry the words from her mouth.

"Indeed. Both she and Hannah thought it should be yours and that I should be the one to give it to you."

Meredith's spirits fell like a stone into a well. "So this brooch . . . is not from you?"

"Well, of course it is. Handed it to you, did I not?"

A heaviness settled in Meredith's chest as she realized why he had given her the gift. It was a test.

Chillton watched as she carefully replaced the brooch into the jewel box. A whisper of a pleased smile quivered upon his lips. "You *don't* like it," he said knowingly. "Told Mother you didn't care for such nonsense. We're of like minds on this issue, I said."

"It is lovely, Chillton." Meredith sniffed back the tears of disappointment that threatened. "However, you are correct. I have no need for it."

"That's my sensible gel." Chillton crossed his arms over his chest and grinned proudly. "You and I are a match in every way." Reaching out to her, he lifted her hand and raised it to his lips before standing. "Must be off now. Business, you know."

Meredith rose and politely followed him from the parlor into the passageway.

When he reached the entry hall, he turned to her matter-of-factly. "No need to delay any longer, Miss Merriweather. Please do me the honor of informing your aunts that I shall call Wednesday next, for I have a matter of great importance to discuss with them."

As Edgar closed the door behind Mr. Chillton, Meredith trudged to the window and watched him board his scuffed phaeton.

It did not take a great scholar to know that on Wednesday next, Chillton would seek from her aunts' permission to marry her.

An odd rawness scraped at the back of Meredith's throat and her eyes prickled. It was ridiculous to feel disappointed in the man for testing her. He was Chillton, after all, and he abhorred risk. She should expect no less from him.

With a sniffle, she wiped her eyes with the back of her hand and moved from the window. What a goose she was being.

Mr. Chillton was going to marry her—the thing she wanted most in this world. This was a time of celebration.

Or, at least, it should be.

She sank down on the settee and, as she rested her forehead in her hand, released a long sigh.

⁓

Three days later, Meredith's mood was bright once again. Her aunts, bless them, had accepted an invitation that would whisk the three of them from dreary London, albeit only for an afternoon, to a fashionable picnic at Brumley Court.

Instead of peering out her window at the tightly packed houses of Hanover Square, twiddling her thumbs and waiting for the days that stood between her and Wednesday to pass, Meredith now strolled atop Brumley Mount, drawing the country air blissfully deep into her lungs. Even from this distance, she could hear her aunt Letitia's booming laugh and it made her smile.

Scores of turreted white tents dotted the rolling green lawns of Brumley Court, on what certainly had to be the most splendid day of the season. The sun shone brightly overhead, and the air was unusually cool, bringing to Meredith's mind a day in mid-autumn rather than late June.

Ladies and gentlemen in straw hats sat on blankets, or on folding chairs clustered beneath the tents, supping on delicacies from wicker baskets. They strolled the hillsides hunting for a few late strawberries that had not been carried off by birds.

As Meredith walked around the perimeter of the glistening lake, she felt more relaxed than she had in weeks, for her future was all but assured. And so she could simply enjoy the day.

She turned and hiked up a gentle slope, where she could observe the picnic and the lake. Laying her paisley shawl on the dark green blades of grass, she sat down and turned her face upward to be warmed by the sun.

She lay on her back and amused herself by guessing which of the white-tufted clouds above might transform into a rabbit or a goose or some other fanciful shape as it moved across the rich cerulean sky.

She had just made out the lines of a horse, when someone passed between her and the sun, eclipsing it. As her eyes adjusted, she saw the dark silhouette of a large man.

Meredith jerked to a sitting position and cupped her hand to her brow in an attempt to discern his features.

"Why, Miss Merriweather," came an astonishingly low, masculine voice. "Your aunts, who were so kind to invite me to join your picnic today, told me I might find you up here."

"Lansing," came her yelp of a reply.

Oh no.

And the day had held such promise too.

She knew, though, that her aunts were only trying to

help, and in their presence, she had vowed to do anything to expose the rake, hadn't she?

Oh perdition!

Drawing in a fortifying breath, Meredith lifted her eyebrows and beamed at Lord Lansing, as if his arrival were a pleasant surprise.

She glanced surreptitiously at her reticule, wondering if she'd remembered to bring her miniature book of notes. No doubt she'd need it the very moment he left.

For there was no time like the present to begin. Besides, she had a question that needed answered: what made a rake advance and retreat?

Why, if a woman knew the answer, she could control the man to some extent, could she not?

First she'd have to lure him close. Simple enough, really. She probably wouldn't even need to utter a word. Then an idea struck Meredith. What if she repelled him with her words, but invited him with her movements? Which cues would the rake read?

This was not going to be nearly as difficult as the other women were making it. They were just letting themselves fall under his spell.

And she wasn't about to make that mistake.

And who knew, by nightfall, she might have another chapter for her guidebook.

Alexander sat down on the grass next to her, perhaps just a mite too close for her ease, but she would suffer his proximity for the sake of her experiment.

"Remember, you agreed at the musicale. . . . 'Tis Alexander . . . or just Alex, if you prefer."

"Very well . . . *Alex*." Her breath was coming fast and she knew she must slow it down if her body was to entice the rake to advance.

"Darling, I just love the way my name rolls off your pink tongue. Say it again. Slower this time." The thin skin around his eyes crinkled with amusement.

Meredith fought back any display of enjoyment: *Repel him with your words.* "No, I do not think I will. Wouldn't want to encourage the notion that speaking your Christian name is an invitation to . . . well, further familiarity." *Well done. Now contradict those words with your body.* Meredith counted to three in her head, then reached out her fingers and patted the top of his hand, before snatching them back.

A delighted little smile burst upon the rake's lips. "And simply speaking my name again would be wrong?"

Interesting. He heard her words, responded to them, despite her touch. Could words be more powerful than . . . The thought burst from her mind as Alexander trailed his hand down her forearm and over the top of her fingers, making her tingle all over.

Test him again. "Indeed, my lord, and well you know it. We've only shared the pleasure of each other's company, oh, perhaps on three occasions. We are barely acquainted." Meredith turned her face toward his and gazed deeply into his green eyes for several moments more than was appropriate.

Alexander worked his throat and swallowed deeply before responding.

That's right, my lord. Let the rake come out and play. Stop fighting your nature, she silently encouraged.

"Oh, I *know* you, darling." His tone was as sweet and slow as clover honey. Still, he did not venture too far. Her touch, her movements, seemed to determine the pace of seduction.

Fancy that. *She* was in control of the situation. Here she was, with London's most skilled rake, and yet she directed everything. Meredith felt almost giddy. La, the feeling of power was, well, rather exhilarating.

But then, Alexander's gaze slid slowly over her body, and when his eyes finally met hers, he smiled wickedly, making her insides dance a little.

She wished he would not look at her that way. Suddenly she was strangely warm all over. At that moment, Meredith felt her command lurch from her grasp. Her heart pattered in her chest.

She had to be in control, or else her experiment would fail.

Straightening her back, Meredith sat up taller. *Stronger words. Use stronger words.* "And . . . there is my Mr. Chillton to consider."

"Chillton?" Alex expelled a small laugh. "Why should Chillton object? You and I are merely new friends." He gazed out over the water beyond. "A friend I value and do so enjoy talking with."

"A friend?" Meredith had not anticipated this turn. Golly, she had to admit, she felt more than a little flattered. She leaned forward over her knees, trying to read his expression. "Truly, you think of *me* as your *friend*?"

⌐～

As she waited almost breathlessly for his reply, Alexander pondered the truth of his avowal. And to his surprise, he realized that in all the years of speaking those exact words—for they instilled trust and tore down a woman's defenses like no others in the English language—this was the first time he actually meant them. He did think of her as a friend.

Imagine that, he speculated.

"I do." He drew back his lips and smiled, feeling quite pleased that he did not have to revert back to his roguish ways and to lie to the woman. "You are a most amiable, intelligent and entertaining companion."

As Alex looked into her teasing blue eyes and at the pleased little smile budding on her lips, he couldn't help but notice that something seemed different. Somehow she seemed much more relaxed and happy this day.

"Well, Alexander, I honestly do not know what to say . . . except I like you quite well also."

Alex glanced around. "Mr. Chillton isn't here? If he is, I daresay I have seen nary a glimpse of the man."

Miss Merriweather's eyes darkened suddenly and she wrenched her hand away to tighten the strings of her reticule. "He is in Bristol, I believe . . . on important business."

"Ah, I thought as much."

She whipped her head around and faced him. "Did you? Why is that, my lord?"

Alex lifted a single brow. "Because your demeanor has changed. Until I mentioned his name, you were once again the Miss Merriweather I met at the stables in Hyde Park . . . more at ease."

Her eyes went large and round. "Sir, I was certainly *not* a tease in Hyde Park!"

"I did not say *a tease*—I said *at ease* . . . within your own skin."

She laid the reticule on the grass beside her and pinned

him with her gaze. "Just what, pray, do you mean by that?"

Alexander gave a small laugh. "You know, I think I'd rather not say. Might cause a bit of strife—and I do not need that."

Miss Merriweather snatched up her reticule, then stood and quickly bent to swipe her paisley shawl from the ground. As she rose up again, her eyes flashed an imperious warning. "I'll give you plenty of strife if you do not explain yourself, for I have the distinct impression that you have somehow insulted me."

"Good Lord. No insult. Just an observation . . . which I will share with you in exchange for leave to address you as *Meredith*." Alexander raised both brows and awaited her reply.

She stared at him, as if pondering the propriety of agreeing. "Fine. Call me Meredith—call me whatever you like . . . though not in the presence of others. Agreed?"

"Agreed, my darling *Meredith*."

She gave her eyes an exasperated roll. "Now that I have given you what you asked, will you please explain your so-called *observation*?"

A grin twitched at Alexander's mouth as he rose and offered Meredith his arm—which she begrudgingly took—for a stroll down to the sunlit lake at the bottom of the hill.

"It is not so great a secret, for I am sure others have made the very same observation as well."

Meredith stopped walking. She yanked her hand from his coat sleeve and folded her arms across her delightfully low-cut bodice. "I have grown weary of your folly, Lansing. Tell me what you mean, *please*."

"Very well." He sucked in a breath, then cocked his head to better observe her shifting expressions. "When you are in the company of Mr. Chillton, you are not the headstrong, mischievous and adorable Meredith I first met."

"I'm not?" Laughter burst from Meredith's lips. "I daresay, this is a bold observation, since we are only new friends and you have only had the occasion to see Chillton and me together at my aunts' musicale."

"That one time was all I required. You were anxious and stiff. You acted as though you doubted your every move. And that girlish white frock you wore—heaven forbid."

"You gleaned all of this from observing me for a few short hours?"

"I've always been a brilliant judge of people. I know when a person is pretending to be someone she is not."

"Then who am I, Lansing, if I am not my natural self when I am in Chillton's company?"

"I—I honestly don't know." Alexander looked deep into her eyes, attempting to make it clear that he was not playing some rakish game. "I do know that you are not the rigid, dreary, manner-cuffed miss I met at the musicale."

By God, from the shocked pallor of Meredith's face, one would think he'd gone and chucked her into the icy lake. This wasn't going at all the way he planned. His intent was to charm her, woo her, make her want him—not to antagonize her. He sought to convince her that Mr. Chillton was not the right man for her. How the bloody hell had everything gone so wrong?

"Y-you know not of what you speak."

"Argue all you like. Though you know in your heart, Meredith, that I speak the truth."

Meredith broke away from Alexander and, turning her back to him, stalked down the earthen path bordering the lake. She walked only twenty paces, as haughtily as she could manage, then stopped and watched the dust she'd kicked up overtake her and swirl about her hem.

What was she doing?

She was supposed to be coaxing him into dropping his gentlemanly facade. Instead, she'd let him rile her . . . make her emotions flare.

Jupiter, his assessment of her was correct, wasn't it? He was right. Otherwise, his words would not upset her so. This rake was too clever. *Damn him. Damn him to Hades.*

Yes, she was different when with Chillton. The man demanded it. . . . Well, all right, he *implied* that he expected better from her. It didn't really matter how he delivered it, anyway, for she'd gotten the message just the same.

Meredith whirled around, just as Alex closed the gap between them. "What is so wrong with a certain amount of decorum and manners, will you tell me that?"

"Why, nothing, darling."

"And will you please stop calling me *darling*?"

"*No.*" Alexander caught her arm and turned her so they could step along the path again. "Please do allow me to finish. There is nothing wrong with decorum and manners. What I find fault with is changing the person you are simply to please another."

"And you believe this is what I am doing?"

"I not only believe it, I know it to be the absolute truth."

Something in the surety of his tone rankled Meredith to her very core. Who was he, after all, to lecture anyone about changing who they are—when he himself was attempting that very same feat! For he was a rake pretending to be a gentleman—she just wasn't sure why he was doing it. Yet.

Granted, she couldn't lob that contrary fact back at him, not without totally ruining her own experiment.

Just then, a gentlewoman, trailing four children, approached on the path. Meredith nodded and smiled a greeting, but the woman's gaze was fixed on Alexander.

"*Scoundrel.*" The woman hissed and narrowed her eyes at Alexander as she passed them by.

Meredith smirked. "Friend of yours?"

Alexander cocked an eyebrow. "Obviously mistook me for someone else."

"They *always* do." Meredith shot him a wry smile.

Catching notice of the wooden-planked dock and the whimsical shell-shaped boats bobbing alongside it, Alexander grabbed her hand and pulled her from the pathway.

"Come with me, my sweet."

He coaxed her onto the dock, and before she knew what was happening, he wrapped his hands around her waist and hoisted her into a ridiculous periwinkle-and-coral-painted rowboat.

"I need your full attention and it simply cannot be had if I must worry that you will bolt from my side again at the slightest pause in the conversation."

Meredith stood in the center of the little boat, her arms folded across her chest, when Alexander leaped into its shallow hull. The wild rocking knocked her abruptly backward and into the Venus shell seat as her captain dipped the oars into the water and pulled them back toward him. Meredith could not manage a single word as the rake . . . Well, he was kidnapping her, wasn't he?

But she had to collect herself and resume her experiment. She'd been observing so many very interesting things—before he set her thoughts awhirl with his claim that he thought of her as a friend. Clever, that ploy. She'd have to make a note.

Meredith sucked in several deep breaths, trying to quell the anger simmering just beneath the surface, as she silently watched Alexander row. Jupiter, she had no idea that the man was so incredibly strong! Why, it took only several forceful strokes to propel the craft what had to be a furlong from shore!

Suddenly a hysterical laugh began to itch at the inside of her mouth. The whole moment was ridiculous. Here she was, sitting in a tiny bobbing shell in the middle of a rippling lake with London's most *horrid* rake as the craft's master and commander. Her cheek muscles pulled high as she fought to rein it back.

But then, Alexander, clearly aware of her struggle, waggled his brows at her. That was it. Tears crowded her eyes and suddenly Meredith could hold it back no longer.

A boisterous guffaw burst through her sealed lips.

There was no help for it. And now he was laughing too. It was all completely ludicrous!

Even more absurd was that at that moment, no matter how hard she tried to deny it to herself, there was nowhere she'd rather be. Nowhere.

How mad was that?

There. They were completely alone, just as Alexander had planned. It was time to begin, correctly this time, the slow seduction of his future wife.

Alex lifted the oars from the water and, turning them on their iron braces, lowered the dripping paddles inside the boat.

Meredith glanced at the picnickers in the distance, strewn across the hillside like so many dandelion wisps. Then clutching the port side, she peered deep into the water below, as if gauging its depth.

For the briefest of moments, Alex actually thought she might dive over the side and swim for shore.

"Considering the obvious quality and expense of your delightful silk walking gown, my dear, if you have a brain in that pretty red head of yours, you won't dare think of diving in."

"That is not what I was thinking, my lord." Meredith raised her eyes to him.

"What were you thinking then?"

"You really wish to know? Very well. 'And so he put her in a shell and there he kept her very well,'" quipped Meredith in singsong manner.

"What was that, a nursery rhyme?"

"'Twas nothing, my lord. I was just thinking what you wish to say to me must be very important, indeed; otherwise, you would not have felt the need to both kidnap and imprison me in this . . . shell." She slapped the flat of her palm twice upon the Venus shell seat behind her, sending a hollow *thump* through the boat's innards.

Although her words were serious, amusement still glinted in her blue eyes.

"You are not planning to seduce me, are you?" The ends of Meredith's soft pink lips lifted, nearly imperceptibly, and Alex had the strangest notion that she was challenging him to do just that.

"I am a gentleman. I do not seduce." He leaned forward, closer to her, and placed his hand on her knee. "I *woo*."

"Do you? And is that why you've rowed me into the middle of this lake?"

Smart girl. Alexander squashed the wicked grin that begged for a moment upon his mouth.

Time to play his hand.

"No, my sweet lady, I have not rowed you into the center of the lake to romance you. Had romance been my intention, I greatly would have preferred the hillside where I found you on your back, staring up into the clouds, thinking of . . . *me*."

Her eyes went round. "You?"

"You could not have been so rapt by daydreaming of your Mr. Chillton. I saw the look on your face. 'Twas thoughts of *me* that so consumed you that my approach went unheard."

Meredith stared mutely back at him for several seconds. "Oh, you would assume that. Actually, I was thinking that the cloud above me looked rather like a horse."

"Which brought you back to thoughts of *me*."

"My, you think highly of yourself. I was *not* thinking of *you* at all!" She exhaled a long breath through her nose. "Sir, what is it you wish from me? Please tell me now . . . then row us back to shore. I daresay my aunts must be ever so worried about me."

"I only want your ear, Meredith, as well as your promise to truly consider my words."

Meredith straightened her back as her hands nervously smoothed the lap of her gown. "Very well."

"I wish for you to reconsider your connection with Chillton."

"W-what?" she sputtered.

"I . . . Well, my staff has gone to considerable difficulty to ascertain your level of connection to the man."

"You did what?"

"And I know that you are not yet betrothed."

Her cheeks reddened and Meredith leaped to her feet, sending the boat rocking uncontrollably. She instinctively spread her feet for balance, but it was far too late. In the next moment, she toppled stiffly forward, like a felled tree, into Alex's awaiting arms.

Her wide eyes stared upward, blinking, and her gaze held his as her moist lips parted.

And at that moment, he knew, with all surety, that he would kiss her.

Imperative Seven

A clever rake will pay a unique compliment to a woman, on something most others will overlook. Beware of false sincerity.

~

It took Meredith only a half-breath to recognize the look in Alexander's eyes as he gazed upon her mouth. Golly, this was a bit alarming. Even more than Alex knowing she wasn't betrothed to Chillton. And that was a fine gob-smack!

For an instant, Meredith thought to lurch back into the shell seat, out of reach of his innumerable seductive charms. But then she recalled the whole reason she allowed herself to be plunked into a fantasy boat by the rotter and rowed out into the middle of the lake. Her experiment.

Without at first realizing it, Meredith glided her tongue slowly across the bow of her upper lip, moistening it as she waited. She'd issued a silent invitation—and he was about to accept it.

She peered deep into his green eyes, and as he leaned over, a faint gasp escaped her lips. Her heart thudded in her ears as his handsome face hovered just above her own.

Good heavens, he was going to do it. *Come on, Alexander . . . just a little lower,* she urged mentally. *Do it.*

"Kiss me."

Good Lord. Had she said that . . . aloud?

Alexander was smiling, a crooked, wicked sort of smile. "Whatever you wish."

Hold on just a tick. This isn't right. It doesn't count if I tell him *to kiss me, now does it? Certainly not scientific.*

Her hand shot between them and slammed against his chest. "Stop."

Alexander's mouth halted a scant finger's width from hers.

My word, she'd corrupted her experiment with her own stupidity.

His brows seemed magnetically attracted in his confusion. "I do apologize, but I distinctly heard you ask me to *kiss* you."

Meredith scrambled back into the cup of the shell. "Kiss you?" She forced a meager laugh. "No, my lord. You misheard. I said . . . er . . . *miss me.*"

Alexander leaned closer. "You said 'miss me'?"

"Why, yes. I was startled when I fell and I thought you would *miss me.*" She smiled as brightly as she could. "You didn't, though. You caught me all right. Good show."

My word, she sounded completely feebleminded.

"Oh . . . well, do forgive me, won't you, Meredith?" The right side of his mouth twitched, and for a moment, she thought he was going to laugh, but he didn't.

It was clear that he did not believe her story for a moment either.

Alex glanced at the softly rippling water, then searched the air until he spotted what he was looking for. "Yes, 'tis a mite difficult to be heard out here on the lake, what with the wind, the sloshing water and, of course, a . . . *scarlet rogue finch* crying above." He jabbed his index finger skyward. "Did you see it?"

Meredith didn't dare look. He was having a little chuckle at her expense. Well, she was not about to play along. He'd let the wriggly worm off the proverbial hook, and for that, at least, she was grateful.

For several long moments, Meredith did not say another word. Instead, she sat primly, staring back at Alex, her pink tongue flicking nervously over her plump lower lip.

But the look in her eyes, only a moment ago, had been plain.

She had wanted him to hold her tight and touch his lips to hers. She had desired the kiss . . . as much as he did, though she pretended otherwise.

Any other gentleman might have retreated in accordance with her wishes, but not Alex. Deep inside, he was no gentleman. And there was nothing like a challenge to set his heart pounding like wooden sticks on drum leather.

How he adored the thrill of the chase, especially with such bonny quarry.

Chillton didn't stand a chance against him.

What was it she saw in the man, anyway? Granted, a woman might find his aquiline features somewhat attractive, but Chillton dressed like a country squire at the best of times. Not like a man-about-town. And damned if the chap wasn't a dead bore.

Not that Alex had any firsthand evidence of this, though after the Feathertons' recent musicale, he had taken a brandy at White's and, out of sheer curiosity, had made a few inquiries about the man. Not surprisingly, none had ever heard of Chillton, and that was as good a testimony of his character as any.

The more Alexander thought about it, the more sure he became, based entirely on his keen instincts, that Meredith was Chillton's opposite in every way.

When he had returned Meredith to her home after the ballooning accident, had her aunts not claimed she was an adventuress, always into some mischief or another? Had he himself not seen her dressed in vibrant gowns cut to fashion's edge? Well, that as much proved his theory. Meredith thrived on adventure, excitement—something *he* could give her in her life. A stiff shirt like Chillton could not.

Meredith was, in fact, his own perfect match in every way that mattered, was she not? Alexander lifted the oars from the water and let the boat drift as he considered this.

Could it be that his father had something when he suggested Alex marry the woman? Married life—a state he must accept if he wished guineas in his pocket—would never be dull with the vivacious Meredith on his arm.

In fact, he should give her an adventure, soon. One she'd never forget. Danger accelerated romance, so there should be an element of it, but he'd keep her safe. Make her rely on him.

Alexander tossed one idea after another through his mind, until he seized upon the perfect plan. Gazing upon Meredith, he studied her for a minute as he fully plotted his strategy.

"I say, Meredith, darling." Alexander lifted the oars and plunged them into the water once more.

Startled by his voice, Meredith's head lurched up.

"You mentioned seeing a horse figure in the clouds."

"I did. What of it?" Her right foot was tapping as if an orchestra were blaring behind him.

Tension still ran tight between them, and Alexander knew he could use that taut cord to draw Meredith closer.

"Got me to thinking . . . Have you come to any decision about the bloodstock we discussed at the stables in Hyde Park?"

Her eyes rounded and she sucked a bit of lip flesh into her mouth. "Hmm . . . honestly, no. I do not feel I have sufficiently . . . uh . . . surveyed the field. I am aware that the best horseflesh to be studied is at Tattersalls. However, as you know, my lord, women are not permitted inside, so I fear my quest for a horse must end."

Ah, now he had her. "Perhaps women are not permitted inside, but that does not mean I cannot get you onto the grounds for a close look at London's premier bloodstock."

"Can you now?" Her eyes lit up at the first hint of a scheme. "This I should like to see."

"Should you? Well, then I shall send my carriage for you tomorrow afternoon."

Meredith's eyes sparkled with excitement and she laughed. "You are mad if you think you can accomplish this."

"Nevertheless, I assure you, I can do it. *If* you do as I say."

"I must admit, I have never excelled at obeying others."

"Those are the terms. I know the terrain. You must do as I instruct, else we may be caught."

Raising her brows playfully, Meredith inclined her chin. "Very well, my lord. Tomorrow at three, shall we say?"

Alexander grinned cockily back at her. "Three 'tis."

Lawk! Just yesterday, on the lake, she had joked that Alexander was mad, but today Meredith held in her hands solid evidence of his complete insanity: a complete gentleman's ensemble of clothing.

Meredith sat alone for some moments inside Lansing's carriage, then looked through the open door to Mr. Herbert, who, she assumed, was his valet. "And his lordship expects me to wear this?" Her nose started to tingle, and her lips itched in want of a good guffaw.

"Indeed, miss. Sent me along in the event ye needed assistance tying yer neckcloth. All you need do is rap on the cabin wall, me brother will rein in the team and I shall descend from the perch to assist ye."

Meredith narrowed her eyes and looked down her nose. "So he actually wishes for me to dress in a moving carriage?"

"Aye, miss. Wouldn't do, he said, fer the Featherton ladies to witness their niece in men's garb—were ye to dress in yer own chambers."

"I see."

The valet, all starched up and perfectly pressed, was so serious—in this, the most ludicrous situation imaginable.

"Very well, Mr. Herbert. I shall—"

"*One.*"

"I beg your pardon? One . . . what?"

"Ye may address me, as his lordship does, by *One.*"

Was it just her, or was everything this day slightly askew? "Very well . . . One. I shall dress on the way to Tattersalls." She looked down at the bundle of clothing. "I am sure I can manage."

There didn't seem to be nearly so many layers as women's wear, after all. How difficult could it be?

~~~

The journey to Tattersalls from Hanover Square took no more than a quarter of an hour—at least twice the time the distance required.

Meredith was thankful for the carriage's snail's progress—no doubt a request from One—since it took her every one of those minutes to rid herself of her petticoats and walking gown and to don the gentleman's ensemble.

When at last the cabin door opened, Meredith stepped out—in her guise as "Lord Stilton," a young gentleman from Cheddar. She'd decided that having made his fortune in cheese, he had ventured to Town to purchase a fine horse.

Upon seeing her, Alexander brought a fist to his mouth, though she could still see the edges of his lips lifting on either side.

"One, did you not offer to tie the neckcloth?"

"I did, me lord."

"And did you tie it?" A snicker of sorts shot through Alexander's nostrils. "For I daresay, I have never seen such a knot in all my days."

"No, me lord, I did not tie it." Then One added far beneath his breath, "How could ye assume such a thing?"

"There was no need for One's assistance." Meredith lifted her chin. "I tied it myself, and I am quite pleased with the result." She proudly flicked the left loop of the great bow that sat upon her throat. "Showed a little creativity, 'tis all. Nothing wrong with that."

"The point, Miss Merriweather, is to slip beneath the notice of the members, not to draw undue attention." Alexander exhaled a long sigh. "'Tis far too late to retrieve a freshly pressed cloth from the house for One to tie for you. The auction is about to begin."

Meredith raised her arms from her sides and turned slowly about. "So, otherwise, am I presentable?"

She did present, actually, Alexander decided, closing the carriage door as he circled Meredith for a more complete impression.

One had done a remarkable job outfitting the tall miss. Her hair was twisted up and hidden into the column of her beaver hat. The gentleman's coat she wore was cut broad in the shoulders, hiding the gentle slope of her own delicate set, while its drape and coordinating waistcoat covered the hourglass pinch at her waist and her other . . . womanly attributes.

"The Hessians are a bit short in the toe." Meredith limped in a small circle to accentuate her discomfort. "Though, I own, I simply adore the breeches." She looked to One. "I say, may I purchase them from you after our little game this day?"

One ignored the comment completely and instead addressed Alexander. "The Hessians are sized fer a young gentleman." He lifted a telling brow and nodded secretly.

Meredith set her hands on her concealed hips. "Are you implying that my feet are overlarge, sir?"

One shook the smallest amount, but his voice remained level. "I only informed me lordship as to the cut of the boot, miss. I beg yer pardon if me comment insulted ye in any way. 'Twas not me intention, I assure ye."

"Very well, then." Meredith kicked the tip of her ebony walking stick and twirled it in a neat circle before returning it to the ground. "Shall we enter?" She started forward.

Alexander grabbed her arm, pulling her back before the carriage. "We have to get a few rules straight before we dare enter."

"Oh yes, the rules." Meredith pulled from his grip and crossed her arms at her chest. "Go on. I did promise, after all."

"First, you do not speak, even if spoken to. Second, *never* look anyone in the eye. Avert your gaze. For while the clothing may disguise your sex"—Alexander ran the back of his fingers slowly across her cheek—"your lovely face will reveal it."

Meredith brushed his hand away and Alexander caught a flash of annoyance in her eyes.

"Is that all, my lord?"

"No, my dear." Alexander urged Meredith from the side of the carriage and toward the gates of Tattersalls. "The last rule is most important—remain at my side at all times. No matter what happens, if anything goes wrong, you stay with me. Understand?"

"Of course, I do." Meredith's face took on a sheen of excitement. "What could possibly go wrong?"

"What indeed?" Alexander carefully tamped down any hint of worry in his reply.

What indeed.

Tattersalls' famed ring was completely deserted, which surprised Meredith. With an auction about to commence, she would have expected to see at least a horse or two being tested by handlers for potential buyers.

Still, Alexander seemed to know where he was going and so she followed him, taking two long strides for his one just to keep up. As she swung her arms, pumping them to remain beside Alexander, she allowed her hand to brush his. All in the name of research, of course. Once, she was so bold as to let her fingers accidentally touch his right thigh as they walked.

Though she doubted a rake would dare attempt to seduce a woman while playing such a risky game as they were today, Meredith wondered if he at least considered it. And though she was dressed as a gentleman, this afternoon she intended to make quite certain he remembered there was a woman beneath the coat and breeches.

Her reasoning for joining him today was twofold, even if a little mad. Firstly, it was a brilliant opportunity to insinuate herself more thoroughly with Alexander. Proximity would bring a more intimate knowledge of the rake, and she hoped this knowledge would enable her to find his weaknesses, which, in turn, would lead him to reveal his true self. Had she been prepared for his surprise arrival at Brumley Mount, and had she not allowed herself to become distracted, she might have accomplished this yesterday. Today, however, would do just fine and she knew her time would be well-spent, whether or not she gleaned any tidbits for her guidebook. For Meredith had a second reason for being here.

It was beyond daring to slip into the "gentlemen only" bastion of Tattersalls. And, admittedly, the mere thought of being the first woman to breach its high gates was more than a little titillating to Meredith.

There were the gigantic horses to consider, which concerned her, but certainly they would all be on lead and she would be safe enough—especially with Alexander at her side.

Her heart thudded as they turned into what she took to be a courtyard with a columned cupola in its center, with a bust of Prinny perched atop it. It was there that Tattersalls' patrons had gathered. Outside the stables was a wide passageway covered by a peaked roof upheld by pale columns. It all looked quite regal indeed.

At least forty gentlemen, many referring to the small folded booklets in their hands, gathered in the open-air passage.

Meredith cuffed Alexander's shoulder, as she'd seen men do from time to time. He stumbled forward a couple of paces, since he'd been leaning to the left for a better view. Turning his head, he frowned at her.

"I only want to know what they are reading," she muttered.

Alexander brought a vertical finger to his lips. "No talking, remember?"

What a ridiculous rule. No one could hear her. "But—"

"Shh!" Then Alexander shook his head slightly and put his lips nearly to her ear. "It's just a catalog describing the horses to be auctioned."

She could feel his warm breath on her cheek and it made her tingle all the way down her spine.

He began to turn, but Meredith caught his lapel and drew him close again. This time, she let her breath caress his face, let her concealed breasts press against his ribs, if only for a moment. "I say"—she lowered her voice, hoping to approximate a young man's timbre, but without much success—"should we not have a catalog as well?"

Alexander raised his brow; then he grabbed her arm and pulled her up against one of the wide columns. He stared down into her eyes for several seconds before speaking. "But you've got to stop touching me." Then a wry grin appeared on his lips. "We've time enough for that later, my dear."

She stared back at him, not wholly sure what she could possibly say in reply.

"Stay here and do not move until I return."

Meredith tipped her head, just like she reckoned a man would, and watched Alexander stamp his way through the dusty graveled courtyard.

She exhaled a sigh. Except for testing Alexander's resolve to act the gentleman, this afternoon wasn't proving to be nearly as diverting as she'd hoped it would. And if she didn't know better, she would think women didn't attend events at Tattersalls *not* because they were not permitted, but because it was too tedious.

By degrees, her gaze was drawn to the roof pitch. Several glassed windows had been set at the outermost slope, allowing large rectangular beams of sunlight to illuminate the passageway.

Suddenly the gentlemen all rushed forward, and Meredith heard the unmistakable clop of hooves on the dry, beaten earth.

Her chest began to clench, and inside, her heart thudded impossibly hard against her ribs.

Horses.

Horses. Oh Lord.

Sweat began to bead in tiny pearls where her beaver hat met her hairline.

Truth to tell, Meredith had known Tattersalls was not the right place to test or observe Alexander. She'd only fooled herself into believing it was. In the presence of so many others, he would never be more than the perfect gentleman.

In reality, she'd only wanted to come because Lansing made it sound so irresistibly daring. And yet, it hadn't been risky or exciting . . . or anything. Why, she'd just walked right in. No one even really looked at her.

Coming to Tattersalls was just plain dim-witted—given her dread of horses.

The earthy scent of the beasts filled her nostrils. She clapped a hand to her chest and struggled for a breath.

Just calm yourself. There is nothing to fear. Nothing. Surely the horses are all on leads.

She swallowed hard. *Be a man. Be . . . Lord Stilton. He would not fear horses. Be Lord Stilton,* she told herself.

Meredith closed her eyes tightly as the clopping grew louder. *Jupiter!* There had to be at least four huge horses in the passage now. Four—just a few yards away.

Her gaze frantically searched the courtyard for Lansing. Where *was* he? By now, her knees had lost all solidity and had been transformed into two wobbly globs of marmalade conserve.

Over the shifting beaver hats before her, she could see the broad back of a fifth horse. Lord above, it was monstrous. Why, it had to be even larger than Lansing's mammoth beast.

Her teeth began clacking together. In another moment, it would be too late to do anything. She'd be paralyzed with fright.

Go now. Now. Her hand slid away from the column and she felt her legs carrying her backward.

From the farthest corner of her eye, she caught sight of the cupola in the distance. At once she knew that she'd be safe there until Lansing returned.

Meredith spun around in the gravel and immediately slammed into a gentleman.

"Oof!" As she struggled to catch her breath, Meredith raised her eyes and readied an apology on her lips.

"Oh *no*."

Meredith swallowed the huge lump that had suddenly formed in her throat. Her heart pounded heavier still and black speckles began to swirl like blue-winged ravens across her vision.

Startled pale eyes stared down at her. "Miss Merriweather?" came her beau's all-too-familiar voice.

She teetered on the heels of her Hessians and felt his long fingers ring her arms, steadying her.

He was *here*. Here . . . at Tattersalls!

"Ch-Chillton," she muttered.

Imperative Eight

A rake knows the appeal of a knight in shining armor.

Chillton's hands slid up to Meredith's shoulders and shook her, whisking away the dark haze descending over her consciousness like a threadbare death shroud.

"What in the king's name are you doing *here*—and dressed . . . so, so shockingly?" His voice was noticeably strained, but he spoke in low tones, to ensure, she knew, that no other would overhear and witness her disgraceful actions.

Meredith could feel her lips moving, and yet no sound was coming from them. There was no way that she could admit what her little charade as a gentleman was all about. He'd never understand.

She peered nervously up at Chillton. "I thought you were away . . . on a business excursion."

"I had been, but was called back to meet with a merchant from India. He was only to be in Town for a short while. . . ." He paused momentarily, as if lost in thought.

"Don't understand why he never showed—the note said Tattersalls, I am sure of it," he muttered before his gaze grew sharp again; then he pinned his attention on Meredith. "My reason for being here is of absolutely no consequence." His mouth snapped shut before he finished, and wrinkling his nose as though Meredith smelled as foul as the dung heap near his foot, he studied her gentleman's garb. "What are you doing here, dressed like—"

"Well, Chillton, my man," the rake's voice called out from behind her, "you've gone and blown the surprise all to pieces."

Meredith snapped her head around to see Alexander striding quickly toward them across the yard.

His gaze searched her face for but a blink of a moment as he pried her from Chillton's angered grip and moved her to the left behind him. Though their eyes had met for only the briefest of seconds, somehow she knew that Alexander had already assessed the nature of her predicament.

She had no choice but to trust him utterly and pray that he could right this odious mess.

For in that moment, her fate . . . and her future had been passed into his rakish hands.

"Why, Lord Lansing." Chillton seemed startled by Alexander's sudden appearance. "Why are you here . . . together with Miss Merriweather? I—I do not understand, but I must, so one of you had better serve up a suitable explanation for this"—he raised his hand and traced his nicked walking stick from Meredith's beaver hat to the toe of her Hessians—"this abomination."

A nervous whimper squeaked through her lips. Alexander turned and drew Meredith up beside him, then laid a gloved hand on her. "Miss Merriweather, you need not try to salvage the situation. Your surprise is ruined. We best tell Chillton, here, the truth."

"The . . . t-truth?" She jerked her chin upward and stared at Alexander, frantically searching his eyes for any hint to his meaning. To her surprise, she saw nothing there but a look of supreme confidence.

"Yes, for I fear we have no choice," he said resignedly. "Wouldn't want Chillton to get the wrong impression."

Meredith leveled a confused gaze at the rake. "Of course, you are right, Lord Lansing." She swallowed hard. "I give you leave to tell Mr. Chillton . . . the . . . um . . . truth."

Alexander hooked his left arm around Chillton's shoulder and his right around Meredith's and began to guide them across the yard. "Perhaps we best take our discussion away from the ears of the other gentlemen, eh?"

"Absolutely." Chillton nodded his head and gave a wary glance at the gathering of the bobbing mass of beaver top hats behind them as they walked.

Alexander did not stop when he reached the edge of the yard, however. Instead, he led them through the gates and outside of the establishment altogether.

He stopped when they reached the packed road, and with a whistle to his driver—who looked . . . Well, she'd be snookered if it wasn't the cranky old valet who wanted to tie her neckcloth earlier—summoned his carriage forward.

When the conveyance barreled before them and Alexander's hand shot out to wrench open the door, Chillton became noticeably agitated. He pressed forward, using his lean form to block anyone from boarding the town carriage. "Now, see here! Neither of you will leave this spot until I have had an explanation."

"And you shall have it, sir, once I have set Miss Merriweather on her way, beyond the reach of any eyes that might still recognize her—after *your* outburst." Alexander nudged Chillton back away from the door, then caught Meredith's arm, pushed her up the steps and handed her into the carriage. "For I would not wish to see *your* indiscretion cast doubt on Miss Merriweather's character."

"My indiscretion?" Gradations of scarlet rose into Chillton's face like the sky above a setting sun. "*She* is the one wearing a coat and breeches, for God's sake."

There was a definite spike of fury in his words and Chillton suddenly lurched forward and reached into the carriage as if to pull her from it.

Meredith slid back into the darkest, farthest corner of the carriage and cowered against the folded bundle of her walking gown.

Alexander caught Chillton's arm and held him back. "Yes, she donned a gentleman's suit of clothes, but she did it for you, dear sir."

Dumbstruck, Chillton swung around to face Alexander. "For me? I do not—"

"'Tis true. She risked all, in a completely selfless act, to please *you*."

Meredith leaned forward over her knees and cocked her ear toward the still-ajar carriage door so she'd not miss Alexander's revelation.

"Don't you see, man?" Alexander began. "She wanted to gift you with a horse—"

"For your new phaeton," Meredith called out helpfully from the belly of the carriage.

Alexander really was telling the truth, as he understood it, anyway. They were at Tattersalls so that she might compare the pedigree and merits of the horses in order to better choose which sort to give Chillton. Actually, it was quite clever of him to be honest in this way. She should have thought of it herself.

"Yes, a horse for your new phaeton," Alexander echoed, casting a secret wink in Meredith's direction. "Naturally, only the best would do for her betrothed—I mean for you, sir."

"Well, that is all fine and dandy," Chillton snapped, "but that does not explain her egregious actions."

"Does it not?" Alexander looked down his nose at the slightly shorter man, and Chillton shifted uncomfortably within the confines of his too tight coat. "Only the best would do, which meant purchasing the beast from Tattersalls—an establishment where women are not allowed."

"So she dressed as a gentleman to gain admittance." Chillton peered dubiously inside the carriage at her.

"Exactly." Alexander straightened his spine.

Meredith saw it then, a slight finger-tug at the line of his neckcloth, the only hint that Alexander was not quite at ease with the confrontation as he let on.

"Of course," Alexander added, "the idea of dressing Miss Merriweather in a coat and breeches was entirely mine."

Chillton's gaze shot inside the dark interior of the carriage for Meredith's confirmation.

"It was indeed," she was compelled to mutter, though she felt like a goose for allowing Lansing to take the blame.

Though, in truth, it *was* his idea. Entirely.

Still, she had agreed to his wild scheme, for her own purposes, of course—her own *entirely noble* purposes, she amended. And for that, Meredith supposed she really did share in the blame. At least, a little bit.

So, being the upright gentlewoman that she was, she

added, "I engaged Lord Lansing to locate the perfect horse for you. When the search led us to Tattersalls, he was perfectly willing to act as my agent in the purchase. I, however, wished to compare the horses myself. I could not be dissuaded. So, Lord Lansing came up with the only possible way for me to enter Tattersalls, without disrupting the auction—for me to dress in a gentleman's clothing."

The crimson had all but drained from Chillton's face when he finally spoke again. "I appreciate your desire to gift me with a fine horse, Miss Merriweather, though your methods for obtaining such a beast are beyond bounds. I . . . I had thought you had matured and put your impulsive nature, which left you at odds with Society, behind you."

A tremor shook Meredith's innards. "I have, sir, I assure you."

Alexander's eyes grew impossibly dark and he grasped Chillton's arm. "Sir, she is not to blame."

Mr. Chillton turned his head and leveled a stern gaze up at Alexander. "Of course, she is not, for she is but a woman."

Meredith felt the pinch of Chillton's statement.

"But you, Lord Lansing," Chillton continued, "are a gentleman, born and bred, and should have realized the jeopardy such an outrageous act would place Miss Merriweather's reputation in."

Alexander cocked a brow and a slow grin spread his lips. "Sir, sullying a reputation was the last thing on my mind. My only thought was to assist Miss Merriweather in any way possible. Never could resist a pretty face."

Chillton's eyes rounded and his jaw set hard. Meredith was sure the conversation would end in fisticuffs, but then a bell in a distant tower sounded. A scattering of gentlemen funneled out of Tattersalls like cattle through a stile, defusing Chillton's fury.

At once, Alexander grabbed the carriage door and slipped his head inside for the briefest moment. "You owe me, Miss Merriweather."

"I know."

"And I always collect what I am owed." Alexander winked at her; then before she could respond, he slammed the door shut. Through the window, Meredith saw Alexander give a quick nod to the driver on the perch and in an instant the carriage jerked and started off down the bumpy road. Meredith scooted forward and pressed her nose against the glass window to peer out.

Both men's gazes were fixed on the rolling carriage. Alexander whisked off his hat and, with a flourish, honored her with a stylish bow.

Chillton merely remained as still and erect as one of the columns at Tattersalls, the look in his eyes as cold as stone.

Heavens. Had her adventure destroyed Chillton's interest in her as a wife? Her skin prickled at the horrid thought.

The carriage rolled onward, transforming Alexander and Chillton into two specks in the distance. Meredith flopped back against the leather squabs and exhaled.

Chillton at Tattersalls. Fancy that.

She began to remove the toe-squeezing Hessians while mulling over their accidental meeting.

Despite Chillton's reasonable explanation for being there, something about the whole incident smelled a little off.

Before Meredith knew it, the carriage turned into Hanover Square and stopped before her aunts' fashionable home.

She'd been distracted by far too many disquieting thoughts. For by the time the frosty-haired driver opened the carriage door, Meredith had done no more to transform herself into a lady than remove her clumsy Hessians.

And so, in her gentleman's garb and shod only in her silk stockings, Meredith gathered up her bundled gown, glossy leather boots and reticule, and raced on her toes up the walk and through the front door of number 17.

She had just pressed the heavy lock closed with a barely audible click, when she turned and came face-to-face with her aunt Letitia.

"Well, now, this is a new look for you, isn't it, dear?" Letitia's snowy brows raised so high that they almost were lost under the folds of her lavender turban.

Drat. Meredith exhaled slowly. "I had hoped to avoid the necessity of explanation."

"Working on your guidebook, were you, gel?"

Meredith nodded resignedly, knowing her aunts would wish to hear the entire story—then help set her to rights again with Mr. Chillton.

Aunt Letitia shook her head slowly, back and forth, as she took in the sight. "Sister will want to see this," she said at last. "Do not leave this spot." With that, she turned and walked down the passage a few steps. Her head disappeared through the doorway of the library and the hiss of excited whispers met Meredith's ears.

Then Aunt Letitia's head reappeared. "Dear, come and have a sit with us in the library."

"Of course, Auntie, just as soon as I remove these clothes and . . ." Meredith started down the passage at full

speed. She'd only just decided to pass her aunt by and se-
quester herself in her chamber, when a cane shot out before her, blocking her way.

"*Now,* if you please." The expression in the old
woman's eyes was bright with amusement. "Come inside,
gel."

Meredith slowly set her bundle on the table in the passage. Removing her beaver hat, she let her curls fall about
her shoulders as she lowered her head and begrudgingly
followed her aunt into the library.

The two old ladies settled themselves in two matching
chairs positioned on either side of a cold hearth, leaving
Meredith to stand before them, hat in hands, and eyes
downcast.

"Odd," her aunt Viola began, "when you left the house
earlier this afternoon, I could have sworn you were wearing . . . a very flattering walking gown." She flicked her
lorgnette, snapping it into place, and peered through it,
studying Meredith closely.

"You are correct, Auntie." Meredith gulped. "I donned
my coat and breeches on the way to Tattersalls. Lord Lansing's valet supplied everything."

"So you were at Tattersalls with Lord Lansing. Did
you hear that, Letitia?"

"I did indeed, Viola." She flicked her eyebrow, almost
as though she were amused. "Most interesting."

Not another word was spoken as the two old ladies
studied Meredith with some interest for several moments.
It was almost as if they'd never seen men's clothing
before.

By degrees, the two old dears' expressions seemed to
evolve from amused to . . . curious.

"How do they wear, dear?"

Meredith glanced up and saw Aunt Letitia eyeing her fawn breeches.

Aunt Letitia cleared her throat. "I daresay, I always imagined that breeches would be restrictive, uncomfortable, you know . . . especially for men."

"I agree, Sister." Aunt Viola nodded. "I always thought the Scots had the right of it. Kilts, you know. Makes more sense for a man."

"Oh, I adore men in kilts, for I do so enjoy the sight of well-shaped calves." Aunt Letitia tittered and clapped her hand to her bounteous chest. "Makes my heart pitter-patter just to think of it."

Aunt Viola's eyes went as wide and round as tea saucers. "Oh, Sister, we should visit Scotland. How exciting it would be!" Her knees bounced with enthusiasm.

"Heavens." Aunt Letitia chuckled. "I don't know if my poor heart could endure it. All those Scots in their kilts—"

"Aunties," Meredith interrupted. She could endure this prattle no more. If she was to be reprimanded, she wished her aunts would speak their minds and be done with it. "Aren't you the least bit upset with me?"

"Upset, dear?" Aunt Viola's eyes blinked in confusion at first; then a smile crept across her thin lips. "Of course not, silly child. Though, for your sake, I do hope no one recognized you in your . . . costume. For if they did, it cannot help your case with Mr. Chillton, now can it?"

Classic Aunt Viola. Daintily getting straight to the crux of the matter.

Meredith glanced down at her stocking feet and distractedly dug her toes into the carpet. "Sadly, the only person who recognized me was Chillton himself."

Her aunts exchanged meaningful glances. *"Oh dear,"* they replied in tandem.

"So he *did* catch up with you," Aunt Letitia muttered so softly that Meredith wasn't quite sure she heard her right. "Chillton didn't do anything rash, did he?"

The two lavender-frocked women traded concerned glances.

"He was not pleased to see me at Tattersalls, that is for certain." She paused for a moment and gathered her courage about her. Then, over the next handful of minutes, Meredith recounted all the afternoon's events precisely as they had unfolded.

"If you've set your cap for Chillton, dear, it cannot be wise to spend your days with the dashing Lord Lansing, no matter the reason," Aunt Viola advised.

"Viola, she is only conducting research," Aunt Letitia snapped. "It is not as if the gentleman is romancing her . . . or an attachment is forming between our gel and Lansing."

At that moment, the queerest thing happened. Both of her aunts focused their lorgnettes on her. A wash of heat suffused her cheeks.

For certain those eagle-eyed ladies would think her guilty—but she was innocent. Completely innocent!

"You need not worry. My interest in Lord Lansing is entirely limited to research for my guidebook."

Then something suddenly occurred to Meredith. She looked from one aunt to the other, crinkling her nose. "A moment ago, you said, 'So he *did* catch up with you.' Why, it sounds as though you knew Chillton and I would meet this afternoon."

"We assumed you might meet." Aunt Viola's head was bobbing like a hen's at feed time. "You see, when Hannah came by for tea, she informed us that her brother was off to Tattersalls for the afternoon."

"But how did you know *I* would be there? I did not tell you about my plans." Meredith peered through squinting eyes at her aunts.

"Oh that." Aunt Letitia wriggled up from her chair, took Meredith's beaver hat into her hand and guided her into her own vacated seat. "It was all quite a coincidence, really. Sister and I happened upon your book of notes last eve—"

"You just happened upon it?"

"Why, yes. It was all quite by accident. Then when it fell off the table and opened, we noticed the paragraph detailing your plans today to go to Tattersalls."

"Serendipity." Aunt Viola nodded her head matter-of-factly. "It was as if the Fates had meant for your paths to cross this afternoon."

"I assure you, Auntie, what happened was not serendipitous. Chillton was shocked by my behavior. I have never seen a man look so sullen." Meredith leaped from her chair and began to pace the length of the library. "Why, had Lord Lansing not intervened, I do not know what Chillton might have done, or said." She turned and looked pleadingly at her aunts. "I have ruined my chances with the man. What am I to do?"

"Shall we fetch the rule book?" Aunt Viola asked, her faded blue eyes blinking with anticipation. "It never failed us before."

"*Rules of Engagement* . . . where is it? I remember it being along this shelf. . . . Ah, here it is." Aunt Letitia pulled a crimson book from the shelf and cradled it in her arms. "It did work wonders for your older sisters."

"Yes, I know, Auntie, and I do appreciate your willingness to assist, but truly, I will come upon a solution by myself, if you do not mind." Meredith chewed the inside of her lip. "Where is Hannah now?"

"Right here."

Meredith whirled around to see Hannah walking through the parlor doorway.

A grin burst about Hannah's mouth. "Meredith, why in all the world are you wearing a coat and breeches?"

"Long story. You may rest assured, however, that I will explain everything to you soon enough."

Meredith crossed the room and took Hannah's hand. "Come with me while I change into something more suitable. I desperately need your counsel."

"My counsel . . . whatever for?"

"Dear, Hannah is so young," came a whine from Aunt Letitia. "Perhaps what you really require is guidance from someone . . . oh, more experienced in the ways of gentlemen?"

Meredith turned and gazed back into the library. Both her aunts looked positively crestfallen that they had not been asked to intervene.

"In another instance, perhaps, Auntie, but Hannah here is Chillton's sister, and who better to help me understand what he might be feeling?" She looked into Hannah's vibrant aquamarine eyes. "Will you help me?"

"I suppose so. If you think it will help."

"I do, but we must hurry. Haven't got much time, you know. We must come up with a way to correct this situation before Chillton calls to retrieve you, else I fear there will be no wedding—*ever.*"

Imperative Nine

Never trust a rake.

✒

Less than an hour later, Meredith and Hannah, their clammy hands clasped tightly together like frightened schoolgirls, crept down the stairs, having heard the low hum of a gentleman's voice coming from the parlor.

Meredith's heart pounded rhythmically in her ears, for she was certain that the visitor was none other than Chillton, come to retrieve Hannah. She shouldn't be so worried. She was just being ridiculous. After all, Lansing had offered a perfectly satisfactory reason for her . . . *unusual* appearance at Tattersalls, hadn't he?

And it was this very reason that Meredith imparted to Hannah. However, after some discussion, she and Hannah had decided it prudent to prepare a supplemental story for Chillton, just in case. It was a good story too, no fat or gristle to chew on to make it indigestible. Chillton would swallow it whole—or so Hannah assured Meredith.

Meredith was hardly convinced, but she had no other

choice but to adhere to their plan. After all, the man was already here and there was no time to twist a stronger yarn.

"Are you ready?" Hannah whispered as they stood outside the parlor door.

"No, though I must do this if I wish to salvage any possibility of a relationship with your brother." Meredith placed her hand on the door latch and had depressed it halfway when she realized that the voice mingling with her aunts' inside the parlor was not Chillton's. The timbre was much too low.

Praise be. Her shoulders relaxed and a sudden lightness seemed to boost her fallen spirits.

The door *swooshed* open, sucking the cooler air from the passageway through Meredith's hair and lifting loose tendrils about her cheeks as she came face-to-face with her aunt Letitia.

"I thought that might be the two of you whispering outside the door. Come in, do come in. For you will never guess who has come to call."

And there he was, standing behind her dear turnip-shaped aunt. "Lord Lansing!"

"Indeed, though you needn't be so surprised, Miss Merriweather. Certainly you did not think I'd pack you off in my carriage, then not have the courtesy to see that you arrived safely home."

The edge of Alexander's lips were twitching a tiny bit. If Meredith had any doubt that he was suppressing a grin, it vanished when, over the top of her aunt's head, he winked at her.

"I am a gentleman, after all." He looked to her aunt Viola and his tone became familiar and confidential. "Though I daresay *some* still find this fact hard to believe, even after not one, but two gallant rescues."

Aunt Viola's eyelashes fluttered as she fell prey to his charm. "I believe you, Lord Lansing."

"So do I," added Aunt Letitia.

Hannah grabbed a handful of her skirt and swished her way beside Meredith. "And I!"

All eyes fell upon Meredith.

The muscles of her cheeks dragged upward. "I reserve judgment until additional evidence is produced."

Flicking her fingers dismissively, Aunt Viola expelled the breath from her lungs in a long sigh. "Well, that's our gel. Stubborn as they come."

"Alex—er . . . Lord Lansing, you may attribute my surprise at seeing you here to the fact that Hannah and I had expected to find Mr. Chillton. He had promised to retrieve her."

"Ah, I see." Alexander offered an elbow to Hannah and the other to Meredith, then led them to the settee.

There was a thumping, and Meredith looked across the room to see Aunt Letitia patting the empty space on the sofa between her and her sister. "Lord Lansing, do have a seat. It is ever so much easier to converse when one does not have to look up all the time." Her hand drifted unconsciously to the back of her neck.

"Quite right." Alexander strode across the parlor and wedged himself, as politely as he could manage given the small amount of space between one bony and one fleshy set of hips. "As I was about to say, Miss Merriweather, Mr. Chillton *was* here, but he left on foot only moments ago."

"My brother was here?" Hannah leaped to her feet. Flames of red licked her cheeks. "And he left me—*again*?"

"Yes, dear. He . . . um . . . stopped by . . . for but a moment while you and Meredith were above stairs." Flapping her right hand in the air, Aunt Viola bade Hannah to sit. "Do not fret, young one, your brother left the phaeton behind for you."

Hannah's eyes narrowed. "How considerate of him."

"It was, was it not?" Viola nodded. "Owing to the lovely weather, he was determined to stroll home. 'Tis not far, you know."

"He said you, Miss Chillton, knew how to handle the reins." Alexander leaned forward slightly. "I would consider it an honor, however, if you would allow me to take the reins for you."

Hannah huffed out her breath. "No, no. He had the right of it. I can drive the phaeton myself. Often do, in fact. My brother was not about to waste good coin on a driver, so I had to learn, didn't I?"

Edgar, her aunts' dutiful manservant, stepped inside the parlor and tipped his head at his employers.

"Now, now. Never you fear, my dear." Aunt Letitia glanced at her sister and the two old women stood, prompting Lansing to his feet as well. "Our carriage has already been brought around. Sister and I will take you home now. One of our footmen will follow in your brother's"—she cleared her throat—"phaeton."

"Why, thank you kindly." Hannah's disappointed gaze flickered over Lord Lansing, and Meredith knew her friend regretted not seizing the handsome lord's offer to escort her home. "I do not wish to impose."

"Oh, have no worries." Aunt Viola took her fichu from Edgar, flashing him a brilliant smile in thanks. "You are not imposing. Sister and I could use the fresh air."

Aunt Letitia stepped into the passage and tossed a soft

lavender shawl over her shoulders. "Come along, child. Your brother will be worrying about you."

"That, I seriously doubt," murmured Hannah as she accepted her bonnet from Edgar.

Alexander followed the women to the door.

Seeing that he meant to leave with them, Aunt Letitia raised her walking stick and held it across her body with two hands, as if meaning to block his way. "My lord, I would be greatly indebted to you if you stayed with Meredith whilst we are away. She has had such a trying day, I would not dare ask her to set foot outside this house again."

"Auntie, he is a *bachelor*," Meredith protested.

"Annie—she is Meredith's new abigail—will be here," Aunt Viola consoled. "So, Lord Lansing, you need not worry about appearances."

A conspiratorial grin bounced from one aunt to the other.

Alexander flashed the elderly women a broad smile. "I am honored to have your grandniece entrusted to me." Then he turned his head and leveled a simmering gaze upon Meredith. "'Twill be *most* delightful, I am sure."

Jupiter. Just what are my aunts thinking?

As the thought piqued her curiosity, Aunt Letitia snagged Meredith's wrist and hauled her along as she hobbled to the front door. "This will be a perfect opportunity for you to conduct a little more research, hmm?"

Ending her words with a decidedly wicked chuckle, her aunt followed her sister and Hannah out the door and down the steps to the street.

Oh dear. A tenseness cinched Meredith's middle as the shocking realization dawned on her. Her aunts had given up on Chillton for her and now they had Lord Lansing lined up in their matchmaking sights.

Meredith stood at the door and waved as her aunts' gleaming carriage, followed by Chillton's ragtag phaeton, rolled from Hanover Square.

As she returned to the parlor and Alexander, she caught a glimpse of herself in the overmantel mirror. It pleased her to see her countenance was calm, almost serene. And yet, the sight amazed her as well, for Meredith felt as on edge and unsure of herself as when she was presented to the queen a few years ago.

"Well, now, Alexander . . . how did you happen to be here, already, when Chillton arrived? Your carriage could not have returned to you so quickly."

"You're right. Chillton gave me a ride. Jolly good of him, considering what had happened, don't you agree?"

"I thought when I left, the two of you were far closer to exchanging blows than pleasantries."

Alexander cocked his leg behind him and propped his foot against the doorjamb. He raised a sly brow. "Then perhaps you don't know Chillton quite as well as you might believe."

Had Alex chuckled at the confused expression that twisted Meredith's normally beautiful face, she probably would have slapped him. And he would have deserved it too.

Of course, Meredith could not have known that it was he who'd secretly arranged for Chillton to return to London. Had she realized that he'd lured Chillton to Tattersalls by hinting at a business opportunity by way of a false letter from a nonexistent merchant, he might have earned a backhand as well.

Though, even if Meredith accused him directly of writing the letter, Alexander still could have claimed innocence—even before a man of the cloth—for, in actuality, it was Georgie—God bless him—who had helped him out with that little detail.

Yes, his plan had worked brilliantly, all right. Heated Chillton's blood to boiling, it did.

"Your Mr. Chillton, my dear, would never allow his temper to drive him to violence." Alexander pushed away from the doorjamb and moved toward Meredith.

She took a step backward, before something inside her steeled. Her chin lifted and she arched a brow, challenging him. "I do not agree with you."

"Then you would be wrong." He moved to her and took her small pale hand in his. Turning it over, he exposed her wrist to the light breaking through the parlor windows. "Why, my lovely, I could touch you like this before his very eyes," Alexander placed the pad of his index finger into the shallow of her open palm and swirled it slowly in a circle, "and he'd do naught but ply me with a few words of caution."

He thought she would pull away then, but she didn't. She only stared at his moving finger.

Her subtle acquiescence sent the blood inside Alexander's veins pumping faster, and the thought of stealing a kiss grew ever large in his mind.

He bent then and lowered his mouth, until he could feel his own heated breath bouncing off her soft ivory skin. She smelled lightly of lavender and rose blossoms . . . as though she'd scattered petals in her bath. *Mmm.* He liked that.

"I daresay, I could even . . ." He raised his eyes and looked deeply into hers before he continued. Still, she did not move.

"You could even . . . what, my lord?" she asked breathily. Her voice was husky, strained. The wide-eyed, wary expression in her eyes told him he walked the edge, but he pressed onward. For somehow—from experience, he guessed—he knew she wished him to.

"I could even . . . do this." He lowered his mouth until his lips brushed the thin skin of her wrist. He could feel her heartbeat throbbing against his lips. Faster. Faster still.

Alexander cradled her elbow in his left hand and held her hand in his right. He pressed his moist lips into the center of her palm, then began to kiss a slow trail to her wrist, over the exquisitely sensitive skin of her inner forearm.

He heard a faint gasp, and yet she did not struggle or protest, though her breathing grew harder, deeper.

Alexander drove onward with single-minded focus. His mouth's journey would not end until he felt her lips against his own.

He straightened as he reached the heavy silk puffed sleeve covering her shoulder. He released her hand and elbow then, and slid his left hand around to rest in the small of her back, while the other cupped her chin.

"Now, were I to . . . kiss your mouth, for you do owe me, darling"—Alexander tilted her chin and brushed her lips with his own—"Chillton might take issue with my boldness . . . but it would be worth it."

Her lips, tasting of tea sweetened with honey, made him yearn to drink in her essence. He pulled her tight, until he felt the softness of the tops of her breasts molding against him, and kissed her, harder this time.

She sighed as his mouth moved over hers and her arms came up around him. "Worth it," she murmured.

Alexander nudged her mouth open with his lips and slid his tongue into the warm smoothness inside. As if by instinct, her tongue mingled with his, as they blissfully suckled and fed on one another.

He felt himself harden against her and knew he should pull away. God, how he wanted her, with a wanton urgency he'd never known. What was it about Meredith that made him desire her like no other?

Perhaps he'd simply gone too long without a woman. It had been two months since his father's edict, after all, and until today, he'd remained the consummate gentleman, ignoring stirrings below his waist, as well as the lusty gazes of women he would have bedded in earlier days.

Of course, this is it. Has to be.

Then suddenly he heard the clop of hooves on pavers, the command of a driver reining in his horses.

His eyes snapped open and both he and Meredith stood frozen, their lips locked fast as they listened. And there it came, the manservant's footfall in the passage, the click of the front door opening.

"'Tis my aunts!"

Alexander and Meredith repelled from each other—one racing to the sofa, the other to the settee.

The parlor door opened.

"Well, now, I trust you had a good visit," Lady Letitia quipped.

"We . . . um . . . we did indeed, Auntie." Meredith tucked a loose lock behind her ear and unobtrusively straightened her skirt. "Quite a delightful visit."

"Oh, then Lord Lansing has told you all about it. Good, good!"

Smiling brightly, Lady Viola crossed the Turkish carpet and sat beside Meredith. "Does it not sound exciting, dear? I shall ask Annie to pack your portmanteau right away."

Meredith's jewel blue eyes darted from her aunt's face to Alexander's. "A portmanteau? Where am I going?"

"I beg your pardon, ladies, but I thought you might rather tell your grandniece the news." Alexander felt a tenseness in his muscles as he waited for the Feathertons to reveal his invitation.

"Oh!" Lady Letitia plunged her walking stick into the carpet and caned her way to Meredith. "Why, dear, we are going to Harford Fell—all of us."

Meredith looked up at Alexander. "Your family home? Might I ask why?"

Smiling uncomfortably, Alexander nodded and had just opened his mouth to speak when Lady Viola interrupted.

"To obtain a horse for Mr. Chillton—from his family's own stables," the old woman blurted.

"W-what?" Meredith's gaze shot to Alexander.

"Miss Merriweather, you do still wish to purchase a horse for Mr. Chillton, do you not?"

Meredith nervously squeezed a fistful of her skirt in her hand. "I have no choice now. No other gift will do, else I fear Chillton will never believe my reasoning for being at Tattersalls."

"*Exactly.*" Alexander released the breath pent up in his lungs. "But a horse from the establishment might only serve as a reminder of seeing you there dressed as a man."

"Sadly, Lord Lansing is quite correct, dear." Lady

Viola took Meredith's hand in hers and patted it gently. "I had not wished to reveal this to you, but now I feel I must. Mr. Chillton was so troubled by your outrageous doings this day, that he feared losing his temper in your presence, and would not even enter our home to retrieve his own sister."

Aunt Letitia bobbed her head. "'Tis true. He simply rapped upon the door, then remained on the outer steps until we were clear about how Hannah was to return home."

Meredith lowered her head and seemed to study the pattern woven into the Turkish carpet. "I . . . I had not realized my actions could affect him so."

"Oh dear, do not fret, for I believe traveling to Harford Fell is the perfect solution for easing you back into Chillton's good graces."

Meredith snapped her head upright. "Really, you think so?"

"Yes, yes, of course!" Her Aunt Viola raised her frosty white brows excitedly. "Surely you have heard that Harford Fell is known far and wide for fine bloodstock."

Alexander knew he almost had her now. Time to cinch it. "And since your troubles with Mr. Chillton are partially my fault, I will sell you a horse for the sum of one guinea."

"One guinea?" Meredith coughed a laugh. "You are joking, surely."

"Well, Chillton will not accept a horse I gave you. If I sell you the horse, however, at a very *reasonable* price, he will think you most thrifty."

"And you know how your Mr. Chillton admires thrift." Lady Letitia slowly walked across the parlor, her gaze fixed on her grandniece.

"You all are mad if you think this will work." Meredith paused a moment and Alexander could see her mind processing the scheme. Finally a resigned smile tipped Meredith's lips. "Oh, very well. I shall accept your kind gift, Lord Lansing."

Lady Letitia plopped onto the sofa beside Alexander. Her walking stick fell to the floor as she clapped her hands merrily. "Oh, is Lord Lansing not the most generous man in all of London?"

"So it would seem, Auntie." Meredith's eyes grew as sharp as a hawk's as she leveled her gaze upon him. "My, my, Lord Lansing, you are just one surprise after another, aren't you?"

"Indeed. But then I enjoy surprises, don't you? Wouldn't do for life to become too predictable." Alexander nonchalantly ran the tip of his tongue over his bottom lip, causing Meredith's cheeks to flush. "How boring that would be, eh?"

Imperative Ten

A wise woman never allows herself to be lured into a rake's home. There she is certain to be compromised.

Two days later, Meredith found herself at ancient Harford Fell, a sweeping stone structure regally perched atop a mountain. Before their arrival, she'd heard her aunts prattle on about the enormity of Lansing's ancestral home. Therefore, she hadn't expected anything less than a veritable castle, but still, her first glimpse of Harford Fell left her quite speechless.

Plump turrets—the sort fairy-tale damsels were always being imprisoned within—bookended either end of the main portion of the house. But, it was the high arches, vaults, slender vertical piers and counterbalanced buttresses that convinced Meredith of its true Gothic origins. Had an addition not been made in the home's more recent past, of French windows and a balcony stretching the entire front length of the house, Harford Fell might have been drawn straight from one of those gothic tales of horror Hannah so enjoyed reading.

Within no more than twenty minutes of their carriage's arrival, Meredith found herself ensconced in an exquisitely appointed, dark-paneled bedchamber.

Here she found herself completely in awe too. Not that all the rooms she had toured weren't tastefully decorated—because they were, of course. Though this chamber in particular was . . . well, special in a way the others were not.

Meredith laid the claret-hued gown she thought to wear to dinner upon the bedstead and crossed to the hearth. It bothered her a little that she could not determine the reason for the room's appeal.

Maybe it was the delightful collection of Sèvres figurines arranged upon the mantel. She lifted a small porcelain shepherd girl and examined its obvious quality for several moments before a bowl of fruit on the hearthside table caught her notice. Plunking the shepherdess down, she grabbed a shiny red apple and bit into it.

Dropping into the wingchair, Meredith gazed upward at five small paintings hanging over the mantel.

Odd, in every other room she'd been privileged to see, a grand portrait of some sort graced that prime spot. But not here. Here was a collection of boldly rendered landscapes—not unlike her own sister Eliza's paintings of Dunley Parish, where Meredith and her sisters were raised.

As she crunched into the sweet apple, remembering fondly how she and her older sisters used to swing on the scarred tree branches in her family's orchard, she realized that it made her happy just to sit here and gaze upon the paintings.

Maybe that was it. Meredith lowered the apple from her lips. The chamber was welcoming.

Just then, the door swung open and Alexander strolled into the center of the room.

"Damn me!" Alexander blinked in astonishment. "I beg your forgiveness. I hadn't heard you'd been settled in here."

Meredith came to her feet. "Have I been placed in the wrong chamber?"

"Not at all. Came in here out of habit, I reckon." At once, Alexander's eye fixed on the little shepherdess on the table beside the fruit bowl.

He swaggered across the room, in that rakish way of his, carefully picked up the Sèvres in his hands and replaced it on the mantel. He started to turn back to Meredith, when, instead, he paused and positioned the figurine toward the window . . . then aligned the six others in identical fashion. "There we are. Perfect."

Meredith crinkled her nose. "I—I do apologize for touching the figurine. She is quite exquisite and I could not help myself." She quieted for a moment, then studied Alexander. "She is yours?"

"Am I so obvious?" Alexander laughed. "It was a gift from my grandmother long ago. All of them were." He joined Meredith at the table and bade her to sit. "This was my bedchamber. Still is . . . when I visit."

She shot to her feet again. "Oh dear. Of course, I will ask to lodge in another room."

"No, no, no. Wouldn't hear of it. I find it the most comfortable chamber in all of Harford Fell, and would consider it a great honor if you were to stay here and enjoy it."

Alexander started to leave the room. "Again, pardon for the intrusion. I'll just head next door, shall I? If anyone asks you why I was in your assigned chamber just tell them what a bloody awful sense of direction, I have. It's true. Ask the staff. They'll tell you."

As he reached the threshold, he bowed politely, then turned and slammed into the wall. "See, what did I tell you? Just awful," he said, grinning, as he quit the room.

Meredith laughed, though she knew he was just having fun with her. Still, he was right about one thing. His bedchamber was most comforting, and, somehow, knowing it belonged to Alexander made her feel all the more at home here.

Lifting the lid of her portmanteau, Meredith withdrew her coffer and removed her book of pages, then slipped the pencil from its center fold.

She glanced out the French windows, past the balcony beyond, to see the sun just beginning to rest in the lush treetops on its way to bed.

Settling at the table once more, Meredith dutifully set herself to the task of recording her successes in bringing out Lord Lansing's true nature.

Though she'd never admit it aloud to anyone, Meredith would be sad when her reasons for keeping company with Lansing came to an end. For recently, she'd felt as at ease with him as she did in his room.

She mentally shook her head. *Bah.* She had to remain focused. Earlier, she'd been far too preoccupied with helping her aunts with packing for their visit to Harford Fell to concentrate on her guidebook. Now that she was here, she needed to get back to what was important.

She dampened the pencil with the tip of her tongue. *Let's see. Might as well start where I left off.* A record of their day at Tattersalls.

Hmm. Well, now, that day hadn't been *quite* the success

she had hoped for. *Oh well.* She'd just begin someplace else.

All right, maybe our . . . visit in the parlor. Yes, much better. The rake had kissed her in there—made her tingle all over. A smile curled her lips at the heated memory.

Meredith lifted her pencil excitedly, ready to record all the delicious details, but then paused again and thought back to two niggling little words she seemed to remember uttering in the passion of the moment.

Worth it. Golly, she'd agreed that his kiss would be worth Chillton's anger.

She gulped down the stone that seemed lodged in her throat. *Oh dear.* What had she been thinking? Aghast at her impulsive words, she cupped her hand over her mouth.

Suddenly it became clear to Meredith the real reason she'd put off recording her results—she had no results to record without impugning herself! Why, she'd ruined every single experiment by issuing her own invitation to him. In no way had he taken unfair advantage of her.

Meredith's breathing slowed as another possibility occurred to her. Was this simply part of his rakish genius? Was Lansing so clever in his seduction that he could convince his lady that he was the innocent and she the party at fault?

Perdition! She was such a fool.

Of course this was his strategy—and she'd allowed it to work brilliantly. Well, no more.

Meredith grinned inwardly. What a fantastic chapter this was going to make for her guidebook.

Now that she was aware of this ploy, the rake would be forced to ply other methods of trickery and seduction, creating great fodder for additional chapters. She just had to remember to keep her head about her.

Pressing the pencil hard to the page, she wrote down a reminder: *Baiting him, permissible. Flirting with him, necessary.* Wasn't it? But breathily accepting his advances: *Wrong, wrong, wrong.* She circled the reminder and drew three arrows pointing to it, lest she forget.

That was a line she must never step across again. She must remain focused and on task—to draw out the rake, to record his methods of seduction without falling victim to them, as she had with Pomeroy.

The door crashed open then, startling Meredith so that she dropped her book of notes on the floor.

"'Ere we are, Miss Meredith," said Annie, her rather earthy lady's maid. "Brought some tea to tide you over till dinner. Oh, will you look at that? I see you've already taken out the claret gown. That one's so lovely. Shows off your curves, it does. Why his lordship won't be able to take his blinkers off you."

"Do you really think so?" Annie's comment warmed Meredith from within, and sent a little dart of excitement through her too. Well, she did have a mission, after all, and looking fetching was key to her success.

"I thought to bring along the garnet pendant and earbobs. Their tones match perfectly, they do, and will bring out the darker strands of red in your hair."

"Why, thank you, Annie." True, her maid might be a bit coarse around the edges, but she knew her fashion. Or *appeared* to, at the very least.

Meredith wasn't sure why, perhaps it was the phrasing Annie used when speaking of gowns or the colors she selected for her, but sometimes she got the distinct impression that her maid's keen sense of style arrived as a missive in the post each week from her former maid, Jenny Penny.

It was no secret that Jenny Penny . . . or rather, the Countess Argyll, since her marriage, was Annie's closest friend and the party completely responsible for her being employed by the Featherton sisters after her own departure.

"What's this?"

Meredith looked up and gasped as she saw Annie whisk her book of notes from the floor and start thumbing through it. She stared in shock as she saw Annie reading it. *Oh no.*

Racing forward, she grabbed the book from the abigail's hands, a little more roughly than she ought, for Annie lurched backward in alarm.

"I do apologize, Miss Meredith. I had no way of knowin' that the book was private-like. Thought it might have belonged to his lordship and had fallen off the table when I set the tea tray down."

"Oh, Annie, I am sorry for grabbing it the way I did. 'Tis only my . . . um . . . thoughts."

"Like a diary?"

"Y-yes. Like that. 'Tis nothing, really." Meredith exhaled through her nostrils as slowly as she could. There, she appeared perfectly calm.

A saucy grin erupted on Annie's lips. "Whatever you say, miss." She bobbed a heavy curtsy and made to leave the bedchamber when Meredith heard her mutter under her breath, "That's the cheekiest *nothin'* I've ever read."

Meredith scolded herself for not taking her usual care in concealing her book of notes. Now it was too late. Annie had seen too much. Still, there was no possible way she could have read more than a few lines. But which lines? That's what mattered.

There was no way she could allow Annie to leave the

room now, not with her grand penchant for gossip and exaggeration.

She had to give the abigail a good explanation, else within minutes everyone below stairs would get a very warped version of the contents of her book.

Why, she could not even imagine what sort of fantastic stories Annie's gossip could spawn. Which, of course, the earl and Alexander would hear in due course, and . . . and—her breath was coming fast—then her reputation would be in the chamber pot. *Again.*

"Annie?" Meredith sucked in a breath.

The lady's maid stopped mid-stride and turned around. "Yes, miss? Would you be wantin' somethin' else? Biscuits, perhaps?"

"No, no. Nothing. I just wanted to . . . get your opinion." Meredith gestured to the caned beech wood chair across from hers.

"My opinion. My, you've never asked what I thought before." Annie smiled proudly and wedged her ample bottom into the chair. "If I can help in any way, miss, you know I will."

Meredith sighed resignedly. There was no other choice but to tell Annie the truth.

"What I am about to share with you is very confidential. It must not be shared with anyone. Do you understand?"

Annie's eyes went wide. She swiped a cross over her heart. "I swear your secret is safe with me, Miss Meredith. Just one question, first."

"Anything."

Annie leaned close and whispered across the table, "Will you be wantin' your aunts to hear this too?" She held up her left palm and poked it with her right index finger. "Because they're hidin' just outside on the balcony."

Meredith rolled her eyes and turned around in her chair. "You might as well come inside, Aunties. I was about to explain my plan to Annie."

~

As the door to the expansive dining room slid open and the gentlemen emerged into the drawing room, Lady Letitia elbowed Viola. "I say we do it," she whispered. "Meredith said she'd do *anything*. La, we all heard her, and I vow she meant it."

"Not *that*, Sister. It's too extreme, even for us, Sister." Lady Viola watched the earl and the handsome Lord Lansing join her grandniece at the card table. She did not miss the interest in the young lord's eyes as he gazed upon Meredith, though her grandniece seemed oblivious. She was evidently too enthralled by what the old earl was saying as he gestured to the largest of the many large gilt-framed Italian paintings hanging against the soaring red walls.

"Do you want to see our gel attach herself to that . . . that Chillton fellow?"

"He is her choice, Letitia. We must respect that."

"Bah! She only thinks she wants the buttoned-up sort." Lady Letitia snorted. "He'll crush her, I tell you. He'll grind her spirit right into the earth."

Viola shivered and tightened her shawl around her shoulders. "No, Sister, he is a kind man. A good man. The only fault I see in Mr. Chillton is his rather frugal ways."

"Frugal? He's a miser, if I ever met one." Lady Letitia raised her finger and pointed it most impolitely in her sister's face. "Mark my words, Viola. If he marries our Meredith, he will control her in the same manner he controls his guineas—with a tight fist."

Tears began to catch in Viola's lashes as she began to see Meredith's future through her sister's eyes. "Do you really think so? If you are right . . ."

"I am always right. And don't get all sniffley, Viola. You'll just call attention to us. Besides, dear, we have a chance, *tonight*, to help Meredith set her life on the correct course again."

From across the wide, luxuriously appointed parlor, Lord Lansing beckoned the ladies to join them. With nods and identical make-do smiles, Letitia and Viola silently accepted his invitation.

Like a moon glade on the blackest sea, the candlelight from the chandelier above the card table gilded every wave of the young buck's ebony hair. Even Viola could not deny that Lansing was probably the most striking gentleman she'd ever laid eyes upon. Yet, there was some question in her mind about his character. Was he still the wicked rake as Meredith claimed, or had he indeed reformed and become the gentleman she now saw before her?

"Letitia . . . are you sure he is the one for our gel?" Viola whispered from behind her lavender lace fan as she and her sister slowly caned their way across the brightly patterned parlor carpet.

"How can you question it? They are kindred spirits meant for one another. Those two lovebirds just don't realize it yet. And yet, they will . . . come morn," Lady Letitia whispered. "I vow it."

By eleven in the eve, Meredith noted that the Earl of Harford was already quite foxed. For some unknown reason, he was aided into inebriation by her own aunts, who seemed to be ever-present at his side, waiting with a full bottle of spirits each time he drained his glass.

Meredith narrowed her gaze at her Aunt Viola, who seemed agitated and skittish the entire evening. Aunt Letitia, on the other hand, remained her own jovial self without having taken one glass of wine all evening. This is what disturbed Meredith most. Her aunts adored cordial—enjoyed it every night without fail. So why were they sipping naught but tea?

Something was afoot.

The earl looked up from his cards and, through his bleary eyes, studied Meredith carefully. "You *are* a bonny lass. Intelligent too," he slurred. "I see why Alexander brought you to Harford Fell." He lifted his gaze from her and turned to Alexander. "It heartens me to see you've taken my advice, son."

Her aunts' heads whipped around and their eyes met. They stared, silently at one another for several seconds, before returning their gazes to their cards. Though they fought to conceal it, there was no stopping the pleased grins that appeared on their painted-on ruby lips.

Alexander cleared his throat. "Father, Miss Merriweather has come to purchase a horse." He pinned the earl with his gaze. "For no other reason."

The earl chuckled. "I do not doubt that." He winked broadly. "Let me know how you find the stallion in the last stable, will you, dear?"

Meredith felt the heated color rising in her cheeks and she hastily reached for her crystal goblet, only to find it empty.

"Dear, allow me to fetch you another." Aunt Letitia looked to Alexander, whose face was set with the most uncomfortable expression Meredith had ever seen. "And a brandy for you, Lord Lansing."

Alexander glanced about the room and, likely seeing no footman in attendance, came to his feet. "Please allow me."

"No, no!" Aunt Viola shrieked. When all eyes fixed on her, she softened her tone. "Letitia does so like to be 'mother' when serving tea—or anything else."

"Well, this eve I shall share the honor of pouring with you, my dear sister." Aunt Letitia waggled her brows at Viola. "Come. Won't you help me?"

"Uh . . . certainly." Aunt Viola slid her reticule from the table beneath the notice of all . . . except Meredith.

As the two old women walked to fetch the libations, Meredith could hear them whispering fiercely. However, with their backs turned to the table, she could not make out a single word. But she knew—oh, she knew—that they were hashing over some sort of scheme.

For several minutes, Letitia and Viola stood on the far side of the drawing room, lifting crystal decanters and setting them back down again, without seeming to pay heed to what they were doing. Each time Meredith glanced in her aunts' direction, they were immersed in their private discussion. Given their proclivity toward outrageous strategies, Meredith was left cold with dread.

At last, her aunts returned to the card table, bearing a salver of assorted drinks.

"Here we are!" Aunt Letitia had affixed a smile on her face as manufactured as the purple paste jewel sewn onto her matronly turban. She handed Meredith her glass of cordial.

"And *this one* is for you, Lord Lansing." Aunt Viola held the brandy snifter out, but the earl, who was already neck deep in his cups, snatched it from her hand, instead. "Oh dear! That one is not for you. 'Tis for *Alexander*!"

Alexander waved his hand and rose from the table. "Not a problem. Drink as you will, Father. I shall pour myself another."

The portly earl mumbled something unintelligible, then lifted his drooping head from his chest and tossed the brandy down his throat in a single draft.

Aunt Viola's eyes bulged in their sockets. "He'd had quite a lot of brandy already." She looked helplessly to her sister, sputtering. "What s-shall we do, Letitia?"

"You need do nothing at all." Alexander took up Viola's hand and patted it. "He'll nod off soon enough. The footmen will see to his needs."

Lady Letitia edged closer and, pressing her hand to Alexander's shoulder, guided him back into his chair. "Lord Lansing, please allow me." She looked pointedly at Viola and jerked her head, beckoning her to join her again.

Meredith's gaze met Alexander's in silent communication as she took a sip of her cordial. Her lips tingled strangely for a moment.

Hmm. She took another draft and dabbed her moist lips lightly together. My, she'd never had cordial like this. Must be from France.

Then she took another sip followed by another and yet another. Now her lips were . . . a little numb. *How peculiar.*

Alexander must have noted the confused expression on her face. "Is there something wrong with the cordial?"

"Oh no. 'Tis fine, really." As she spoke, Meredith realized that now her cheeks were numb too.

"Father makes it a habit to acquire only the best."

A low humming called Meredith's attention to the earl, who was smacking his lips together . . . in his sleep. She looked to Alexander. "Well, I wasn't going to comment, but the cordial is far sweeter than I've tasted before. And—"

Before another word left her lips, Alexander snatched up her glass and took a sip. He swirled the liquid around in his mouth, then paused and looked back at Meredith.

"You're right. In fact, I can almost taste . . . almond, is it?" He drank again.

"Are your lips numb too?"

Alexander shook his head.

"Take another drink. You'll see."

And so Alexander did. In fact, so perplexed by the queer effects of the cordial was he, that the young lord swallowed down every last drop.

Her head was spinning furiously now, and Meredith knew, if she did not seek out her bed soon, she would be too dizzy and disoriented to make it to her chamber at all.

"Do forgive me, Lord Lansing. I don't know what has come over me. I am so tired, I find I must retire for the evening."

She glanced up at her aunts, who were watching her almost expectantly.

"I shall assist you, dear." Aunt Viola helped Meredith from her chair. La, her legs felt weighted, though her head seemed to float somewhere near the vaulted ceiling.

As her aunt led her through the parlor door, Meredith glanced back at Alexander, who was patting his cheeks and laughing.

"Can't feel them." He looked up at Letitia. "Go ahead,

give them a good hard smack. I vow, it's the oddest thing, but I won't feel a thing."

Then she saw her aunts' expressions change from concerned frowns to pleased grins.

Heavens above. What had they done?

~

Slam!

Meredith awoke from a very deep sleep to see a large dark shape break from the shadows of the door. Her heart began to pound. She opened her mouth to scream, but there was no sound. None at all.

Then she realized why. Of course. She was dreaming. And it was one of *those* dreams. The sort where if she crawled out of bed, she'd just find herself wallowing slowly through space as if she were drowning in a hogshead of molasses.

She was still groggy as she slid up against the headboard to await the arrival of whatever it was stalking closer. She pulled the coverlet over her head, then lowered it just enough to peer over.

The shape grew larger as it drew up beside her bedstead.

Just a dream. Just a ridiculous dream, she chanted inside her head, even as her breath came faster and faster.

The coverlet moved. It was being pulled back.

Something heavy pressed down on the mattress beside her.

Oh God, the *thing* was in the bed with her. The blood pumping through her inner ears drowned out all other sound. Her legs shook madly.

Just a dream! Just a dream!

A hand, a man's hand, touched her face gently. She stilled at once.

Wait. She knew that touch. Knew that slightly musky, manly French scent.

Her heart slowed and her legs quivered beneath the covers as she realized who'd joined her in bed . . . in her dream.

"Darling?" came a low, heady voice.

Alexander.

Imperative Eleven

A rake will take advantage of confusion, then act.

❧

After a few attempts at speaking, which resembled a dormouse's squeak far more than words, Meredith found her voice. "You've got the wrong bed. You must go!"

She tried to give him a good hard shove, but the cordial still flowed sleepily through her body and, instead, she fell against his side.

"Oh botheration." Meredith tried to push up, but she was just too exhausted. So she lay there, poking his ribs with her fingertip, hoping he'd do the gentlemanly thing and leave.

"I do apologize if you find my company shocking, Meredith; nevertheless, I am not leaving this bed tonight."

"You must! What if my aunts find you here? Viola is just across the passage, and Letitia is in the very next chamber. I will be ruined." *Again,* she added silently. "Your chamber is just on the other side of that wall. I will help you to the balcony door. You can enter from the outside."

"Meredith, if you wish to leave, you may, but I barely made it here. I have no motive for remaining in this bed with you other than my legs are like pudding and I can hardly keep my eyes open."

His arm came down around her as he pried off one boot, then the other, using his heel and toe for leverage. "Damned cordial. Never felt anything like it. Must have been off. . . ." His voice grew languid. "P-poisoned us both, I reckon."

"More likely my aunt slipped something into it." Her eyes were growing heavy again. "Into your father's glass too. He fell asleep almost right away, didn't he?"

When there was no reply, Meredith quieted and listened in the darkness. Alexander's breath was slow and she could feel his chest rising and falling in the gentle rhythm of sleep.

As he slept, the slow drugging heave of his chest, coupled with the intoxicating warmth of his body, made it impossible for Meredith to keep her lids open.

So, she decided to rest her eyes for just a moment. Then she would get up. Yes, that's what she'd do.

～

Her dreams were not frightening this time. This time they were bliss.

She was lying on the hillside at Brumley Court, staring up at the white fluffy clouds when suddenly she detected the slightest smell of French musk. She turned her head to see Alexander standing over her, blocking out the sun. She smiled at him, but instead of doing his utmost to provoke her, he slipped his hand beneath her loose locks and dragged her mouth to his.

Someone would see them, she was sure, and Meredith broke from the kiss to look around. But there was no one at all. No white tents dotting the rolling green hills. No pink shell boats floating on the sun-stroked lake. They were alone. *Completely* alone.

A glow of excitement flooded her senses, and courage . . . or maybe it was recklessness . . . surged through her in rapid pulses. Without a thought to propriety, Meredith pulled Alexander to the grass, then rolled him atop her and slid her fingers through his hair as she kissed him.

As her mouth moved against his, all the emotions, all the longing she'd suppressed since the day they met, came flooding unbidden to the surface.

This was a dream, after all, a lusty fantasy in which she was in total control. Here there was no right or wrong. No Society to impose rules of conduct. Only passion. Only need.

Alexander eagerly met her kiss with a desire so fierce and wicked that she shuddered. As she accepted his tongue deeply inside her mouth, her body trembled with excitement and she knew without a doubt that she would soon welcome his hard body into hers . . . completely.

And somehow, she was aware that he knew this too. For he took her mouth skillfully with a single-minded drive.

She felt a tugging then at the neck of her silk shift. And for the briefest of moments, it occurred to her that she seemed to be wearing nothing else. The thought was fleeting, and hardly worth her notice. Then, in the very next moment, she felt a burst of cool air as her breasts were exposed. Just as quickly, Alexander's mouth came down upon one nipple, calling forth a ragged gasp from her lips. His hand cupped the roundness of her other breast, and suddenly a rush of molten fire erupted within her.

His mouth traced a moist line from peak to peak, taking each nipple into his mouth in turn. Each time, he teased her gently with his teeth, before closing his lips and swirling his tongue around her nipple, making her shiver with pleasure.

This wasn't like the last time, her first time, when her former betrothed, to celebrate their engagement, had coaxed her into giving herself to him. There was no fear, no apprehension, no pain.

Only desire. Only the wish for more.

Her hips bucked against him. God, how she wanted this man.

Alexander lifted his mouth from Meredith's body and cradled her face in his hands. His head was spinning, and for the life of him, he could not understand how he came to be lying atop her. Sweet, soft Meredith. Strangely, he really didn't seem to care.

All he knew was he wanted this woman, but he had to see her eyes. Had to know that she wanted him as much as he needed her.

Her smooth hands travelled down his sides and he felt his lawn shirt being pulled free of his breeches. Then her fingertips were on his skin, touching, tantalizing him as they ran in small yet widening circles across his back.

"Take it off," she whispered huskily. "I need to feel your skin against mine."

His arms were heavy, but he pushed up from her and

whisked the shirt from his body. He nudged her legs apart and moved his own between them, bracing his weight on his arms as he stared down at her beseechingly.

In the darkness, he could barely make out her mass of red hair fanned out across the white linen pillow. Still, in a silver wand of early-morning gray light, he could see her eyes.

A pleased sigh broke from his mouth.

He had his answer.

Meredith rested her palms on his collarbones, then eased them slowly downward, through the wiry curls and over the defined mounds of his broad chest.

Though his face was cloaked in shadow as he remained poised above her, balancing his weight on hands braced on either side of her shoulders, she knew he watched her.

Turning her gaze to his, she ran her fingers over his ribs, across his hard stomach, then to the two buttons on either side of his front-fall.

Instinctively he sucked in his breath as she pressed each brass button through its hole and lowered the fall. She brought her hands together and felt for the closure that separated him from her. She touched the row of buttons and felt the bulge of him straining the button stitching and the fabric as well. He wanted her, clearly, as much as she wanted him.

The tightness of his breeches made it difficult as she twisted and forced each button to release.

He groaned as the last of the restraints gave way, and she wrapped her fingers tightly around him. She drew her hand from the nest of hair at the base of him to the plum-shaped tip, making him gasp at the sensation of it. His skin was smooth and his shaft pulsed erotically in her hand, his obvious desire driving heat to pool between her own legs.

Her hips, seemingly of their own accord, thrust upward, toward him. Her mind focused on one single thought . . . to feel him inside her.

There was no question in his mind. Her need was clear. She panted softly beneath him, all modesty abandoned.

All at once, the shift that separated him from her essence incensed him. He leaned far back on his heels and clawed the silken swath and dragged it down over her hips and her pale thighs, then off her, tossing it to the floor.

He knelt between her legs once more and looked down at her. The cool morning light illuminated her face now. Her breathing was hard and she reached out a pleading hand to him.

"Alex," she breathed. "Come to me."

Her words seemed to revive his senses. "Darling, we should not—"

"Shh. Let us not think. We are alone. *Please*." She reached out her hand and touched him again, guiding him forward toward her moist center.

He felt the beast, the rake inside him, stir and rouse. And Alex knew that in a moment more, there would be no chance of turning back.

"Come to me," she whispered seductively as she caressed him.

As her hand slid over him, Alexander was lost in sensation, helpless to do aught but what she asked.

　　　　　　　　⌐

She gazed at Alexander through the ripples of her dream as his hand moved up her thigh and touched her between her legs, just there. His fingers moved in tight circles, making her body quiver under his skilled command.

She bit her lip and pressed wantonly down upon his hand, wanting to feel the fullness of him inside her. Wanting more, needing more. "Alex, *please*."

He moved over her then and she felt his large hands grip her hips and position himself before her. In the thin light, she saw him close his eyes briefly. When he opened them again, his intent was clear.

Squeezing her eyes closed, Meredith sucked in a breath, waiting for the inevitable pain to come as he thrust firmly into her. But there was none. She blinked in surprise.

He paused for a moment, a queer expression glimmering in his eyes as he seemed to watch her. Then he began to move inside her, slowly at first; then his thrusts became harder, faster.

Meredith threw her head back and arched her back, her breasts jutting upward. Twisting her hips in a circular motion to meet each of his powerful thrusts, she tried to claim something that felt just out of reach.

Alexander slipped a hand between them and touched the nub between her thighs as he drove into her. Meredith gasped and her hands flew to his waist.

She pulled him toward her, wanting to feel his weight atop her, but he resisted. Instead, he urged her legs around his waist as he slid deep within her, again and again, as his finger touched her, teased her most intimate of places, tightening her, driving her closer and closer to madness. She was writhing now, her body begging Alexander to release her from this blissful torment.

Alexander pulled his hand from her and slipped it beneath her buttocks, pushing her hips to him. He pressed impossibly deep inside her—once, twice—and at the third time, she felt her muscles contract and hold him.

Warmth flooded her body and she cried out, shuddering with the sensation.

Alexander tensed then and Meredith felt his body explode within her.

As his chest came down over her, Meredith clung to his damp body as her head and body reeled.

⁓

"God save us all! Miss Meredith, what have you done?"

Meredith woke with a start. Annie, her abigail, stood at the edge of the bedstead with her hands clapped to her mobcap in horror.

"Lord have mercy. We've got to get him out of here afore your aunts wake." The abigail whirled around briefly to turn the key in the bedchamber door's lock. "This was not supposed to happen. Oh, this is a mess, this is!"

"Annie, calm down. What are you talking about?"

"I would guess she's talking about . . . *me*," came Alexander's voice from behind her.

Meredith tried to roll over. Instead, she hit an immovable object. It was then that she noticed a man's muscled arm draped over her bare waist, his hand resting atop hers.

She blinked with astonishment as she realized, not only was she completely naked, but an equally naked man was pressed as closely against her as two spoons in a silver chest.

"Um . . . Alexander!" Meredith sputtered. She shoved his arm from her and yanked the coverlet to her chin. "What in the blazes are you doing in my bed?"

Movement caught her gaze, and Meredith looked up to see Annie hurrying toward the wardrobe in the far corner of the chamber. The abigail, for once choosing to do the proper thing, focused her eyes and attention inside the cabinet and kept to the task (or pretended to) of selecting a frock for her mistress.

Meredith turned her head. The rake grinned sleepily back at her, then propped his weight onto one elbow, allowing the covers to fall away from his well-muscled chest.

Meredith's gaze fastened on the dark band of ink ringing his muscled arm. "Good heavens. What is *that*?" She slipped her hand from under the covers and touched his arm with her fingertip.

"Ah, this?" Alex glanced at the tattoo. "The mark of the rake, didn't you know? We *all* have them. Though, now that I have reformed, I am at a loss as to how to remove it."

At first, Meredith actually believed him, having never seen a naked rake in the daylight. But then he flashed one of those crooked smiles of his and she knew he was only teasing her. Then, without warning, he leaned close and kissed her bare shoulder. Shivers of delight skittered across her skin, making her accidentally sigh with pleasure.

"Stop that!" Meredith shook off the sensation and

pulled the covers high so only her head stuck out the top. "'Tis quite unseemly."

"Really, darling? You didn't think so last eve."

"W-what do you mean?"

"Meredith, how can you not remember what happened? 'Twas a night *I* will never forget."

"I haven't the faintest notion of what you are speaking, sir." Then suddenly a clutch of erotic images flooded her mind.

Oh no. Oh please.

Her own eyes widened. "Alex," she whispered, "tell me 'twas a dream. I didn't . . . I mean, *we* didn't—" She shook her head from side to side, hoping upon hope that he would mimic her.

But he didn't.

"Alex, please say something. God, say anything!"

Alexander glanced downward, then drew in a deep breath and raised his eyes to hers again. "Marry me."

"*Please* be serious."

"I am serious. Marry me."

Meredith looked him in the eyes, expecting to see laughter there, but there was none. There was a confidence in his gaze, a sureness of purpose. It suddenly became quite clear to her that Alexander was perfectly sincere. She gaped at him.

Alexander took her hand and brought it to his mouth. He kissed it gently. "I admit, I did not ask you to Harford Fell to give you a horse. I wanted my father to know you. I wanted to be permitted to be with you, to walk with you, to talk for hours on end. I wanted time, something unmarried gentlemen and ladies are not afforded in abundance in London." Alexander turned her hand over and kissed her wrist, then looked deep into her eyes. "I did not mean for this to happen between us. On my honor, I did not, yet I do not regret it. I never will. You mean everything to me. Marry me. Say you will."

Annie quietly returned to the bedside. She swiped Meredith's shift from the floor and, keeping her eyes down, discreetly handed it to her.

For a time, Meredith did not move. She just peered back at Alex. Then finally she dived beneath the coverlet and, after wrestling with the silken garment for several seconds, emerged, at least partially dressed. "My dressing gown, Annie. Quickly, *please*."

Alexander's lips curled as Meredith self-consciously fought her tousled curls. "I can obtain a special license and we could have the deed done within a day—two at the most. Marry me."

Meredith stared back at him. "I cannot marry *you*!"

"Well, I am afraid you have little choice. . . . I have ruined you." When she continued to stare, he added, "Physically."

"You?" Meredith softened her voice. "Lord Lansing, y-you did not ruin me."

"I do beg to differ." He sat up in the bed beside her, and even as shocking as her situation was, she could not help but follow the trail of dark hair from his chest to where it disappeared beneath the coverlet.

"Alex . . ." She looked up and peered deeply into his eyes, then bowed her head to study her twisting fingers as she spoke. "I have not been a . . . maiden for nigh on two years now."

"What did you say?" Alexander blinked at her, then raised his hand before her and glanced away momentarily. "No, no, I heard you. I just—" He seemed to struggle for the right words to finish his thought, but none came.

"I—I thought you knew, Alex."

"I knew about Pomeroy . . . but not"—he lifted his head and gazed into her eyes—". . . and yet the ton—"

"I was left at the altar. Made a fool of by a rake." Meredith felt her throat quiver and heard her voice begin to shake. "Had my aunts not had the money to ensure my debaucher's silence, as well as enough influence within the first circles of Society to make certain my disgrace at St. George's was virtually overlooked, I most certainly would have been barred from every drawing room."

Annie cornered the bed with Meredith's dressing gown. "'Ere you go, Miss Meredith."

Meredith had just slipped her arms through the sleeves when she felt her eyes begin to heat. No, she would not cry. Not in front of Alex. Not ever. She fixed her gaze on the door to the passageway and threw her legs over the edge of the bed. Alexander grasped her wrist.

"Do you not understand, Meredith? I don't care a damn about your past. I only care about you. *Marry me*."

Meredith could not meet his eye. She didn't want his pity . . . his charity. "I told you, I was not a maiden. You owe me nothing. Please just leave." She looked down at his hand upon her wrist. "Or at least free me so that I may go."

"I will return to the chamber next door, once you tell me why, even after we have lain together, that you will not consider accepting my troth." His voice was suddenly thick.

Confusion licked at Meredith's mind. Why, after bedding half the women in London, did he suddenly feel the need to marry *her*?

She raised her gaze to his. "Because . . . of Chillton."

"Are you claiming that you are in love with him?"

Alexander laughed skeptically, but it sounded forced to Meredith's ears. "Darling, I know you. You no more love him than I love—" His words died miserably on his lips.

"What were you going to say, Alexander? That I no more love him . . . than you love me?"

"No." Alexander lowered his head. "I didn't mean that."

"Yes, you did." Meredith yanked her wrist from his hold. "A rake never gives his heart. So, please, let us not pretend that you have."

The doorknob rattled and Meredith's eyes darted to Annie's.

"Meredith?" Aunt Letitia called through the mahogany door. "Open up, dear. Sister and I wish to speak with you."

Meredith turned to Alexander and with her eyes implored him to leave.

With a nod, Alexander crawled from bed and bundled up his clothing and boots; then with a shiver borne of the cool morning air, he walked naked through the French windows onto the balcony.

"Oh, my word!" The shock in her aunt Viola's voice was clear as her words sailed into the bedchamber from the balcony. "L-Lord Lansing."

Meredith raced to the window to find Alexander in the middle of the balcony, his clothing bundled over his sex, staring straight into prim Aunt Viola's eyes, who stood there as well.

"So sorry, my lady," Alexander was saying. "Just went for a swim in the lake this morn. Thought I was heading back into my chamber."

Aunt Viola was clearly dubious. "Oh really? I thought you were coming *from* Meredith's bedchamber."

Alexander grinned sheepishly. "No, no. Heading for my own."

Taking five wide strides backward, Alexander pulled at the handle of his chamber's French window. When the latch depressed, he quietly stepped through. "Damned sense of direction, you know. Found the right chamber now, though." He bowed his head. "Good morn."

Aunt Viola stepped inside, headed straight for the interior door, and turned the key she found poised inside the lock to let her sister into the room.

The pair silently sat on the edge of Meredith's bedstead, watching her.

"Well, gel?" her Aunt Letitia began. "Do you have something to tell us?"

Meredith gulped. "I . . . I—"

Aunt Viola, quite unbelievably, was suddenly smiling brightly.

"What Sister is asking is . . . have you chosen a date for the wedding?"

Imperative Twelve

*A rake will pay boundless attention to a lady one day,
then seem to forget her the next. This is intended
to tip the lady from her footing, making her wonder
what she did or said incorrectly, while keeping him
in her mind for days.*

❦

"Annie, please help me dress." Meredith crossed the bedchamber to the basin and ewer. Pouring some well water
into the blue-and-white bowl, she splashed her face, then
began to wash, shivering at the icy temperature.

Her Aunt Letitia cleared her throat. "You wouldn't
rather have a bath?"

Meredith looked over her shoulder at the two Featherton ladies, who were still sitting, side by side, on the edge
of the bed, watching her.

Aunt Letitia gave her a sweet, grandmotherly smile.
"After last night . . . you know."

Meredith twisted her face into a scowl. "There isn't
time enough. We must leave at once." She turned her head
to her abigail, who had one foot outside the French window and was peering toward Lord Lansing's chamber.
"Annie! Come back in here at once, please."

Annie stepped back into the chamber with a disappointed sigh and turned the twist latch on the window, locking it. "I was only trying to get a better look at that rake's mark of his." Then she saw the angry look in Meredith's eyes. "For my own safety, you see. Now I can recognize a rake straight away . . . if I see his mark, I mean."

"Please, Annie. Just throw everything into the portmanteau. I cannot stay here a moment longer."

"I beg your pardon, Miss Meredith, but if I just throw everything in, as you said, all your clothing will be wrinkled and crushed."

Meredith stopped washing her left underarm. "I don't care. I have to get out of here before *he* comes back."

"Well, I care, miss. 'Twill double my work when we get back to London, it will," Annie cheekily informed her. "So if you don't mind, I will wrap and fold your things. Won't take but a minute more. You'll see."

Both aunts chuckled at Annie's gall. It was clear neither of them was in any rush to leave Harford Fell.

Meredith dropped the cloth and soap cake into the basin, sending a swell of water over its edge. She glared at her aunts. "Do not pretend innocence with me. I know that whatever you stirred into my cordial is to blame for what happened last night."

"And what was that, dear?" Aunt Viola asked, appearing all wide-eyed and innocent.

"Y-you know very well what happened!" Then Meredith lowered her voice to just above a whisper. "We . . . shared a bed." She drew her brows close. "Really . . . *shared* it."

"When you say 'shared it' . . . do you mean the two of you were intimate?" Aunt Letitia asked.

Annie pretended to be packing, though it was obvious

she was listening with great interest. Meredith shot a glare in her direction too . . . just for good measure.

"You of all people should know," Meredith snapped as she snatched up a morning dress from the pile beside the portmanteau. "'Twas the fault of your drug. What was it, some sort of Chinese aphrodisiac from your apothecary?"

Aunt Viola was already nodding. "Oh yes, the powder was from our trusted apothecary, but—"

"I knew it!" Meredith pulled the gown over her head, then gestured for Annie to tighten her ribbon cinch at the back.

"But 'twas not meant to arouse," her aunt continued. "'Twas only my sleeping powder that we mixed into your refreshments."

Meredith could not believe what she was hearing. "What do you mean?"

"Dear gel, if you and the young lord felt the undeniable urge to make love, 'twas not due to the effects of the powder. That longing came from the two of you."

Hot red dots burned on both of Meredith's cheeks. "Are you saying I *wanted* to bed Lord Lansing? If you are, I vow you are quite mad."

Aunt Letitia laughed. "Then send us to Bedlam, dear, for the only aphrodisiac in play last eve was in your minds."

Meredith gasped as Annie gave one last tug at her ribbon and tied it off. "Why, then, did you put the powder in our drinks? It makes no sense to me."

"So the two of you would end up in bed together—too drugged to move—so you'd *have* to marry each other. I should think that fact is quite clear." Annie cupped her hand over her mouth. "Beggin' your pardon, Miss Meredith. I did not mean to speak out of turn."

"No, no, Annie, I am glad you did." Meredith crossed her arms over her chest and looked down her nose at her aunts. "I thank you for being honest, for it is obvious to me that my aunts would not have been so willing to supply the truth."

She walked toward the bed and stood before the two old women. "So, is Annie's story the truth of the matter? Were you hoping to force a marriage between Lord Lansing and me?"

The Featherton ladies nodded sheepishly.

"But why?" Meredith unfolded her arms and brought a hand to her forehead. She began to pace. "Why would you wish me to marry Lansing when you know my cap is set for Mr. Chillton?"

"Why Chillton, child?" Aunt Viola rose and put a comforting arm around Meredith's waist.

Meredith looked up at her aunt, dumbfounded. "You, of all people, should know the answer to that. I—I am *ruined*! When Lord Pomeroy left me, my fate was sealed. Were it not for the two of you, I was to be a spinster living my life with eyes cast downward in shame."

Aunt Viola gave her a look of pure pity. "Dear, you needn't feel shame. You did nothing but follow your heart."

"I wish Society felt that way, Auntie, but we both know better. Mr. Chillton, however, can save me from such a fate. It matters not to him that Pomeroy set me aside. In fact, he refuses to even discuss my past. Our union is perfectly logical—I will be able to hold my head high again and he will have the advantage of a Society connection for business."

"And what of Lansing?" Viola watched Meredith pensively. "Can he not save your reputation as well?"

"Yes, he could. He is to be a respected earl. He needs a respected wife. Not me." Meredith turned a teary gaze upon her aunt. "Do you not think I have heard the ton's derisive whispers? My past would only shame Lord Lansing." She wiped the back of her hand across her eyes. "No, it is Chillton I will marry."

Aunt Letitia slid from the bed and her plump slipper-shod feet hit the floor with a double thump. She came and stood at Meredith's opposite side. "You may have your mind made up that Chillton is your man, but your heart is not in agreement."

Meredith pushed free from her aunts and turned back to face them. "What do you mean?"

Aunt Viola stepped forward and took Meredith's hand. "Haven't you realized it yet, child? You are in love with Lord Lansing."

Meredith opened her mouth, then closed it just as quickly. A flush of heat rose up and colored her cheeks and ears. "He is an untrustworthy rake—a rogue, a debaucher."

"Is that so, dear?" Aunt Viola lifted her fluffy white brows. "You have studied him, tested him. Have you truly found him to be so despicable?"

Meredith thought about it for several moments, but knew deep down that, had she flipped open her book of notes and reviewed every single page, she would never find clear evidence of rakish deceit on his part.

Could her aunts be right?

No, no. The thought is preposterous.

Alexander mightn't be untrustworthy or unfeeling or cruel, but he had seduced her . . . sort of. Though, the seduction might have been somewhat . . . mutual, now that she thought about it.

Well, no matter. He was a rake of the first order and one does not fall in love with a rake.

Ever.

Why would her aunts not understand?

~

Moping and gloomy-faced, the two brooding Featherton sisters reluctantly began to board the carriage that would soon be headed back to London.

They were certainly taking their leisure, Meredith noted, as she and Annie waited behind Aunt Letitia for their turns to climb up the steps.

"Miss Merriweather!"

At the sound of the male voice calling for her, Meredith, against her better judgment, glanced over her shoulder toward the house. Perdition, it was Alexander, shouting from a far window on the upper floor!

She had hoped to make a clean escape and thought, until this very moment, that they had managed just that.

They had left a note of appreciation to their kind host, who had been abed still when they crept down the passageway with their bags, as well as a hastily scrawled missive with One, Alexander's dutiful valet. That letter had been handed to Mr. Herbert by Meredith herself, along with strict instructions that it not be delivered until their party had left the house.

Those instructions obviously had been ignored, for here was Alexander, calling to her.

So Meredith did the only thing she could. She ignored him.

"Auntie, *please* do hurry." Her aunt had bent to retrieve something she'd dropped upon climbing into the carriage and her rather wide hindquarters were now blocking the door.

Meredith groaned, fighting the intense desire to press her aunt's backside through the narrow carriage door.

"Viola, I can't reach my reticule," her aunt was moaning, her voice raspy from the exertion of bending. "It's nearly under the bench. Can you reach it?"

"I shall fetch it for you." Meredith looked back at the house's upper window again. Alexander was gone. "Just, please, take your seat. I fear Lord Lansing is coming down."

Letitia straightened and turned around to face the house. "No, not the young lord, I fear."

"W-what?" Meredith whirled completely around only to see the earl barreling toward them.

He was wrapped in a dressing gown and wearing India gold brocade slippers with their toes pulled up in tasseled curlicues. He was quite breathless by the time he reached the carriage.

"Jolly good. Thought I'd missed seeing you off," he huffed. "Wouldn't want to be a poor host, now would I?"

As Aunt Letitia descended the steps to the earthen drive, the carriage bounced on its coils as surely as it were traveling the pocked and pitted road north. "Forgive us, dear sir, for attempting to leave before bidding you farewell."

"Is all well?" the earl asked, reaching out to take Letitia's plump hand. "We have not offended you in some way? Please tell me we have not."

"No, no, no. Heavens, you and your son, and indeed all of Harford Fell, were delightful."

Meredith froze where she stood, furious that her aunt was chatting away the morn with the earl.

"Then why, pray, must you leave so soon?" the burly man asked with all sincerity.

Letitia gestured to the carriage. "You may see for yourself."

At first, the earl did not seem inclined to do as her aunt bid him to, so Letitia tugged him forward. As the earl was pulled toward the carriage, Meredith saw that her Aunt Viola's eyes had grown wide; then suddenly she collapsed dramatically on the leather squabs.

The moment the earl set eyes upon the wilted lady, Letitia added, "You see, my sister has taken ill."

The earl released Letitia's chubby hand and lurched backward several feet. "What is wrong with her?"

"Sadly, we do not know." Letitia barged forward and grabbed his arm. "Perhaps, if you took a closer look—"

Then the earl's eyes bulged in their sockets. "I? Why would I know what ails her?" The earl wrenched his arm away and instantly began to gasp. "Geminy. You don't suppose it's catching . . . whatever felled her?"

My, my, Aunt Letitia is a clever one, Meredith mused, *playing on the earl's fears of becoming ill.* For certain, he would have no quarrel with their leaving now. The way her aunts were carrying on, one might think poor Viola had come down with the pox—or worse. It was time, however, to put an end to their performances.

"Auntie, we mustn't tarry." Meredith drew her aunt back to the carriage steps. "We should see Aunt Viola to her own physician at once." She turned her head to the earl and caught, from the edge of her vision, Alexander racing from the house toward them. "Good day, sir," she said, hurrying to follow her aunt up the stairs.

The footman closed the door as Annie boarded behind her, just as Lord Lansing reached them.

"Miss Merriweather—" he managed to say before Meredith rapped her fist on the forward wall of the carriage.

At the crack of a whip, the team jerked the carriage forward. Alexander ran alongside the window. "Meredith, what about the horse? You've not even seen the horses. What will you do?"

Meredith leaned her head out the window as Alexander fell behind. As the wheels of the carriage rounded the bend in the drive, she waved good-bye. "I will manage, Lord Lansing. I always do."

⁓

Meredith sat in her aunts' beloved library, trying her best to focus on the scattering of papers that detailed every plan for her aunts' upcoming special musicale.

Her aunts had given her the task of paring the guest list so all might fit within the confines of the Featherton sisters' Hanover Square home.

Still, after twenty minutes with her eyes on the same page, Meredith had not the slightest notion of the names she'd read. No doubt this mindless chore was simply a means to distract her from weightier thoughts.

It was finally Wednesday, after all. The fated day of Mr. Chillton's much anticipated private meeting with her aunts—which was occurring just across the passage at that very moment.

Meredith was not surprised that he had kept the appointment, even after their last disastrous meeting at Tattersalls four days earlier. Chillton was nothing if not reliable. If he said he would be there, he would be.

She'd left the door open to the passage, hoping perhaps to catch a word or two from Mr. Chillton as he discussed his matter "of great importance" with her two great-aunts.

Though her chances for an offer of marriage were all but dashed—to her way of thinking—Meredith still held out a modicum of hope that Chillton would see beyond her abhorrent behavior to the logic of a union. It made sense, after all, for both of them, for she would regain her respectability and he would gain a wife with Society connections—which could only benefit his import business. And the fact that he actually arrived at the house ten minutes early—a possible gauge of his enduring enthusiasm—did bode well for her, did it not?

Meredith thrummed her fingers on her knee, then leaned forward in her chair to catch a glimpse of the tall-case clock in the passage.

He'd been in there for nearly thirty minutes now. What could be taking so long?

Knowing Chillton as she did, he was likely exchanging pleasantries with her aunts rather than coming straight to the point. He was always polite that way. At first, this annoyed her, for she always preferred it when people spoke plainly and said what they meant. Soon, though, Meredith realized that Chillton, as a businessman, found it best to begin with niceties. He put his partner in conversation at ease before tackling important matters that might cause tension.

Suddenly there was a swell in the tone of conversation; then the parlor door opened. Both of her aunts spilled out into the passage, with Mr. Chillton bringing up the rear.

Meredith caught Aunt Letitia's eye, but she saw no clue there. She looked to Aunt Viola. Her face was expressionless too as she passed Meredith on her way to see Mr. Chillton out the front door.

Mr. Chillton paused when he saw Meredith and extended his hand to her. "Lovely to see you, Miss Meredith. I trust your day has been pleasant." He glanced at the door Mr. Edgar held open for him.

Meredith cinched her brows. "Um . . . yes, my day has been lovely." Was that it? A few empty words and he was leaving? She looked helplessly to her aunts for assistance, but they seemed as eager for Chillton to leave as the gentleman himself. "Mightn't you like to stay and join us for tea?"

Mr. Chillton forced a smile. "Another time, perhaps. The tea I just enjoyed with your aunts was quite enough to quench my thirst."

"Oh." Meredith peered through the parlor doorway and saw the silver tea service glinting in the light. *I am such a nitwit.* Of course, they would have had tea.

"Must be off." Chillton turned to Aunt Letitia. "Thank you for your graciousness concerning my Hannah."

Aunt Letitia graced him with her very best hostess smile. "You are quite welcome, Mr. Chillton. We do adore young Hannah."

Then, with a curt nod in her direction, Chillton skipped down the steps, untied his mare's reins and boarded his phaeton.

When Mr. Edgar closed the door, her aunts silently turned and disappeared inside the parlor once more.

"Aunties!" Meredith raced after the two old women. "Will you not tell me what he said? You must know I have been on pins and needles since he arrived."

Both her aunts looked as though they had been sucking on lemons, for their lips were puckered, the expressions on their wrinkled faces pulled.

"Dear, he did *not* ask for your hand, if that is what you

want to know. In fact, he did not speak of you at all. I am sorry." Aunt Viola revisited her teacup and drank down its cooled contents—likely to avoid having to say anything more.

Meredith looked to Letitia, trying to keep the jolt that seemed to shake her body from reaching her voice. "Very well." She swallowed deeply. "If I was not the topic of conversation, what was?"

Aunt Letitia gave her a long, consoling look before she spoke. "Hannah."

"He spoke of Hannah?" Meredith felt her mouth gaping most unbecomingly after the four words spilled from them; she snapped it shut.

"Yes, dear, it seems that Mr. Chillton is seriously considering a three-year journey to India," Aunt Letitia began. "Some business arrangement or another, I believe. He'd leave late July . . . that is assuming he shall go at all."

"India? Why, he never said a word of this to me." Meredith's heart was racing as she felt any chance of marrying Mr. Chillton slip from her grasp.

"We were greatly surprised by his announcement as well, child. But even more taken off our heels by his request to take Hannah under our wing—and find her a husband."

With all of her shocked staring, Meredith's eyes were becoming dry. She plopped down onto a chair beside the hearth. "He . . . he wants the two of you to act as Hannah's duennas whilst he is away—and he never spoke a word about marrying me?"

"Shows a lack of manners, if you ask me." Aunt Letitia bobbed her head overtly, until her sister took her meaning and echoed the sentiment.

"I agree. Still, we cannot deny his request," Aunt Viola added. "You see, Meredith, his mother has a great fear of leaving their family home in the country. An illogical fear, which of late prevents her from venturing out of her own bedchamber."

Meredith squinted her eyes as she took in her aunt's words. "I've never heard of such a thing."

"Nor have we, child, though we dared not question Mr. Chillton further on it. He did seem quite distraught over his mother's . . . condition." Aunt Letitia rose and, jabbing her walking stick into the carpet, came to Meredith. "So you see, we could not refuse his request."

"No, no," Meredith began. "You did what was right. I am just a mite shaken that he did not mention me at all." She looked up at her aunt. "Were my actions at Tattersalls so egregious that it destroyed my suitability as a wife entirely?"

"Dear, if so, then clearly Mr. Chillton was never the man for you." Then her aunt Viola added, "Perhaps you might look to Lord Lansing with new eyes, eh?"

Meredith sprang from her chair. "No, no! I was so close to receiving an offer from Mr. Chillton. I cannot believe all is lost." Meredith began to pace the parlor with several firm strides before stopping in the center of the room. She raised a single digit in the air. "I will not give up. I *will* marry Mr. Chillton. Just you wait and see."

Imperative Thirteen

*Smiling is the most potent weapon in a rake's arsenal.
A charming smile has the power to put
an unknowing lady at ease, when instead
she should be backing away.*

Sitting in the shadows at the top of the stairs, Meredith propped her chin on her knees and tapped her leather book of notes on the toe of her slipper. She blew out a long sigh, feeling very sorry for herself as she peered miserably down at the crowd collecting below for her aunts' musicale celebration.

Why couldn't Letitia and Viola have canceled the wretched event once they realized there would be no engagement to celebrate—no pending nuptials to toast with their secret booty of French wine from Champagne.

It would have been easy enough to simply slip the Austrian pianist the mound of guineas promised for regaling the frosty tip of Mayfair Society with his famed—yet *dreadfully* dreary—sonatas. In fact, Meredith had even offered to pay the man herself.

However, for a reason known only to their two cotton-topped heads, the Featherton ladies had decided that the special musicale must commence as planned.

Meredith's suspicions had begun to build earlier that evening as they supped on a roast of beef, pigeon pie and spring beans. Her aunts, who normally would have been chatting excitedly about the musicale, were unusually quiet. More was said with their darting eyes and averted gazes than with their words.

Having been unable to rouse her own appetite, Meredith had left the table and a plate of steaming food behind, preferring the solitude of her chamber. She had had her fill of half-formed sentences and giggles, and she'd left the dining room with naught but a bellyful of worries about the night to come.

And now, as she sat upon the top stair, watching her aunts scurry back and forth between the parlor and the music room, she was more sure than ever: the Feathertons had a plan.

"Meredith? Is that you sitting up there in the dark?"

Meredith glanced down to the figure beside the newel post at the bottom of the stairs.

There, Beth Augustine stood, her hand cupped to her brow to reduce the glare from the chandelier's candles. "Why are you skulking around up there like a child? The music is about to begin. Come down and join us like a big girl."

A couple who'd just handed off their wraps to the footman chuckled at Beth's quip, and Meredith suddenly felt quite ridiculous. A rash, borne of nervousness, erupted on her chest, which, of course, would be immediately visible to her *dear* friend Beth.

"Are you coming down, Meredith?" Beth persisted. "Honestly, what are you doing up there?"

Meredith rose and, thinking quickly, tucked her notebook under her arm, then toyed with the brilliant dangling at her ear. "I dropped my earbob. Found it, though. See? Here 'tis."

She descended the stair treads; then, as she passed by the pointed gaze of Beth Augustine, she covertly pushed her book of notes to the back of the entryway table. It would be safely out of view of their guests there.

Glancing in the mirror, illuminated by matching sconces affixed to the wall on either side, Meredith appraised the flat smile she'd applied to her lips especially for Beth. Yes, she decided, her expression was just chilly enough to suffice.

"How is the babe, Mrs. Augustine?" Meredith peered at Beth's eyes and shook her head. "It appears he is not giving you much sleep. Just look at those dark circles."

It wasn't much, but even that little jab felt . . . well, quite *good*.

Beth grinned saucily. "'Tisn't the babe keeping me awake at night." She smirked at Meredith. "Although, not being married, I don't assume you would know of such things . . . or would you?"

Oh! Now that smarts. Especially tonight. What had she been thinking? Meredith should have known better than to cross swords with a master.

"And now that we are on the subject, dear Meredith, when might I expect an invitation to your wedding to that merchant . . . Chillton, was it? Last we spoke, the engagement was but a breath away."

Hurt, wreathed in anger, welled up inside Meredith. She sucked in three deep breaths in an attempt to calm herself, but it didn't work. Nothing would. Too much had happened that day. She was going to explode.

"Do you really want to know, Beth? Well, I shall tell you—*never!*" Something clenched in Meredith's stomach. "Mr. Chillton did *not* offer for me, after all. So there you are. Are you completely satisfied, now that you have humiliated me in my own home?"

Beth slapped a hand to her chest and staggered back a step, though a hint of a pleased grin touched her lips momentarily. "Heavens, I was only asking. Of course, I meant no harm. My fondest wish is to see all my friends as happily married as I."

Meredith stared with disbelief at Beth and began to feel all hot about her face.

What a grand liar Beth was.

She didn't care a fig about anyone's happiness but her own. Why, Meredith guessed, the only thing that could make Beth happier than she was this very moment would be to see Meredith's cheeks wet with tears. Well, by golly, she wasn't about to give the wench the satisfaction.

Then Meredith felt her bottom lip tremble.

Oh no.

Then the back of her eyes started to prickle.

Now her throat felt thick and a little raw. *No, no!* She would not cry.

"Now, if you will please excuse me, Mrs. Augustine, I promised my aunts I would see to"—Meredith's gaze darted through the open doorway for anyone she recognized—"um . . ."

"*There* you are, Miss Merriweather."

The faint scent of French musk tickled her nose. Meredith looked up. Alarm shook her body as she realized that Alexander stood at her side and was smiling at her.

Smiling. After she'd gone and run off from Harford Fell, leaving him in a cloud of road dust.

"Alex—" she breathed. She peered into his eyes, searching them apprehensively. His gaze did not so much as hint at anger or at pain. His green eyes sparkled with adoration as he peered down at her.

The emotion that had pinched the back of her throat only moments ago began to fade away as she stood in Alexander's reassuring presence.

Her knight had come to rescue her—again.

"I am sorry, my dear, but I was only able to find two seats together near the rear of the room. I hope you do not mind." He reached out and gently took Meredith's hand and laid it in the crook of his arm. "Though our position might be an advantage, for the music room is already quite warm, and we'll be much nearer to the doors . . . should we wish to take the air."

Meredith felt a tug at her sleeve and she turned belatedly to find herself pinned beneath Beth's annoyed gaze.

"Are you not going to introduce me formally to your gentleman friend, Miss Merriweather?" She moved before Alexander and bequeathed him a grand smile; then she dropped a curtsy. "I know you, my lord, by reputation, of course, though we have never been introduced."

"Oh . . . Lord Lansing, may I present Mrs. Augustine—a neighbor."

"Oh, much more than that," Beth added. "You needn't be shy. You see, Lord Lansing, Miss Merriweather and I are bosom friends from Miss Belbury's School for Girls."

Meredith coughed to cover her gasp of disbelief. *Oh yes, just the best of friends.*

"Madam." Alexander, being ever astute, glanced briefly in Beth's direction and tipped his head slightly to her. "Augustine. Hmm. Don't know any Augustines, I'm afraid."

Beth actually blanched, and for a moment, Meredith thought she might fall right off the heels of her shoes.

Ha! That put "Mrs. High and Mighty" in her place. Meredith couldn't leave it at that, however.

"Mrs. Augustine, my family just returned from visiting his father, the earl, at Harford Fell. Do you know it?"

"Do I know it? Why, what a question! I have connections, y-you know," Beth sputtered. A sardonic gleam came into her eye. "So you, Lord Lansing, are truly a friend of the *Featherton sisters*?" She looked at Meredith smugly.

"Indeed. I met them through my dearest, here." Alexander looked back at Meredith and flashed a most charming smile. "Shall we go inside?"

"Absolutely." As they began to walk away, Meredith could not resist a parting glance back at Beth, who appeared suitably gobsmacked.

Ha-ha! A little swoop of elation lifted Meredith's spirits.

"Lord Lansing," Meredith said softly, "I am forever in your debt." She gazed into his eyes, expecting, now that they were no longer in Beth's company, to see a hint of pain or even anger. But only amusement flickered in his green eyes. Nothing more. If only she could feel at ease with him once more—but too much had passed between them in recent days for her to relax.

"Really? *Forever?*" he replied. "Being the wretched rake that I am, I shall have to think of a positively wicked way for you to repay such a great debt." His dark slash of an eyebrow flicked up playfully.

"No doubt you will think of something." Meredith gave a nervous grin back to him.

Somehow, every horrid thing that had befallen her today had been whisked from her memory, the very moment Alexander came to her side.

Meredith had to admit, the man's timing was perfect. She supposed that timing was an important skill for any rake to possess. Yes, she could see how it could remove a man from all sorts of strife.

As they passed her Aunt Letitia, who was standing by the glass door to the music room, Meredith leaned close. "If Lansing's appearance here tonight is your scheme, I thank you, Auntie."

A tiny smile twitched at her aunt's lips. "I am sure I don't know what you mean, but if you are happy, dove, then so am I."

As the pianist's fingers massaged the ivory keys, releasing his melody into the still air, Meredith's knee bounced nervously in approximate time with the music. And yet, when the music ceased and the pianist turned to accept claps of appreciation from the audience of twenty-four Londoners, her knee danced onward.

Without looking away from the pianist, Alexander reached out and lifted Meredith's hand, then placed it firmly atop her agitated knee, patting it twice.

Alexander obviously was aware that she was not at ease with his sudden appearance at the musicale, but she was grateful. Very grateful, for he had put a quick end to Beth Augustine's intent to humiliate.

Now what? How could she even pretend to be enjoying the music with Alexander sitting so close to her? It was impossible to put aside the fact that just two nights past they were lying naked together, in each other's arms, their bodies merged and moist with exertion.

The rash on her chest began to itch, and Meredith looked down to see that the earlier wash of pink rising out of her bodice now resembled a trim of crimson lace. And there was no way to conceal her outward display of anxiety, for she had been so angered by Chillton's rejection of her that she'd given every fichu she owned to Annie and bade her to donate them to the poor that very afternoon.

Stupid that. Should have kept at least one, for instances just like this.

Meredith flipped open her cutwork fan and waved it over her chest, hoping the cool air would reduce the flaming color of the tiny bumps strewn across the upper slope of her bosom.

"Shall we slip outside in the courtyard for some air?" Alexander whispered to her. "If we are quiet, no one will even notice we've gone."

Meredith thought to decline the offer, but the back of her neck was sprinkled with tiny beads of perspiration. Her chest now felt as though it were covered with pinching ants. "For a moment or two. That's all."

Alexander nodded, then took her hand back into his; then they both, stooped at the waist, sneaked out of the music room into the passage, then through the French windows at the back of the house.

Meredith sucked in a gulp of cool evening air as they poured into the courtyard. "Lord above, I thought I would suffocate if we stayed in the room a moment longer."

"'Twas a tad warm."

"And crowded too. What could my aunts have been thinking to invite so many to squeeze into such a small glassed-in room?" Meredith walked across the brick pavers and collapsed upon the iron bench beneath the old oak tree.

"Perhaps they were thinking that they had something to celebrate." Alexander came and stood directly before Meredith.

She could not look at him, though she knew it was rude not to. "I wasn't sure if you overheard that part of my discussion with Mrs. Augustine."

"I am sorry, Meredith." Alexander pivoted slightly and rested his weight on the bench beside her.

She turned her head and peered up at him then. "You are sorry? I thought you would be pleased to learn that Mr. Chillton did not offer for me."

"Oh, I am. I am." She had expected him to hoist one of those cocky grins of his, but he didn't. "I am only sorry that he hurt you—that he broke your heart."

"Oh." Meredith looked down at her lap, where the fingers of both her hands were twisting like warring spiders.

She didn't dare tell him that Chillton hadn't broken her heart.

Feeling no pain over this blow was odd, she knew. And it surprised her. She had set her cap for Chillton and everyone knew it. She'd devoted herself entirely to becoming his wife. And when he did not ask for her hand, though by all indications she'd believed he would, she felt naught but . . . humiliation. Embarrassment.

His rejection did not drive her to her knees as Lord Pomeroy's had when he left her standing at the altar. It did not send her, quivering and sobbing, into her chamber.

She felt no shame, as she had when the rake had all but destroyed her years ago.

In fact, Meredith realized quite suddenly, Chillton's rejection had not touched her heart at all. It just left her cold, not knowing what she would do now that she'd failed at the task she set for herself more than a year ago.

No, she'd not admit any of this to Alexander. She didn't wish for him to see her as heartless—which she certainly must be, for she didn't shed one tear over her loss. Not one!

"Put the bastard out of your mind, as you should have done long ago."

Meredith's head shot up. "I—I beg your pardon."

Alexander slipped off his gloves and touched her cheek with the back of his fingers. "You never loved him."

"Lord Lansing, you overstep." Meredith's words held no conviction. Even she could hear that.

"You love me." Alexander leaned close, and she knew he meant to kiss her.

She let his lips touch hers. Softly, briefly, before she turned her face away. "Sir, you have gall. I give you that."

"You know you love me. I see it in your eyes. Feel it in your kisses, in the way your body responded to mine at Harford Fell."

Meredith hurried to her feet, but Alexander caught her hand and pulled her to his lap. She did not struggle against him, though she knew she should.

"Don't run from me, Meredith. We belong together and you know it . . . know it in the very depths of your heart."

His mouth came down upon hers and ignited the embers of need that she'd managed to bank since the day she left Harford Fell.

She felt his mouth opening hers and the roughness of his budding beard on her face. Alex's arms rose up around her and pressed her tight against his body.

Her breath caught in her throat, and all at once she realized her hands were beneath his coat, running over the ridged muscles of his chest.

His mouth separated from hers then, leaving her lips tingling and wet, wanting more.

"Marry me. Say you will."

There was a click followed by a whine as someone opened the French windows. Meredith froze and her eyes met Alex's stunned gaze.

"Oh dear!" babbled Beth Augustine. "F-forgive me for intruding. Have an ache in my head. Thought some cool air would help."

Meredith hesitantly turned her head toward the French windows. Beth was purposely averting her gaze, fingering the tight buds of the rosebush nearest the gaping door.

"I just wanted to tell you good eve."

Meredith narrowed her eyes. The wench had not just stumbled upon them. For heaven's sake, the door was made of at least twenty lights of glass. She had to have seen them, even in the darkness of the courtyard. Beth had wanted to interrupt.

Meredith raised her chin. "Good eve, Beth. Do forgive me for not rising."

Beth looked up then. Her eyes rounded, a shape echoed by her mouth. She studied them both briefly; then, as if realizing she had failed in sending them scampering to their feet, she spun around and charged back through the door.

When Meredith looked back at Alexander, she saw

that one edge of his lips was pulled higher than the other in a roguish grin. "Now, where did we leave off?"

Meredith pressed a palm to his chest and used it as leverage to stand. "My aunts, or another guest, might come out and find us at any moment. We must go back inside, please."

Alexander was upon her in an instant. He cupped his hand behind her neck and pulled her mouth to his. "Is that what you really want . . . to go back inside?"

"No." Her eyelids felt heavy and she wanted more than anything to lean close and take the kiss she wanted so badly. Instead, she twisted away from his grasp, turned and walked into the house.

As the last guest left the house late that evening, Meredith stood with her aunts waving farewell.

Thankfully, it seemed that Beth Augustine had not reported finding Meredith and Alexander in a couple's embrace in the courtyard. Or, at least, her aunts had had the good grace to refrain from mentioning it.

"Well, I am off to find my pillow," Aunt Viola announced as she started up the staircase.

"Pillow, bah! I want my bed. My feet haven't throbbed so badly all month." Aunt Letitia started to cane her way up the stairs behind her sister, when she paused and looked around at Meredith. "We shall discuss your . . . progress with Lord Lansing in the morning, shall we?"

Meredith looked up at her aunt and smiled. "Yes, Auntie. Good night."

What progress had she made, though? The more she tested and studied the rake, the more she seemed to yearn for the man. For certain, she wasn't thinking as clearly as she normally might. After all, he had turned her to jelly with a duo of fantastic kisses less than an hour before.

Oh! She just had to stop thinking about those kisses. She needed a distraction. Best review her notes. Slowly she walked over to the entryway table and reached around the vase of spring flowers for her book of notes. After all, as any student of the sciences knows, she appreciated the importance of interpreting results in a thorough and unbiased manner.

As her fingers slipped across the polished table, she felt nothing.

A little tremor started in her hands as she whisked the heavy vase into the air. To her horror, she saw nothing more than her own startled expression peering back up at her, blurred and wavering in the glossy cherry wood surface. Plunking the vase back down, she fell to her knees and began scrabbling around the shadows beneath the table.

It wasn't there.

The book where she'd recorded all of her notes for over two years, all of her experiments—all of her observations of London's rakes—was gone!

Imperative Fourteen

*Do not be fooled by pristine starched neckcloths
and gloves. A man who wishes to dance with a lady
truly wishes to bed her.*

By eight o'clock the next morn, Arthur Chillton had heard
the most disturbing news about Miss Meredith Merriweather. She had replaced him with another.

He'd been standing at the counter in Fortnum &
Mason, waiting to pay for a bag of coffee. It was a purchase he was loath to make.

Arthur had flushed each measure of grounds with boiling water at least six times over the past weeks, but now
his morning cup resembled dishwater more than a dark
brew. Time to replenish.

He'd been trying to decide between the black glossy
beans, which might result in a richer flavor—therefore
lending itself to more uses—and the nut-colored coffee,
which mightn't last nearly as long, but was twenty pence
cheaper.

He'd just made up his mind to go with the nut-hued
beans, deciding he could make do with lighter coffee be-

cause . . . well, twenty pence was twenty pence, after all. Right then, a curly-haired woman with a bright green feathered hat entered the establishment.

As he pushed a coin forward to the shopkeeper, he heard something that snared his attention.

"I tell you, Mrs. Augustine was at the Feathertons' musicale. She told me everything. Saw it all for herself," the woman in the frivolous hat was telling the woman at her side, a rounder lady a good ten years her senior. "Miss Merriweather, the little hoyden, has somehow—oh, I do not know how, so do not even ask—snared Lord Lansing's heartstrings."

"What? You cannot be right. She was all but ruined just two years past." The older woman was clearly aghast, or at least making a good show of it. "Certainly the heir to an earldom could do far better for himself. Why, the man hails from one of the oldest families in the realm."

"Be that as it may, she has done it. The rumble is, she had set her cap for a merchant of some sort, but he pushed her aside. It was not the first time she'd been summarily jilted, and, I daresay, she must have decided it would be the last time ever. Well, Mrs. Augustine stumbled upon the lord and Miss Merriweather canoodling in the Feathertons' courtyard—during her great-aunts' musicale, no less!"

Hearing this flustered Arthur Chillton so deeply that he snatched up the cotton bag of coffee beans and charged out of Fortnum & Mason, completely forgetting the tuppence in change he was due.

How could this be, he wondered as he set off walking the ten or so blocks back to Russell Square.

Yes, it was true he hadn't actually spoken to Miss Merriweather herself since the incident at Tattersalls, but he was only trying to teach her a lesson. Surely she could understand that. Any woman worthy of being his wife could not conduct herself in such an outrageous fashion.

He had even planned to speak with her again on the first of next week, thinking that a sennight of silence was appropriate, given the circumstances.

In no way had he intended to jilt her. He had been quite clear about his wishes with her aunts Wednesday past. At least, he thought he had.

Arthur Chillton clenched his fist as he stalked down the flagstone walkway, but then straightened his fingers again, thinking better of it. The day was warm, after all, and he did not wish to soil his gloves with perspiration.

He had to acknowledge that this bit of gossip was quite bothersome, indeed. He needed Miss Merriweather—there was no way around it. Needed her name and Society connections for business. He had been darned lucky to find her, or so his mother oft said. How many nearly ruined, available debutantes did one of his class come across in a lifetime, anyway?

And now Lansing was sniffing around, was he?

Well, the rake wasn't going to win Miss Merriweather from him.

Arthur just had to find a way to cut in on Lansing's waltz. And, not being as skilled in turning the ladies' heads as his lordship, he had to remember that it might take a little bit of time.

Perhaps the Featherton ladies would assist him. They were quite an amiable pair, those two. And he knew they liked him. Why else would they so eagerly agree to become Hannah's duennas next season?

Yes, he would ask them for their assistance in this matter as soon as he was able.

Miss Merriweather *would* become Mrs. Arthur Chillton.

He smiled then as he imagined slipping his mother's ring over Miss Merriweather's knuckle, with a shocked Lord Lansing looking on.

In fact, he so enjoyed the lift the musing gave him that he held it in his mind slightly longer than he should have. For he became so consumed with this rousing thought, he walked blindly out into the road.

He never heard the jingling of bridles as horses bore down upon him.

In fact, he never saw what hit him at all.

Around that same time, Meredith and the Featherton house staff had searched every nook, cupboard, loose floorboard and mouse hole for the missing book of notes.

"A guest from the musicale stole it." Meredith folded her arms over her chest and plopped down on the settee next to Aunt Viola, whose full skirt puffed up like a great pumpkin before slowly beginning to deflate.

"*Stole* is a very strong word, dear," Aunt Letitia, who was entering through the parlor, reminded her.

"I daresay it is the perfect word," Meredith replied. "When I could not find the book last eve, I still held out hope that one of the staff might have stumbled upon it and put it away. And yet, Mr. Edgar has interviewed every member of the staff, including those brought in to assist with the musicale."

Worry was making Meredith breathless. "We've searched the house four times, from top to bottom. The book has been stolen. There is no other explanation."

"Who would do such a thing?" Aunt Viola's wide, innocent eyes blinked across at Meredith.

"Beth Augustine, that's who." Meredith narrowed her eyes as she remembered Beth standing in the foyer, waiting for her as she descended the stairtreads and slipped her book of notes onto the table. "She was the only guest still in the foyer when I hid the book."

"Why would Mrs. Augustine do such a thing, dear?" Aunt Letitia spread her feet and leaned on her cane, then tipped herself back into the wingchair. The chair's front feet bucked in the air for an instant before slamming loudly down to rest on the wooden floor again.

Meredith shook her head. "I've given up asking why Beth does anything. It's as though she has a vendetta and is bent on seeing me run out of Town."

"No, dear. If Mrs. Augustine has your book, I am sure she picked it up by mistake." Aunt Viola rose and walked over to the rosewood secretary and opened the drop front.

She glanced back at Meredith briefly, then very purposely pulled out a card, opened the silver inkwell and dipped a nib into it. "I shall send over a card to let her know the book is missing. If she has it, she will be under the impression that we know it is in her possession and will no doubt return it promptly."

Meredith coughed her doubt. "Or she will see it published in the *London Times*."

Aunt Letitia chuckled at that. "My gel, you do have quite the imagination." Then she grew quiet and thoughtful. "Though . . . you did mean to see the book published."

"Not in the *London Times*! It was meant to be a helpful guidebook for young ladies." She lowered her head then.

"Besides, after my latest . . . experiments, I am beginning to wonder if I was right, after all."

Aunt Viola set her card on the flat of the desk and turned around. "Right about what, dear?"

Meredith slowly raised her head and met her aunt's gaze. "Maybe . . . just maybe, 'once a rake, always a rake' is not quite true. Perhaps . . . they can reform."

Aunt Viola's gaze crossed the room to where her sister reclined near the hearth.

Had Meredith not followed the path of her aunt's gaze, she might have missed the flash of excitement that blinked for an instant on the elderly sisters' faces.

⟶

Alexander was dressed, but he lay atop his bed, staring at the drape of the velvet draperies. His arms were propped behind his head when One entered his chamber with a silver tray of tea, toasted bread with butter and a mound of sliced apples.

"There ye are, my lord. I thought I heard ye come in, a few minutes ago."

"Aye, I was out for a ride earlier. Made some calls. Nothing like cool morning air to revive a man's sense, eh?"

One nodded, then grimaced when he tripped over something lying on the floor at the foot of the bed. Murmuring something unintelligible, he lifted Alexander's discarded boots and begrudgingly set them beside the door for cleaning.

"I would have come down, One. I was going to wash up first." Even as he said this, Alexander was sliding up in his bed and allowing One to prop pillows behind him.

"Aye, my lord. *Arms*."

Alexander raised his elbows and One flipped open a crisply starched serviette and spread it across his lap. "I say, has the post arrived?"

One retrieved three missives from the glistening silver tray and settled them into Alexander's open hand before the last syllable of "arrived" had tumbled from his lips.

"Very good." Alexander eyed the missive with the heavy green seal—which looked very important, indeed—broke the wafer open and unfolded the thick vellum.

Several darkly inked words leaped out at him: *The Duke and Duchess of Euston*—two of the most boring people in all of England—*request the honor of your presence, on the occasion of a ball*. Could this invitation be any worse? No. Impossible. The rest of the wordy invitation was just broth in which to float the meat.

Alexander dropped the vellum, flicking his fingers as if the invitation were a bit sticky. "One, would you fetch some paper and ink, my good fellow?" Alexander took a quick bite of toasted bread, then washed it down with a swig of tea. "I want to send a note round to the Featherton house right away. No doubt, with their long friendship with the duchess, they too have received an invitation."

Within a moment, One had placed beside him a fine mahogany lap desk with ebony inlays. Alexander flipped open the lid and set about writing. "Bit low on ink."

"Bit low on everything these days, my lord," murmured One.

Alexander glanced at the butler. "Hmm, yes. So we are. Well, I hope to remedy one situation quite soon."

Very soon, in fact. The Eustons' annual ball was to be held at Euston Hall, home of the esteemed duke and duchess of Euston. He knew this without actually reading anything more, for he'd successfully skipped the event, despite his father's protests, for the past ten summers.

But he was about to put an end to that right now.

Yes, the first card would go to the duchess of Euston, thanking her and accepting her gracious invitation to the ball.

Alexander grinned as he touched ink to paper, for he knew his acceptance would do wonders in the eyes of his father. It would prove his worth as head of the family, and would serve as yet another solid example to all that he had indeed reformed.

The duke's boundless acres abutted the Lansing family lands, and as he grew up, it had been no secret to Alex that his father had always coveted the duke's wealth and had wished some connection between the families.

The duke's lone daughter, Ursula, was a true beauty, indeed. For a time, Alexander shared his father's hope that some connection would lie in their mutual futures. That is, until they were seated beside one another at a gala supper one eve. Alexander realized then that the chit's beauty and, sadly, great interest in him far exceeded her intelligence.

The night was surely the longest in Alexander's memory, for the girl seemed not to possess a command of more than nine words. And though his father was displeased that his son did not take a fancy to the lovely young miss, neither could he fault him for passing her by. Alexander, after all, reminded him that such a union would produce Lansing heirs who may or may not inherit their mother's wit.

He handed the first card to One, then began his second. This one was for Meredith, asking her—nay, *beseeching* her—to join him in a carriage ride to Hyde Park this day—for he had something of great import to discuss with her. The third card was for the Featherton sisters, inquiring about their intentions to attend the Euston ball— with Meredith. He could scarcely coax the idea from his mind. How he longed to take her hand and dance with her before the appreciative gaze of all. He fought the urge to sigh as the image played out in his mind.

He wasn't quite sure why he so strongly desired her attendance at that particular event, and he pondered it for several moments.

Perhaps, he wanted his father to see the future . . . and to be pleased.

Perhaps, he really had reformed, and after troubling Meredith at Tattersalls, then ruining her bodily at Harford Fell, he owed her the chance to hold her head up again— *Owe her my name.*

Or . . . perhaps, it is because—Alex's eyes suddenly widened. *Well, now, this is quite the surprise, isn't it?*

He shoved his hand through his hair and exhaled, knowing he had indeed come upon the shocking truth of the matter.

It was because, damn it all . . . he loved her.

~

Beth Augustine handed the reins of her curricle to the waiting footman, hurried inside her home, then turned the key in the lock.

She rushed up the stairs to her bedchamber and filled the ewer with water. She dropped a cloth in the chilled liquid and slapped her hand to it, sinking it to the bottom of the bowl and swirling it about before hauling it out again.

She looked up in the mirror over the wash table and a pale ghostly visage peered back at her. Wringing out the excess drips of water from the cloth, she briskly rubbed it over her face, then looked into the mirror again.

Meredith was right. There were deep, shadowed crescents below her eyes, making her look at least five years older than her two and twenty years.

"You made me do it, Meredith!" Beth hissed at the mirror. "Why should you be the one to keep your youth . . . to marry a peer? You don't deserve it. You *had* your chance."

Her words were too loud, and she realized it at once, for in the next room, her baby let out a grating wail. Anger gurgled up inside her.

"Mrs. Redding, can't you quiet the babe?" She pressed the cloth to her head, then sat down on her mattress as she waited for the wet nurse to see to her duties. The woman seemed to be taking her sweet time about it. "Hurry, will you! My head is pounding."

Beth gazed out the window to the square below. Looking out at the square, and the memories it held, always calmed her.

She closed her eyes for a moment and slowed her breathing; within seconds, she was remembering . . . remembering a beautiful evening only two years ago. The night when Lord Pomeroy had kissed her and touched her, and made all sorts of sweet lover's promises to her—Beth's eyes snapped open then—before offering for Miss Merriweather the very next day. And she knew why too.

It was all because of her *Society connections.* Just because the Featherton ladies, Miss Merriweather's great-aunts, were daughters of an earl, everyone seemed to be under the impression that Meredith's blood was blue as well. Except it wasn't. She was little more than a milk-maid, fresh from the countryside.

A splash of red snared her notice and she narrowed her dark eyes to focus. Roses . . . just beginning to bloom on the far side of the square's wrought-iron boundary fence.

A slow smile spread over her lips as the vibrant color brought to mind a certain red book that had recently—quite fortuitously—come into her possession.

Meredith's scandalous secret book of notes.

Well, Beth pondered, chuckling softly, *it isn't going to remain a secret for much longer.*

She'd seen to that little detail that very morn.

Imperative Fifteen

A rake never says, "I love you," for it leaves him no possibility of escape.

❧

Meredith smiled as she read the card from Lord Lansing. For a morning that began so abysmally—her worries about the missing book of notes had left her weary and not at all eager to leave her bed—the afternoon promised a basket of delights.

"I am to await your reply, miss." Herbert . . . oh yes, who preferred to be addressed as One, stood before her, as starched and pressed as ever. Meredith could not help but be impressed by the man's industry and loyalty to Lord Lansing. Why, it seemed Alexander counted upon the man for everything, whether it be dressing a woman as a gentleman, driving a coach, or . . . as it would seem, delivering cards to ladies.

"Very well." Meredith hurried into the parlor, opened the secretary and readied the ink bottle.

Miss Merriweather graciously accepts Lord Lansing's invitation for a stroll in Hyde Park.

And then she finished off the card with a large, swirled flourish of an *M*. Alexander ought to like that. Showed her true self, did it not? Or at the very least, the part of her he wished to see more of.

Meredith returned to the front door, where Mr. Herbert waited patiently. "Here you are, One." She held the card out to the white-haired servant as Mr. Edgar opened the door to the square.

One did not take the card right away. Nor did he move. He paused for several seconds. "Oh, I'm not One. Though I see why you might think it."

There was a shout from the street, and Meredith looked up to see *another* Mr. Herbert sitting on the coach perch. "He's Two. I am Three. One is tendin' to his lordship just now," called the man atop the carriage.

"I beg your pardon." Meredith felt all of her facial features constrict as she stared at the Mr. Herbert who stood before her. "There are . . . *three* Mr. Herberts?" She looked at the man in the dark suit standing before her.

"*Four*, if ye truly want to know. Except our youngest brother—a reverend—is not in service like the rest of us."

"And you are all . . . identical?"

"No, miss. Not truly, though we all greatly favor our da, so people often mistake us fer one another."

Meredith looked very closely at the man before her, then at the carriage driver. If they were not twins, they certainly could be. There was nothing different about them—except their clothing. "So you are not One, the valet. . . . You are—"

"Two, the butler . . . and footman when his lordship is conductin' important business." Two long, gloved fingers shot out and snared the card between them. "Me thanks, miss. Oh, and this would be a card for the two ladies—

from his lordship, as well." He handed her the last card, then bobbed his head in a manner that almost had her believing he'd bowed, and headed down the walk and boarded the carriage with the Lansing coat of arms emblazoned on its side.

Three tipped his hat and grinned before he set the team into motion, then edged the square on the way to Brook Street.

Meredith started up the stairs for her chamber, when her Aunt Letitia tottered into the passage.

"Did we have a visitor, dear?" Aunt Letitia poked her head into the parlor. Then, obviously finding it empty, she looked back to Meredith, perplexed.

"Lord Lansing sent around a card. He wishes an interview with me this afternoon. He thought we'd stroll through Hyde Park. Oh! Wait a moment. There is a card for you and Aunt Viola as well." Meredith leaped down the two steps she'd climbed and snatched the card from the entryway table. "Here you are."

Aunt Letitia caned her way into the parlor and took her lorgnette from the secretary. Meredith did not move from the marble threshold as her aunt's eyes whisked this way and that across the crisp card.

When her aunt looked up, there was an elated sheen in her eyes. "It seems our Lord Lansing wishes to ensure our attendance at the Euston ball on Friday . . . for he has an announcement of some import to make."

Meredith's brows pulled toward the bridge of her nose. "What sort of announcement?"

"He might have mentioned something about it when he paid a call early this morn, but I am old, gel, and cannot recall." Aunt Letitia's white brows arched artlessly.

Meredith squinted her eyes at her aunt, as if doing so

might enable her to see through the clever woman's mask of innocence. "Lord Lansing was h-here this morn? I did not see him. Where was I?"

"Still abed, I fear. But he was most determined to speak with you, which is why, I own, he sent around his numbered men with these cards." Aunt Letitia waved Lansing's cream card, to and fro, through the air.

"Why do you believe he so urgently wishes an interview?" Meredith's skin seemed to go a bit clammy, for in truth she had a very good idea of why he wished to see her.

"Who can say what goes through a young man's mind when he is in love?" Aunt Letitia glanced sidelong at Meredith, and the corner of her mouth twitched cheekily.

Meredith raised her chin and cast her most serious-looking gaze at her aunt. "Lord Lansing is most certainly not in love with me."

"Whatever you say, gel. Of course, Sister and I will attend the Euston ball, for I do not wish to miss this so-called announcement." Aunt Letitia's mouth was wriggling like bait fish in a barrel as she tried not to smile. "Of course, you will join us, love, hmmm?"

Meredith held her reply on her tongue for several seconds, but saw no reason why she should sit at home while her family merrily kicked up their heels at a Society function. "Now that Mr. Chillton is no longer in my future, I would be delighted to attend the ball. Besides, staying at home would only give Beth Augustine something to gloat about."

"No doubt."

Meredith knew that her aunt was just humoring her now, but she just couldn't seem to stop rationalizing her reasoning for going to the ball. "Good spot for research too, you know, even without my book of notes. I should think there is bound to be one or two rakes there, don't you agree?"

"At least *one* we know of will be there."

"Indeed." Meredith smiled weakly at her aunt, then turned back and started for the staircase. *The only one who matters.*

As Meredith slowly ascended the stairs, she was sure she heard an excited giggle coming from the parlor.

⁓

Three turns of the hour hand later, Meredith was dipping the plump brown end of a cattail into the Serpentine. She turned away from the dripping, soggy head of the reed to look at Alexander, who was sitting on a rock at the water's edge.

She furrowed her brows. "My aunts have already agreed?"

Alexander pitched a flat stone and watched it skitter across the water. "First thing this morning; so you see, there is no reason why we should not marry."

Meredith returned her gaze to the cattail. She forced a hard laugh. "Except for the obvious one."

Sliding from the rock, Alexander drew up behind her and gripped her shoulders. He nuzzled his mouth just below her earlobe. "And what might that be?"

The hum of his voice at her throat made her feel warm, and without really thinking about it at all, she leaned back against him and closed her eyes. "Oh . . . well, that we don't love each other."

His arms came around her and held her snuggling against him. "Is that so?"

"'Tis." She spun around in the wreath of his arms. She gazed up at him through her thick lashes and set a saucy little smile upon her lips. "Because, Lord Lansing, rakes *never* fall in love. And I have taken an oath *never* to fall in love with a rake."

"But, darling, have you forgotten? I have reformed."

"Have you now?" She looked quizzically up at him. "So, I should simply reverse my belief: 'Once a rake, always a rake'?"

Alexander leaned in and kissed her, and there went her knees, as weak as the soggy reed. Something in the back of her mind sounded in warning, and she halfheartedly heeded it.

Meredith snapped her head back. "No, no, no. You cannot change my mind." She pushed against his chest and broke his embrace with a smirk. "You see, it is a rule with me. I cannot divert."

"Ah, you mock me." Grinning, Alexander caught her wrist as she sought to whirl away, making her drop the sodden cattail. "I am certain I have reformed, for there is no other explanation." He cupped Meredith's chin and positioned her mouth beneath his.

"Explanation for what?" She gazed up at him, waiting for some cocky retort. Instead, he just stared down at her.

"Because, Meredith, I adore you. With all my heart and all that I am, I adore you."

Adore? Adore . . . not love. "Oh" was all Meredith could manage.

"And I know you adore me as well. Do not even try to deny it. If my years as a rake and rogue taught me anything, it was to know the look of adoration in a lady's eyes when I see it."

He kissed her gently, yet passionately, and gazed down

into her eyes. And she knew what he was really seeing in them. Because she felt it.

Love.

She did love him. *Damn it all.*

Meredith suddenly felt very uncomfortable. Why, here she was, the soon-to-be authoress of a cautionary guidebook on rakes—in love with the most notorious of them all. "S-so is this why you brought me here?" she stammered.

"Partially." Alexander took both her hands into his. "I wanted to tell you, that at the Euston ball, I want to announce our betrothal."

"What?" It took several seconds for Alexander's words to soak into her mind. "So . . . so I have no choice in the matter? My aunts have agreed; you wish it—so we are to be married? Just like that?"

Alexander threw his head back and laughed. "No, my dear, of course not."

Meredith expelled her pent-up breath in relief.

"Do not be ridiculous. You have three long days until the ball. That should be plenty of time to decide to marry me."

Suddenly, though her lungs were burning, Meredith could not seem to draw another breath.

⁓

The three long days Alexander had promised Meredith passed more quickly than she could have ever imagined. At the encouragement of her aunts, she'd spent those days, sunup to sundown, frantically searching every crack, crevice and shadow of the house for her missing guidebook. Of course, her rummaging had been futile—

for Meredith knew Beth Augustine had stolen the book during the musicale, though her aunts would not believe it.

Her mind had never been on the search, however. She was far too distracted by Alexander's proposal, and the answer she owed him.

She had hoped Alexander would call upon her at least once, and do something hurtful or dreadfully rakish, so her decision of whether or not to accept his troth could be made simple. But he did not cross the threshold of number 17, Hanover Square. He hadn't sent a letter or even left a card. Devil take him.

Now Meredith sat before a dressing table, peering into a candlelit gilt mirror, in the overcrowded ladies' withdrawing room at Euston Hall. Around her, gray-haired matrons and frustrated abigails chattered, clucking and fussing over young misses, while her own great-aunts pestered the staff for a spot of sherry to ease their travel-weary nerves.

"'Ere, have some punch, Miss Meredith." Annie, her abigail, whom her aunts insisted accompany them to help with Meredith's dressing, set a glass of golden liquid on the table before her. "Might settle you in a bit."

"No, thank you." Meredith pushed the glass to the side, out of her sight. Truth to tell, she was feeling more than a little queasy. All it would take was one sip of the sweet swill and . . . well, Society would be talking poorly about her for another two years, at least.

"Are you feeling unwell, Miss Meredith?" In the mirror's muted reflection, she could see Annie standing behind her, brows arched in the middle like one of the hillocks they passed in the carriage as they came in from Town earlier that afternoon.

"Just a little anxious is all."

"I heard." Annie nodded her head knowingly. She glanced around, as if to be sure no one could hear their conversation, then bent down to whisper in Meredith's ear. "And I don't fault you for feelin' a wee bit edgy. It ain't every day a miss from Dunley Parish is betrothed to an earl—I mean . . . a lord who'll be a grand earl, you know, as soon as his pa meets the Reaper."

Meredith twisted around in her chair and stared, shocked, at the abigail.

Annie, who never failed to overstep the bounds of the servant-mistress relationship, straightened and set her hands on her wide hips. She chuckled softly.

The merriment died on her lips the very next moment when the Featherton ladies drew up on either side, bookending her. Annie stuffed a sparkling paste sapphire pin into Meredith's hair, then brushed her hands together. "Well, now, that ought to do it. You'll be the loveliest woman in the ballroom." She glanced around at the other young ladies in the withdrawing room then, as if to be sure of the truth of her statement. "Yes, truly the most lovely."

Aunt Viola critically appraised Annie's handiwork, taking in the deep blue silk gown and the twinkling of brilliants in Meredith's burnished copper locks.

She didn't need to say a word. Meredith could see it in her eyes. And la, if she didn't truly feel beautiful this eve . . . even if the gown's neckline was carved lower than certain *more conservative* parties might deem appropriate.

Meredith smiled at the whiteness of her generous décolletage, sure—and quite pleased—that Alexander was *not* one of that lot.

"Are you ready, dear?" Aunt Letitia looked every bit as apprehensive as Meredith felt, but yes, she was ready.

She was sure.

That surety, however, hadn't come easily. She'd settled upon it only after several days, pacing and fretting and searching for her notes. It came only after nights spent tossing and turning, wondering if accepting Alexander's troth was the best thing to do.

At first, the only thing she knew for certain, knew in the depths of her heart, was that she loved him.

Oh, she'd tried not to—because heaven knows that she, of all women who'd been burned by love in their youth, was all too aware of the folly of offering such potent emotions to a man of Alexander's roguish background.

But she had had no choice.

After careful consideration, and discussions with her aunts, she finally listened to her Aunt Viola, who advised her that to live cautiously, to live without trust, was to hardly live at all.

And so tonight, she would entrust her heart to Alexander and agree to become his wife.

A little zing shot through her limbs as she stood and turned to take her aunts' gloved hands.

"Yes, I am ready." Meredith drew in a deep breath and blew it out slowly through her lips. "At long last, I am ready."

Standing at the edge of the sweeping Euston ballroom, Alexander gazed at the pocket watch his mother had given him when he left Oxford, three days before she died.

To his great surprise and consternation, he had not seen or heard from his father in two days. Still, Alexander knew the earl was more than likely just undergoing a cautionary examination by the physician he retained at Harford Fell, given the imagined exertions a ball was sure to inflict on his body.

"Quite the coxcomb this eve, aren't you?"

Alexander snapped his watch closed and slipped it into his fob pocket. He looked up to see Georgie, with some tasty morsel, whom Alexander had never met, on his arm. "I shall tell you only once more: One will never leave my household, so you might as well resign yourself forever to being the *second* best-turned-out gentleman at any gathering."

Georgie laughed, and his confused-looking, blank-eyed miss followed suit. "So is it true then? You will announce your betrothal to Miss Merriweather this eve?"

A jolt raced through Alexander. "Where did you hear that? From my father?"

"Damn me, Lansing, you'd think it was a secret by the way you are acting."

"It *was.*"

"Might have been at some time or another, my man, but the entire ballroom is abuzz with the news."

"What?" Alexander blurted out.

Georgie exhaled an uncomfortable laugh. He laid a hand on Alexander's shoulder and leaned close. "Hate to be the bearer of bad news, but you've made the book at White's."

"The hell you say."

"'Tis true, I am afraid. In fact, I'd venture to say that half the gentlemen here tonight are in on the wager—odds are against you going through with it. You know: 'Once a rake, always a rake.'"

"What did you say?" Alexander swallowed deeply. Hadn't Meredith made the same claim?

"Come now, can't be a surprise."

"Well, I daresay it is. For not only have I truly reformed, but I fully intend to make Miss Merriweather my wife before year's end."

"Lansing, this is *me* you're talking to—" Georgie's grin fell away from his face when it became clear that Alexander was quite serious. "Damn me! You're going to do it. You are really going to do it."

Alexander tugged at his neckcloth and straightened his spine. "I am."

"No, you are not," came his father's voice from behind. "I forbid it."

Alexander whirled about. "Sir. I—I did not see you arrive." Stunned, he stared at the portly earl, who was standing just behind him, proud as a peacock, in his outmoded turquoise blue frock coat. Surely he misheard his father. There was no possible reason he would forbid a marriage to the Feathertons' grandniece.

"Come with me, son." His father grabbed his arm, rumpling Alexander's coat sleeve. "I have an urgent matter to discuss with you."

"Sir, Miss Merriweather should be down presently. Perhaps our discussion might be postponed until after—"

"This cannot wait." The earl's tone was firm and the look in his eye sober.

Alexander looked to Georgie and gave a shrug. "I hope you didn't wager against me, man. For I *will* marry her. You can take that bit of news back to White's."

～⌐

Meredith and the Featherton ladies entered the ballroom with elation in their hearts, but curious stares upon their persons.

Still, Meredith didn't much care. Interested eyes had followed her for two years now, wherever she appeared. Well, she was finished with walking with her eyes cast downward. She was through with caring what others thought of her.

For tonight, she would proudly take Alexander's hand before the entire assembly and accept the troth of the man she loved.

Her heart was buoyant and she could scarce wait to find Alexander. Her gaze flitted excitedly about the ballroom, waiting to alight on Alexander's handsome face.

Her feet were light, and she danced a little on her toes as she rose up to scan the room.

"Calm yourself, gel," Aunt Letitia teased. "Your man will be along presently, I am sure."

Even Meredith had to admit that her face smarted a bit from the broad smile tugging at her cheeks, but she couldn't deny her feelings any longer. "Oh, Auntie, how can I possibly calm down—for this eve, there is certainly no happier woman in all the world."

~

"Please take a seat, son."

"What is this about, Father?" Alexander settled uneasily into a tufted chair beside the saloon window. "I must return to the ball. Meredith will be looking for me."

The earl motioned for Alexander to remain seated; then he withdrew a red leather book of notes from his coat pocket. "There is something you must see."

Imperative Sixteen

Silence is his answer. Hear it.

As Meredith waited at the edge of the dance floor, desperate for Alexander to appear, she nervously twisted her fan. Dark pangs of doubt punctured her airy mood, deflating her spirits as surely as the balloon that had fatefully sent her crashing into Alexander's life, uninvited.

"Don't fret, poppet." Aunt Viola took Meredith's hand, which was now trembling just a bit, and squeezed it. "Your Lord Lansing will be along soon enough."

Meredith wasn't so sure, though she wished with all of her heart that she could believe her aunt. Still, this eve was beginning to feel eerily similar to the morn she stood inside St. George's . . . waiting for another, who never appeared.

A tapping on the ballroom's parquet floor redirected Meredith's gaze to her Aunt Letitia, who passed straight through the middle of a well-populated quadrille to reach her. She was quite breathless when she drew alongside Viola.

"There now, you see, gel? Everything is going to be all right," Aunt Letitia began. "I just spoke to the duchess and she told me that the earl has taken his son to the saloon to talk." She puffed her cheeks and rounded her eyes, then expelled a little chuckle. "Weren't we being a flock of geese, worrying for nothing? *Nothing,* I tell you both. No doubt the earl is just imparting some last-minute fatherly advice. This is a momentous occasion for Lord Lansing too, you know."

Meredith smiled a little. "I . . . I am sure you are right, Aunt Letitia. And I should not worry." She stood straight and tall. "I trust, Alexander. *I do.* He will not leave me standing alone. He loves me . . . and I love him."

~

The earl thrust out his wobbling triple chin and shoved the red leather book of notes toward Alexander. "It belongs to your Miss Merriweather."

Alexander did not take the book, but merely peered at it through squinting eyes. "Yes, I have seen the notebook before." He turned his confused gaze upward to his father. "Why do you have it?"

"Came in the post today. Don't know who sent it or why, but the timing could not have been more fortuitous."

"How so? I do not understand."

Seeing that Alexander was not about to take the book, the earl heaved his body into a large armchair opposite him. He tapped the notebook nervously upon the buckle of his knee breeches. "I knew I was familiar with the Merriweather gel's name when you first spoke it. I thought it itched my memory because she was kin to the Featherton ladies, whom I've been acquainted with—peripherally, of course—for many years."

"And now?"

"Now I recall why her name is so fresh. . . . She was the talk of Society, not two summers past."

Alexander exhaled. "Is that all? Father, I know Miss Merriweather was left at the altar by that jack-a-dandy Pomeroy. That was hardly through any fault of her own."

"Perhaps you do not know the story in its entirety."

"Sir, I believe I do. Lord Pomeroy, the gentleman— and I use that term very loosely in this instance—was a fortune hunter of the most ruthless sort. Miss Merriweather was naught but an innocent who was taken advantage of."

The earl leaned back in the chair. "That does not excuse her actions."

"*Her* actions? Father, her so-called ruin is entirely the doing of Pomeroy." Frustrated, Alexander rose, folding his arms over his chest.

The earl sighed. "Son, I know 'twas I who insisted upon your connection with Miss Merriweather—"

"And I thank you for that," Alexander interrupted. "Had you not guided me, I would never have learned what an exceptional woman she is."

His father raised his hand. "Allow me to finish, if you will. I no longer believe that marrying Miss Merriweather is prudent. Connecting the Lansing title with . . . her sullied name, well, I'll not have it. I just won't."

"*You* won't have it?" Rage exploded within Alexander. "Sir, the decision is not yours to make."

The earl's heavy jowls flushed red, and he shoved the book toward Alexander again. "Read this, and tell me if you still insist on wedding the chit. I daresay, this notebook will change that stubborn mind of yours."

When Alexander made no move to take it, the earl flung it at him. It hit his chest hard, just below his throat, and fell to the floor. "Nothing will change my heart, sir. I love her, and she loves me as well. I shall marry her."

"Loves you?" The earl forced a breathy laugh. "You really should read her notes. She no more loves you than she loves me. You are naught but an experiment to her, a test, borne of some misguided effort to spare other young women the pain of ruin at the hand of a London rake."

A cold prickle raced across Alexander's skin. "W-what do you mean?"

"Sit down again, and I shall tell you the whole revolting truth of the matter . . . or you may read it yourself, if you still doubt me."

Alexander gaped at his father, unable to gain purchase on a single word.

The earl bent and staggered a bit as he retrieved the notebook. Then he thumped his thick index finger on the leather cover and looked Alexander dead in the eye. "It's all here, the whole damning plan to make a fool of you . . . written by her own hand."

❧

Almost half an hour had passed since she'd come down from the ladies' withdrawing room, and Meredith still had not had even a glimpse of Alexander.

"I am going back above stairs. I'll find Annie and will sit with her until Alexander arrives." She sounded very calm, even to her own ears—though, in truth, she felt so unsteady that she wasn't confident of her ability to climb the staircase. "Will you send someone for me . . . when he comes?"

The two Featherton sisters exchanged worried glances. Then, suddenly, a huge smile burst upon Aunt Letitia's lips.

"Look there, 'tis the earl!" Her aunt gestured to the far end of the ballroom.

By golly, she was right. Meredith took a deep sniff of air and exhaled with relief. *Thank God.*

In that instant, the earl spotted her and her aunts as well, giving a nod of recognition. He began edging his way through the bustling crush of the ballroom, seeming perturbed by the delay this created in reaching them. But at last he did just that.

"My lord, very good to see you this eve." Meredith bowed her head and dropped him as elegant a curtsy as she could muster on her still-wobbly legs. Straightening, she smiled, thankful that now at least she would know what had delayed Alexander.

The earl did not return her greeting, or her smile. In fact, he did not even bother to acknowledge her aunts, who stood on either side of her. Instead, he shoved something at her.

Meredith grappled for whatever it was, not realizing, until she turned it over in her gloved hands, that it was— *no, it couldn't be*—her book of notes!

There was a collective gasp from her aunts as they saw what the earl had thrust at her.

Meredith turned her gaze up to the earl. She was totally mute. Finally a sound crawled up from inside her throat. "I . . . I . . . I can explain."

The earl raised his pudgy hand, squeezed his eyes tight for a moment and turned his head away. "Explanations are not necessary. I think your plot to mock my son speaks for itself. I am just thankful someone thought enough of Alexander to send the notebook to me before it became too late."

Aunt Letitia pounded her cane to the floor angrily, but, to Meredith, the sound could not drown out the beating of her own heart. With each throb, Meredith's head grew lighter, her breathing shallower.

Taking charge, her aunt stepped forward until her round body was not more than the book's width from his. "What do you mean . . . *too late*? Just where is Lord Lansing?"

The earl tried to edge back and away from her aunt's formidable figure, but already a small, curious gathering of guests was beginning to cinch around them all.

"I have spoken to my son and made my views clear. I told him he will be disowned if he continues with this imprudent notion of marrying Miss Merriweather." The earl paused then and looked straight into Meredith's eyes, as if to make sure she understood the stakes completely. "And despite what you may believe, Miss Merriweather, my son is no fool."

Meredith was stunned from her silence. "You must believe me. I do not think your son a fool. I greatly esteem him. I . . . I love him."

"So Lord Lansing . . ." Aunt Viola's voice was trembling too severely to finish her sentence.

"Need I be any clearer—there will be *no* wedding. Ever!"

A muffled gasp rose from the crowded ballroom. Meredith looked past the earl at the mass of shocked faces, and indeed some knowing grins.

Tears began to push at the back of her eyes and a

tremor shook her limbs unbearably. How could she endure this . . . yet again?

The fan she'd earlier twisted to breaking fell from her fingers to the floor. There was nothing more to do. So, bending slightly, Meredith snatched up her skirt, whirled around and ran for the doors.

Behind her, she heard the hurried clicks of her aunts' canes.

~

In less than a quarter of an hour, the Featherton carriage had been brought up, Annie and the dressing case brought down, and the Featherton sisters and Meredith had burst out through the front door.

Within moments, the driver had snapped a whip above the lead horses' ears and the beleaguered group was on their way back to London.

No one had tried to stop them.

The earl was a powerful man. No one would have dared.

~

Alexander sat in the saloon for nearly an hour, with no other company than a decanter of the Eustons' marginally good brandy. At this point, the quality meant nothing to him. It was the numbing effect of the liquor he sought.

Still, no matter how he tried, he could not wrap his mind around what his father had told him. He simply could not believe that Meredith sought to humiliate him, not when she knew the feeling so well herself.

This, however, did not diminish the pain.

In the back of his mind, it occurred to Alexander that nearly an hour had passed since he first entered the room to hear his father out.

Meredith would be wondering where he was, why he had not come to find her among the Eustons' many guests. But he had needed time to steady himself. He did not want to confront her in the heat of emotion.

He brought the glass to his lips one last time and came to his feet.

Alexander shoved a shaky hand through his hair.

Time to do what he must. Lord, help him.

Imperative Seventeen

There is a good and responsible gentleman waiting to make you his wife. Look past the handsome, untrustworthy rakes, and there you will find him.

❧

After a grueling four-hour flight through the darkness from Euston Hall, and the short remainder of the night spent tossing and twisting within her bedcovers, Meredith was completely drained.

Still, being unable to capture even a wink of sleep, she made her way to the dining room at first light. Neither of her aunts had roused, nor did she expect them to for several hours, for indeed they were surely as weary as she, if not more so due to their advanced years.

As she descended the stairs, her nose caught the soothing aroma of fresh baked bread and steaming chocolate. Her stomach growled with hunger as she approached the hunt table, laid for any early riser to break her fast. Meredith gathered a cup, a silver pot of chocolate and a slice of toasted bread with strawberry jam—favorites that in her childhood never failed to bring a smile to her face.

She was aware, however, that no smile was to be had

today, or for many days to come. Meredith knew this from experience.

Settling her morning meal onto the linen-draped table, she slumped into a chair and released a forlorn sigh.

To her, it felt as though she had somehow been whisked backward through the months, only to land on the morning after she'd been abandoned at the altar. Except this time, she felt far worse.

The pain was unbearable this time, as though a dark raven had swooped down and clawed her heart from her breast with its sharp talons.

When Pomeroy had left her, she suffered the effects of humiliation far more than loss. True, she had thought she was in love with him, but in all honesty, Meredith knew now that what she had felt was nothing more than girlhood infatuation.

Now she understood that until she met Alexander, she had no comprehension of what true love was.

"Good morn, dove," chirped Mrs. Penny, the Feathertons' longtime housekeeper. "Shall I pour for you?"

Meredith raised her eyes to the housekeeper's kind face and simply nodded, afraid that if she spoke, she'd break down and lose herself in grief.

"Don't you worry none, child. Annie told us what happened. We'll take care of our gel, don't you worry." The housekeeper reached into her wide pocket and withdrew a missive. "In fact . . . I've got something that might cheer you up a crumb. Came for you just after you and the ladies left for Euston Hall. It's from Miss Chillton."

Meredith took the paper from Mrs. Penny and released it from its folds. She rubbed the dampness from her eyes with her napkin, then read the hastily scrawled words.

"Oh no. *No!*" Meredith leaped from her chair, startling

the housekeeper so that she slammed back into the hunt table, sending the serving platters rattling.

"Please send Annie to me at once, Mrs. Penny, and then ask Mr. Edgar to send for the carriage. I mustn't tarry."

"I'll fetch Annie for you right away." Mrs. Penny dashed for the door, but then turned her head. Her eyes were wide. "Miss Meredith, what shall I tell your aunts when they ask where you've gone?"

Meredith dropped the note onto the table. "Tell them that my . . . Mr. Chillton has been injured and Hannah fears for his very life! I shall send the carriage back to fetch them. But I must go *now*. I cannot wait for them."

Heavens, she only hoped she wouldn't arrive too late.

~

"Oh, you've come at last!" Hannah took Meredith's hand and led her into an austere sitting room, deplete of furnishing except for two wooden slat-back chairs and a settee, upon which Mr. Chillton lay.

"Of course I have come. I daresay, I am sorry for arriving so late, but my family was not in Town when your message was delivered." She didn't dare tell them why her family was not at home, or what happened.

As horrible as she felt, responding to Hannah's plea offered some measure of distraction from the weight of what lay upon her heart and her mind. Here she did not have to feign bravery. For if she did appear distraught, well, it would appear completely natural, wouldn't it? Chillton had been injured, after all.

Meredith looked at Mr. Chillton, who gazed brightly

upon her from the settee. She rushed to his side and knelt beside him. "I heard that you were hurt."

"Indeed. Trod upon by a horse . . . or *two*. Maybe more. I never saw them coming." He glanced at the window, through which a light breeze fluttered, then back at Meredith, with a peculiar expression on his face. "I did not see your aunts. Are they still in the passage?"

Meredith slowly came to her feet. "No, sir, I came alone. I did not wish to delay another moment."

"You came *alone* . . . to a bachelor's home?" His voice was harsh. "Tongues will wag if you were observed; you know this, do you not?"

"Arthur!" Hannah snapped. "I asked her to come. I own, I was quite beside myself when I penned the card, what with mother too . . . *ill* to leave Brookside. I had no notion what to do. None at all."

"Well, you didn't waste a moment sending for a physician, did you?" Mr. Chillton complained. "I could have told you my ribs were broken. Didn't need to spend five guineas to have someone else tell me that."

"I was worried, Arthur." Hannah set her hand on her hip.

"Well, I was damned lucky you came along when you did."

Meredith felt a bit confused. She looked across at Hannah. "*You* brought him home? Do you mean someone ran him down and then . . . just left him in the road?"

"I was out shopping. I had taken the phaeton, thankfully."

Meredith squinted at Hannah. "And you just happened along?"

"N-no, of course not." Hannah turned away as she spoke and dragged the two wooden chairs before the settee. "I knew Arthur was after a pound of coffee beans, so when I finished my shopping, I took the horse round to Piccadilly to see if he would like to ride home with me."

"How very fortunate for Mr. Chillton that you came along when you did!" Meredith graciously took the chair she was offered. "Did you see the accident? Who hit him and left him . . . possibly to die?"

"I wasn't about to die," Mr. Chillton protested. "Have a stronger constitution than that. I was knocked out, 'tis all."

Hannah took her seat, then leaped up again. "Shall I fetch some tea?"

Meredith studied Chillton's sister for a long moment. Something wasn't being said. "Hannah, did you see who did this to your brother?"

"I was too upset to see anything other than Arthur lying in the road." Two dots of pink appeared on Hannah's cheeks. "Well, now that I have mentioned it, I cannot make do without a cup of tea. I shall return in a moment."

Meredith rose as well. "Allow me to assist you, dear. You must be ever so worn from looking after your brother, all on your own."

Hannah flushed an even deeper hue of crimson. "No need."

Meredith laid a hand on the girl's upper arm. "I insist."

"Oh, Hannah, let her help you," Mr. Chillton hissed. "I won't wither away and expire if I am left to myself for more than two uninterrupted moments."

"Very well." Hannah looked sheepishly at Meredith as they walked together into the kitchen.

"Hannah, what happened?" Meredith asked as she settled the kettle onto the pothook and pushed the crane over the cooking embers. "It is quite evident to me that you did not just *happen along*."

All of a sudden, tears welled in Hannah's eyes and she collapsed upon the bench by the worktable.

"Oh, Meredith," Hannah sobbed, "it was all a horrid accident . . . and I've had to hold it inside, for you were gone and I knew no one else would understand."

Meredith hurried around the table and sat down beside the girl, cradling her in her arms and offering what comfort she could. "I say, dear! What is this all about? Whatever happened cannot be so bad as to warrant all of these tears."

"Oh, it is bad. Very, very *bad*." Hannah pressed Meredith back a few inches and looked up, her vibrant eyes already streaked with red from her salty tears. "It was me. *I* did it."

Meredith searched her friend's gaze for an answer. "What? What did you do?"

"I ran Arthur down!" she wailed, then clapped a hand over her mouth until she was able to soften her tone between gasping sobs. "He doesn't know. He can *never* know."

"It was an accident. Surely he will understand."

"That's just it. It wasn't an accident, not really. I did it . . . *on purpose*."

Meredith drew back slowly and studied Hannah's face. "You ran him down on purpose? My God, Hannah, why?"

"I did not mean to hurt him. I just wanted to . . . *startle* him a bit. I just knew he was going to lose you to Lord Lansing—what with all his meaningless delays. I kept asking him when he would offer for you, and he always had some excuse. 'Once the silk shipment comes in.' 'When Mother is well enough to leave the house.' It was *always* something."

Meredith shook her head. "I still don't understand why you ran him down."

"I wanted him to realize that he didn't have an infinite number of days on this earth. I wanted him to cease with his delays and offer for you—before it was too late. Telling him so did nothing. I knew I had to show him. So when he went into Fortnum and Mason, I waited in the phaeton just down Piccadilly. When I saw him come out of the establishment, I cracked the whip and started the phaeton toward him." Hannah sniffed back her tears. "I only meant to startle him, but it was as if he were blind and deaf, for he walked straight out in front of Prunnie, our horse."

"Hannah, you have to tell him."

"No, I won't! You see, even though my plan got all mucked up along the way—it worked."

"How?" Meredith wasn't quite sure she really wanted to hear the answer.

"Since he awoke, he has talked of nothing else except marrying *you*."

Silently Meredith rose and, taking a cloth from the basket on the table, removed the teakettle from the fire, setting it down on the trivet. "I don't know what to say. This is all . . . so unbelievable." She looked across the table at Hannah.

"When he offers, just say 'yes' and we'll be sisters." Hannah came to her feet. Hannah's eyes were now brilliant with desperate hope.

Meredith sat very still for several moments; then she smiled at Hannah.

"So you will accept him?" She cupped her hand over her mouth for a moment. "I can't believe it."

"Gels?" came Aunt Letitia's voice from the top of the servant staircase. "Are you down there?"

Hannah's gaze fixed on Meredith's face.

"Do not worry." Meredith held her voice to a low whisper. "I asked them to come . . . in case you and your brother needed assistance."

Hannah nodded, then called back to the sisters. "We are, my lady. We are coming with the tea."

"Very good, child. Sister and I will wait for you and Meredith in the sitting room with dear Mr. Chillton," added Viola.

Hannah hurried to snatch a plain white service and the tea caddy from the pantry. "Oh, you cannot know how happy you've made me." She grinned then. "We shall celebrate by using an entire pot of *fresh* tea leaves . . . Just don't mention it to Arthur."

Meredith returned a weak smile and wondered, in the back of her mind, if Hannah was somehow related to her two absolutely mad—but well-intentioned—aunts.

⟡

"It is what I've dreamed about for over two long years now." Meredith leaned forward and peered out the window in the carriage door, her thoughts one tangled mass of contradictions.

"So you will accept this offer of marriage *from Mr. Chillton* . . . and join him in India?" Aunt Letitia seemed highly doubtful.

"Of course. Why shouldn't I?" Meredith replied without falter. Never mind that at least one solid reason banged painfully around inside her head—she was in love with Alexander.

Aunt Viola, who sat directly across from her, leaned forward and touched the tip of her finger to Meredith's knee. "Dear, your wounds from the Euston ball have not yet had a chance to heal. Perhaps you are rushing into this."

"Hardly. I set my cap for the gentleman long ago. And you know as well as I that Mr. Chillton is a good and responsible man. Very dependable."

Meredith caught the chary look Aunt Letitia shot her sister.

"He *is*. Mr. Chillton would never—" Meredith abruptly stilled her tongue.

"Leave you at the altar?" Aunt Letitia finished for her. "Leave you standing alone and humiliated at a ball?"

Grimacing, Aunt Viola tapped her sister's leg with her reticule. "That is quite enough, Letitia."

And it *was* quite enough. Too much. Tears started gathering in Meredith's eyes and she tipped her head back just enough for the liquid to well within her lashes, instead of coursing down her cheeks.

"No, it is not," Aunt Letitia snapped back. "We've all danced around this for hours, but I cannot bite back the truth any longer." She turned a solemn gaze upon Meredith. "You have not even tried to explain your book to Lord Lansing. I know you were hurting, gel, and needed to leave the Euston ball right away, but before you bet your future on . . . on a man you do not love, you owe it to yourself to speak with Lord Lansing!"

"I do not." Meredith's voice quavered despite her best

efforts to bolster it with conviction. "You heard the earl. Alexander was given an ultimatum: set me on a shelf, or have his livelihood cut off." She narrowed her eyes. "And he made the choice that any rake would. *He chose money.*"

"How do you know that for sure, dear?" Aunt Viola asked.

"W-why, we were all there. Surely you heard the earl. He said it all quite plainly. 'There will be no wedding— *ever.*'"

Her aunt nodded slowly. "Yes, yes. I heard the *earl* . . . but I did not hear *Lord Lansing* speak those words."

"Perhaps not, but his silence . . . his unwillingness to even face me, said it all."

The carriage fell into utter silence as Meredith swallowed the deep sob forming in her throat.

"An offer has been made and I shall accept. I cannot and will not be dissuaded. I will marry Mr. Chillton. I will."

Meredith's heart seemed to fold in upon itself. She turned slightly and stared out the window helplessly as a torrent of tears cascaded down her cheeks and dripped from her jaw to her lap.

Imperative Eighteen

A rake is impeccably groomed, bathed, smoothly shaved and lightly touched with an alluring French scent, all to draw a woman into his grasp.

Alexander returned to London late the next evening, eager to call upon Meredith the next morn and set the whole situation to rights.

Bathed, shorn and set-out with a neckcloth expertly tied in the Irish style, he allowed One to assist him into his dark blue cutaway. He knew wearing it for luck was naught but folly, but it was the very same coat he wore when Meredith tumbled from the sky and into his life.

"Well, do I cut a fine form?" Alexander raised a brow at his valet.

"Sir, ye are more finely cut than a crown jewel," One droned in that bored tone of his, which for some reason always made Alexander wonder if his valet was just telling him what he wanted to hear. And yet, he *did* look quite dashing today. The cheval mirror had confirmed it, if he had had any doubt; so at least this afternoon, he was confident that One was being truthful.

"Me lord." Two entered the room with a sour expression on his wrinkled face and a newspaper upon his silver salver. "I've been followin' the Society reports in the *Times,* as ye requested, and I believe there is a snippet ye will wish to read." He extended the tray toward Alexander.

Glancing first at the newspaper page on the tray, ironed free of any folds the way he liked it, Alexander shrugged. "No doubt just an *on-dit* report of the Euston ball." He took his hat from One. "I believe I shall pass on reading it, Two. I do thank you, however."

The valet opened the front door and Alexander started through it and toward his waiting carriage.

"Sir. I daresay, I may be oversteppin', but ye must read this before ye call upon Miss Merriweather." Two seemed most insistent.

Alexander turned on the heels of his freshly polished Hessians and, feeling exasperated by the delay, pinned his butler with the sternest of gazes. "What is it, Two? You've read it. Save me a moment, won't you? Tell me what the damn newspaper says."

"'Tis a rumor of Miss Merriweather's betrothal— leaked to an *on-dit* columnist, 'twould seem, by the Featherton ladies of yer acquaintance."

Alexander chuckled. "Well, perhaps the notice is a tad premature, but no matter. I shall make my offer today and have the papers drawn up tonight. All will be right."

Inwardly he gave himself a smug little smile and patted his upper arm, where the Celtic band, which matched his Scottish grandfather's own and indeed the men of his clan, ringed his bicep in bored-in ink.

Today, Alexander was thankful that the Viking-Scots blood ran thick in his veins.

It was true that the old Highlander embarrassed the

hell out of his father—who was ashamed of his Scottish roots and who held impossibly high standards for propriety—but Alexander loved his grandfather, for a more self-assured man he'd never met . . . and never would.

The old man never bowed to anyone's dictates. Never cared what anyone thought of the life he chose. And neither would Alexander. He would marry the woman he loved, no matter the cost. His heart would have it no other way.

"Begging yer pardon, me lord." Two shifted his weight from one foot to the other. "But . . . 'tisn't a column about *yer* troth—'tis regarding a Mr. Chillton's, of Russell Square."

"The hell you say!" Alexander charged back into the house and snatched the newspaper from the tray. Emotions he could not even name flooded his senses as he blindly scanned the page.

Two poked a helpful finger to the lower left corner. "Just here, me lord."

And there it was:

Lady Letitia Featherton and Lady Viola Featherton have confided in this columnist that Mr. Arthur Chillton, of Russell Square, shall indeed wed their grandniece Miss Meredith Merriweather, of Hanover Square, both parties late of Mayfair, by special license, ten o'clock in the morning on July 1 at St. George's Church, Mayfair.

Alexander stood for some seconds, as stunned as if he'd been punched in the face, then crushed the newspaper in his fist. Chillton had wasted no time. Nor had the Featherton ladies in announcing the wedding to all of London.

He looked at Two. "Our arrangements have been made?"

"Aye, but I can cancel now if ye wish—"

Alexander looked down at the crumpled paper in his hand. "No. Do not change a thing." Turning, Alexander dashed out the door to his carriage, with the balled paper still in his hand.

Meredith was *not* going to marry Chillton—wasn't going to wed anyone but *him*. He would see to it.

~

"No, no, go ahead without me. I cannot manage today— my gout, you know. It is going to rain, anyway. Go on now." With a wary glance to the gray sky, Aunt Letitia flicked her fingers at Meredith and Viola, shooing them through the front door and toward the carriage waiting for them on the square.

"Very well, but you may not challenge our choices," Aunt Viola called back to her sister. "You will have given up your authority to veto any gown we choose to have made." The footman let down the steps and she took his hand and began to board.

Meredith blew out a breath through her pressed lips. She did not want or need a new gown for her wedding. Thanks to Annie, her industrious lady's maid, she already had an exquisite ball gown she'd never even had the opportunity to wear.

Aunt Viola wouldn't hear of it, however, and had planned an afternoon with her and her sister's favorite modiste in all of London. Here was a stylist who seemed to specialize in lavender frocks, judging from the selection of gowns she regularly fashioned for Meredith's aunts.

Aunt Viola was just ducking her head into the town carriage when her sister's voice boomed from the front door.

"Shut the carriage door—*now!*"

The perplexed footman did not hesitate.

"Viola, lock it!" came her next order.

Still standing in the walkway, Meredith wrenched her head around in time to hear the metallic click of the carriage cab's inner lock.

Aunt Viola peered quizzically through the window at her sister, who appeared to be jabbing her index finger at something in the distance.

Meredith followed her aunt's line of sight. *Oh . . . my . . . word.* A carriage, led by a team of six stunning equines, had just entered Hanover Square from Brook Street.

"Alexander," she gasped.

She looked frantically at the Featherton carriage and flung herself at the locked door. "Let me in!"

Her aunt Viola had scooted across the leather bench and obviously now understood why her sister had wanted her to lock Meredith out. She turned and smiled, shaking her head.

Whirling around, Meredith raced for the house. She had no sooner reached the porch when the front door slammed in her face with such energy that the knocker was sent beating double time against its rest.

"Drat!" A string of other words, stronger words, unfurled in her mind. This was just so like her conniving aunts! Why, they likely sent for Alexander and had this planned all along.

The second carriage drew to a stop just before number 17. The door opened and Alexander descended. "Meredith," he said. "We must talk."

Good gravy, she wished he didn't look so incredibly handsome. It would make it so much easier to remember how deeply he had hurt her if he didn't make her swoon so.

"I have nothing to say," she snarled.

"I think we both have quite a lot to say . . . and to explain." Alexander started toward her.

Yes, yes, they did. But not now. The pain was still too raw within her breast. "Just go away." She spun around, unable to face him, and instead stared off into the distance.

She felt his hand on her arm, and her body turning. "Alex, you—you should know I am b-betrothed to Mr. Chillton," she stammered, hoping he would leave her be now.

"I know, which is why I must speak with you now. You left the ball before I had my say."

Meredith narrowed her eyes. "You have quite a lot of gall, sir. I stood alone in the ballroom waiting for you, because you promised me you would be there. Still, you never appeared. Instead, you sent your father to deliver your blow!"

"You've got it all wrong, Meredith. Come with me now, in my carriage, and I can explain."

"I remind you, I am promised to another." Meredith's voice was low and steady, which surprised her since her legs were quaking beneath her skirt. "How would it appear if I were to be observed boarding a *rake's* carriage?"

Alexander flinched ever so slightly. She knew her words stung. But then, they were meant to.

"I do not give a bloody damn how it looks." He grabbed her hand then and started back to his carriage.

"Let me go, Alex!"

"Never." Lord Lansing gave a curt nod of command to his footman, who obediently opened the cabin door.

Without a warning, he lifted and carried her the remaining distance to the carriage, hoisted her inside and crawled in after her.

Even in the dimness of the cab, Meredith could see his eyes were flashing. A protest would be sheer madness, but so was allowing herself to be abducted—even if it was by the man she loved.

Unable to resist him bodily, Meredith resorted to the only defense she had at her disposal. "What will your father think of this? Sullying your family name by keeping company with a *ruined* woman?"

"What my father thinks is absolutely none of my concern. My only concern is you."

He pounded his fist on the forward wall and the carriage jerked forward. "We are going to talk and I shan't return you to Hanover Square until I have said what I must."

"W-where are you taking me?"

He paused for a heavy moment; then the most wicked, rakish smile Meredith had ever seen lit up his face.

"Someplace where you can't escape me."

⁓

Alexander did not say a word for the clutch of minutes it took the carriage to arrive at Hyde Park. He glanced out the window and scanned the length of Rotten Row for any sign of the giant red balloon.

Somehow, when he had Two make the hasty arrangements earlier that afternoon for a balloon ascension, Alexander had thought Meredith would find it very . . .

romantic of him. Thoughtful, and generally very un-rakelike. Why, he'd even worn the exact blue cutaway he'd worn when they first met. How quixotic was that?

Despite the unpleasant occurrence at the Euston ball, he thought she would be eager to repair the rip in the fabric of their relationship. For she had to know he loved her. And she did claim to love him as well.

He did not count on her aunts having to lock her out of the house, or that he'd have to resort to kidnapping her, just to convince her to listen to him.

Somehow, Alexander never thought offering for a lady was going to be this bloody difficult.

When the carriage halted, and the footman opened the door, Alexander climbed out quickly—in the event that Meredith had a thought of making a mad dash. He glanced up at the ashen sky and sighed. Still, the rain was holding off, and even if the sky burst, it would not change his plan. It was too late for that, for not twenty feet from the Serpentine was the red hot-air balloon.

The massive, inflated bulb was clearly newly sewn, rather than just patched. And so it should have been, for he'd paid the amount the pilot demanded from Meredith—which had so disturbed her that she had fallen unconscious the day they met.

Bloody hell, for the amount he'd paid, he would have thought the Irishman would have replaced the basket as well, and yet he hadn't. Fresh reeds had been woven into the side where the oak branch had gouged the basket, after tipping Meredith from its pot. Oh well.

Meredith blinked her eyes in the gray light as she emerged from the carriage. "Why are we here?" she asked warily.

"Shall I be honest?"

"Absolutely." Meredith folded her arms across her chest. "If you can manage it."

Alexander winced at that. "I had thought you would find a balloon ascension romantic."

Meredith's face screwed up into a scowl. "*Romantic?* I thought you said you would be honest."

"I assure you, I am."

"Ha!" Meredith spun around and tried to climb back into the carriage, but Alexander caught her arm and held her firm. "You only seek to humiliate me," she accused him, "the way you and the earl believe I sought to *humiliate* you!"

"I—I have no notion what you are on about." Alexander's patience was wearing thin. He tugged her forward. "Come with me. We're going up."

"You cannot deceive me, Alexander. You read my book of notes and you know that our meeting was no accident— I was spying on you from this very balloon!"

"You *what*?" Alexander was incredulous. "What nonsense is this?"

Meredith opened her mouth, but then Alexander suddenly had a better idea and laid his fingers across her lips, silencing her. "Just a tick, my sweet."

He reached over the lip of the basket and, with one hand, gripped the pilot's collar. "*Get out.* I shall take it from here. Just leave the tether handler. I'll need him."

"'Ere now! This is *my* balloon. I'll not leave my *Betsy* to you or anyone, until I'm cold and stiff in my grave."

Alexander looked the Irishman dead in the eye. "That, sir, can easily be arranged."

The pilot gulped loudly. "You don't frighten me, your lordship."

"*Really?*" Alexander opened one of his hands and dug

down inside his pocket. His fingers touched upon a small leather bag of coins, which he withdrew and pressed into the pilot's hands. "Perhaps, then, you can be gently persuaded. I only want to borrow your *Betsy* for a short while, after all."

The Irishman opened the bag's cinch and peered inside at the gold coins. A wide grin parted his lips. "I'll just take the second tether, if you don't mind. Just call when you wish to come down."

Meredith began struggling wildly. She was not going to get into the balloon willingly, so Alexander did the only thing he was able. He looped his arm tightly around her waist, climbed into the basket, then dragged her over its lip with him.

With a nod to the pilot and his handler, the balloon lurched into the air.

When the balloon swayed on its tethers a good fifty feet above the ground, Alexander released Meredith.

"Now, darling, what were you saying?"

Imperative Nineteen

*Give over your heart to a man who truly loves
and respects you. Only then will you be safe
from heartache and ruin.*

Had everyone in her life gone completely insane? Meredith had certainly asked herself this very question enough times over the past few weeks.

As the balloon sailed higher into a rumbling sky streaked with gray, Meredith was fairly sure they were all mad. Her aunts, Hannah and Chillton, Alexander . . . *all* of them.

Looking over the worn lip of the basket, she saw that two handlers were letting out more and more rope from their thick coils. In another few minutes, she and Alexander would be dangerously brushing the low-hung clouds in a tattered basket that was scarcely as wide as the measure of a lady's outstretched arms.

Alexander casually leaned back against one of the thick corners of the basket. "Are you ready to listen to me?"

As Meredith whipped her head around and glowered

at him, her hair tumbled loose about her damp face. "Have I any choice?"

"Not unless you suddenly fall deaf." Alexander winked at her then. "All right. I know you have something to say to me, so why don't you begin?"

She groaned, and looked away again.

"Shall I help you then?" he asked.

Meredith said nothing.

"You mentioned that the day we first met, you had been spying on me." He paused for a moment, then shot her a curious look. "Is that why you carried the brass telescope?"

Meredith sighed. *Oh perdition! Why not? Why not get this all over and finished now?* It was not as if she were going anywhere . . . but up. "Yes," she muttered.

"So, you were not truly studying the ever-elusive *rogue finch?*" A half-grin flickered on Alexander's lips, but somehow she got the impression that his levity was forced.

Meredith gave an exasperated growl. "Do not pretend ignorance with me. It was all laid out plainly in my book of notes."

"But, Meredith, I never read your book. Other than a couple of wild accusations my father made—which I must admit caused me to doubt your true feelings for a time—I have no notion as to what you recorded in that little leather book of yours. And, Meredith, I had no right to doubt you. It was wrong of me. I only needed to stew awhile on it to know that the truth of your feelings is plain in your eyes, your touch, your kiss—no matter what was written in that damned little book."

Her head told her he lied.

Rakes always lied if it suited their own ends. Or so her research proved.

However, as she gazed upon Alexander's innocent expression and clear eyes, she knew in her heart he was indeed telling the truth.

"So, you didn't read a *single* page?" she asked shamefacedly.

"*No*." Alexander reached out and tentatively trailed his fingers down her sleeve, as if he weren't sure if she would allow his touch. "I knew that the notes were your private thoughts—and not meant for public consumption."

A little culpable snivel slipped out of Meredith. The air was thick and smelled of coming rain as she turned her head and peered out over the swaying treetops. "That is where you are wrong." She forced herself to turn back and look at Lord Lansing straight on. "It *was* meant to be read by the public—eventually. At least part of it."

Alexander straightened and impulsively pushed up from the basket corner. It was a struggle to stand upright upon the swaying floor. He grabbed the rail lip nearest Meredith for balance and peered at her with a genuinely confused expression. "Perhaps you best start from the beginning, from the day we first met."

"Very well."

And so she did.

Meredith explained her reasoning for wishing to write *A Lady's Guide to Rakes*—her ruin by Lord Pomeroy and her desire that such pain never touch another innocent.

Surely he knew the details of her ruin. It seemed all of Society did—or at least the part her aunts could not conceal. Still, Alexander seemed most compassionate and truly able to understand her hope to spare other women her ill fate.

Next she explained her assorted schemes and experiments to learn more about rakes, rogues and cads, one after another, as Alexander dutifully, yet silently, listened to her prattle on.

He raised his hand, trying to stop her, more than once. She wasn't sure if he meant for her to pause and clarify a point for him—or simply to stop talking because he could bear to hear no more.

Either way, it really didn't matter. Meredith could not have stopped the spill of words, even if she cupped her hand to her mouth.

But as the words came pouring forth, she could breathe easier, she felt so much lighter—for she was finally free of the deception that had weighted her heart. It was as if with each confession, she had taken one of the heavy homespun bags of sand sitting in each corner of the basket and flung it over the side.

Geminy, it felt so good to confess! She wanted him to know everything—needed him to know every last detail so that nothing more would stand between them.

And then, she had only one more thing to say: the few healing words, of all she'd flung into the wind, that might succor the wounds she'd inflicted.

"You must understand, once I trusted you—*once I came to love you*—the book no longer mattered to me."

Her heart thudded at least a dozen times as she awaited a response—a word, a sigh, a frown. *Anything.* Alexander did not reply.

Her gaze studied his striking face, but his expression offered no insight into what he was feeling. Ever so hesitantly, she reached her arms out to him, staggering across the basket like a babe taking her first two steps, seeking acceptance . . . forgiveness in his embrace.

And he gave it.

Powerless to do anything but press against him, Meredith hugged Alexander close. She inhaled his scent, which, until now, she hadn't known she'd missed so very much.

His hand came up behind and pressed the small of her back, bringing her closer.

Meredith shuddered as his touch raced through her like a rare bolt of lightning, making the hairs at the nape of her neck rise.

She turned her face up to his, expecting him to speak, to tell her everything would be all right. Instead, his mouth came down upon hers, surprising her, and a storm began to build within her.

Alexander turned slightly and leaned her back against the weave of the basket. Lifting her slightly, he leaned into her, his thighs straddling hers.

She gasped softly as he pressed against her and she felt his hardness between them. She instinctively answered by pushing her hips hard against him.

Wanton heat surged between her legs, and as if he knew this was happening, he responded with a low, carnal groan.

The wind whipped up around them then, and dived deep inside the basket, blowing high any part of Meredith's skirt hem not pinned by Alexander's hard body.

The reviving breeze swirled about her thighs, startling Meredith, and she broke away from his kiss. Sucking in a deep breath, she hoped for at least a moment's reprieve— for the chance to beg him to stop, since she seemed unable to do so.

No matter what she felt, no matter what she wanted, she was promised to another.

Good, responsible, *trustworthy* Mr. Chillton.

And instead, here she was, clinging to Alexander, wanting to feel him inside her. Wanting to sate the tempest within.

"You'll be needin' to come down now!" came a frantic shout from below.

Alexander glanced at the handlers on the ground. "Not yet."

The trees seemed to shudder then, and the balloon whipped and lurched, flinging them both to the floor of the basket.

Alexander fell onto his back, his knees crooked upward within the tight confines of the basket.

Yelping in surprise, Meredith fell atop Alexander, landing in a most unladylike position, straddled over his lean hips. She wrapped her arms around him and held tight. Her senses reeled with terror, but her body only knew need.

A drop patted the top of her head, then another slapped her cheekbone. Meredith leaned back and looked up at the blackened sky and the slants of rain coming down as the balloon violently tugged and twisted against its tethers.

Fat drops of rain beat at her chest, sending rivulets coursing between her breasts. Bending toward her, Alexander ran his hand along the mounds of her breasts. The warmth of his palm against the coolness of her wet skin sent goose bumps across her chest.

He took the low neck of her damp gown, catching the chemise between his fingers at the same time, then dragged the fabric down, fully exposing her breasts to him. He glanced up into Meredith's eyes, then lowered his mouth and took her nipples, hardened by the cool rain and need for him, one into his mouth, the other between his hot fingers. He sucked on one, and squeezed the other gently. It hurt a little, but in a way that only made her want him more.

Meredith moaned, but the sound was muted by the growl of the sky and pounding of the rain. At that moment, Alexander grabbed her hand and pressed it against the straining fabric between his legs. A little jolt made her tremble as she felt the hardness of flesh beneath her hand.

Then the basket jerked. The handlers were pulling it down.

"Alex, the balloon—"

"At this rate, we'll be on the ground in ten minutes."

Meredith looked into Alexander's eyes and saw his were searching hers as well. She answered the question she saw there with a deep kiss. *Ten minutes.*

As their tongues swirled together, Meredith hurriedly fumbled with Alexander's wet buttons.

He shoved her hand away and tore up his buttons, then guided Meredith's unsure hand inside.

He pushed his hips forward as she tightly gripped the hard smoothness of him. He closed his eyes, for but a moment, and sucked in gulps of moist air as she moved her hand up and down the now rain-slickened length of him.

The basket lurched again, and now, just above the rail lip, Meredith could see the uppermost leaves of the writhing treetops. She looked frantically at Alexander. With a look of determination, he forcefully grasped her hips and lifted her spread thighs over him.

Meredith pulled her skirt and chemise toward her waist as he positioned her above him. She felt the heat of his tip teasing her, dipping just barely inside her. They hadn't time for this. The balloon was coming down, and so was she.

Meredith slapped splayed hands to Alexander's chest; she pressed down and took him fully inside her. If it was possible, she felt him grow inside her. She wriggled for position as she rose a bit on her knees, then thrust down atop him again.

It took her a moment to find her pace as she moved against him, but Alexander held her hips firm and met her, thrust for thrust.

Suddenly she felt one of his large hands release her, and then, starting at her knee, slide along her inner thigh until he found the tiny sensitive nub between her legs. With his thumb, he circled the bit of flesh as she rode him, while he pushed deep into her.

Meredith looked down at Alexander and he nodded re-assuringly; her confidence grew.

He reached his other hand upward then and pulled her closer. His mouth closed over her nipple and he began to thrust harder into her. Meredith began to tremble, and each breath became a gasp.

The basket lurched to the side again, knocking Alexander's mouth from her. Then the balloon dropped several feet, lifting Meredith's knees from the floor for an instant, then slamming her down on top of Alexander again, face-to-face.

Her head was spinning, her body throbbing madly as she looked up through the driving rain and saw the lower canopy of the trees beyond.

She turned her gaze back to Alexander as she lay straddled over him, her weight barely supported by her hands, while their bodies thrummed and pumped together.

Suddenly a sensation, like a crash of lightning, ripped through Meredith and she cried out as Alexander caught her hips and thrust furiously into her, again and again.

Then a wave of wet heat pulsed inside her, and Alexander squeezed his eyes tight and inhaled sharply. When he opened his eyes again, he smiled as he pushed his fingers through her tangled, wet hair and kissed the rain tenderly from Meredith's face.

"I love you, Meredith," he said softly.

Meredith's eyes widened. She sat upright on his hips. "But rakes *never* say that! It's one of the primary tenets of . . . of rakehood."

"Then need you any more proof that I have reformed?" Alexander propped himself up on his elbows and looked directly into her eyes. "I love you."

"Just another few feet and we'll have you down, all safelike," the Irishman yelled up from a distance not too far beneath the balloon. "Don't you worry none, my lord!"

Meredith stared at Alexander for another moment, then lifted up from Alexander and sat in the corner of the basket, hurrying to straighten her clothing.

Lord above, what am I to do now?

⌐

They didn't talk on the short ride back to Hanover Square—or rather, Meredith didn't utter a word. Alexander, on the other hand, had tried out a number of arguments for Meredith's jilting of Chillton and marrying him, instead.

Meredith just rested her dripping elbows on her sopping knees and peered out the carriage door window as the horses clopped their way into Mayfair.

She could not jilt Chillton. Yes, she might have been hurt and therefore accepted his proposal rashly, but she could not cry off. Why, it was against everything she believed in.

She would not destroy another's self-worth, the way hers had been. Meredith knew she was better than that.

Without moving her head, her gaze sought out Alex and she felt a tug at her heart—for she didn't love Chillton. She loved Alexander—a man who loved her too. . . . So much did he love her, he was willing to give up everything just to be with her.

Tears budded in her eyes and trickled down her cheek.

Alexander sat bolt upright on the bench. He laid his hand on her knee. "Are you crying?"

Meredith exhaled a false laugh. "Certainly not." She pushed a damp lock of hair from her face. "My hair is wet and dripping. I am perfectly fine."

Alexander looked doubtful. Concern was plain in his eyes.

"*Really,* I am," Meredith chirped.

What a terrible liar she was.

⁓

The carriage entered Hanover Square a mere two minutes later, much to Meredith's great relief.

When the footman opened the door, and Alexander made to get up, Meredith thrust out her hand and slammed it to his chest, stopping him.

Alexander's fingers folded around her wrist. "I am

going with you. We need to explain to your aunts—" Alexander protested.

"No, *please*." She released the pressure against his chest and looked up at him. He opened his hand and she pulled her arm back. "I am more than capable of explaining everything on my own. We were caught in a shower, 'tis all. Nothing more."

Alexander's eyebrows migrated toward the bridge of his nose, making him look dreadfully stern. "'Tis not the dampness of your gown I wish to help you explain."

"I know." Meredith lowered her head, then slowly raised it to look at him again. Her lower lip quivered and she drew in a shaky breath. "It is too late for us, Alex. I am promised to another. And you . . . you will lose everything you hold dear if you defy your father and marry me."

"I don't care." Unlike her own, Alexander's voice was sure and steady.

"I know, my love." Her voice broke. "But *I* do." Meredith stood as best she could inside the carriage, then leaned toward Alexander and lightly kissed him.

"Meredith," he breathed. "Marry me—"

She touched the four fingers of her shaking right hand to his lips. "Shhh. Let me go. *Please*."

Turning quickly then, she ducked through the open carriage door and hurried down the steps.

Clutching her wet skirt in her left hand, she raced up to the front door and, thankfully finding it unlocked, rushed inside. She pressed the door closed behind her, then threw her back against it and squeezed her eyelids tight. Unbearable pain filled her heaving chest and a loud sob burst through her lips.

"Dear me, Meredith. What is wrong?" came a horribly familiar voice.

She wrenched her head around and opened her tear-filled eyes, at once wishing she hadn't. For there was Beth Augustine standing with her aunts just inside the parlor door.

Imperative Twenty

Once a rake, always a rake.

As Beth Augustine's dark-eyed gaze, brutally patronizing and pitying, met her own, fury scalded away all remnants of pain inside Meredith.

"You stole my book of notes." Meredith pinned Beth with a look as sharp as a finely honed blade. "You sent it to the Earl of Harford."

Rounding her mouth, Beth gave a fair approximation of astonishment. "I have no inkling of what you are on about, Meredith."

"Yes, you do." Meredith wiped away her tears with the back of her hand. "And you will be happy to know that your plan worked brilliantly. Hats off to you, Beth." She whirled her hand in the air, then bent briefly into a mock bow.

"Meredith, I—I can see that you are distraught, but on my honor, I do not know what you mean."

"On *your* honor?" Meredith scoffed.

"Dear, you and Mrs. Augustine have been due to have a conversation for years now," Aunt Viola began, "and though this mightn't be the most opportune time, it is nevertheless the time that has chosen you."

Meredith stood dumbfounded as both her aunts came to her and kissed either cheek, then started for the library.

Aunt Letitia turned back for an instant and raised a single finger. "Just send for us if you are in need." When Meredith nodded, her aunt smiled. "That's our strong gel. I'll just send Mrs. Penny with some nice, hot tea."

"Well?" Meredith straightened her back and gestured for Beth to follow her back into the parlor.

"I do not know what your aunts mean. I have nothing to discuss with you." To Meredith's surprise, Beth actually looked confused.

"You mightn't, but I do. I have quite a lot to say to you, as a matter of fact."

Beth followed Meredith to one of the two chairs situated on either side of the hearth, which had been set to a low burn to stave off the chill from the rainstorm.

As the rain hammered against the tall parlor windows, Meredith, oblivious to her dripping wet condition, recounted her years of emotional torture at Beth's hand at Miss Belbury's School for Girls. And then, how Beth had ridiculed her when she had been left at the altar.

Beth did not try to argue her innocence, which greatly amazed Meredith, but instead sat silently listening, seemingly astonished by every word spoken.

The door opened just then, shattering the tension that pervaded the parlor, and both women looked up.

"Don't mind me," quipped Annie. "Don't mean to disturb you none, but I brought a dressing robe for Miss Meredith so she don't catch her death." Annie held the heavy brocade up. "Will you stand for me, Miss Meredith?"

Meredith knew she should not say another word until Annie, sower of house gossip, had left the room, but she knew too that if she quieted now, she'd never summon the courage to do this again.

"And now"—Meredith pulled air into her lungs to better propel her next words into Beth's face—"you deliver my private book of notes to the Earl of Harford! My life will never be the same again. Why did you do it? *Why?*"

Beth's eyes rounded like two drops of India ink. "I never!"

Annie turned her head and gave a dismissive glance to Mrs. Augustine. "Yes, you did. Saw you with my own eyes. You took it, all right."

"What?" Meredith gasped. "You saw her take it?"

"Oh yes."

"H-how can you believe a . . . a maid over me, Meredith?" Beth stammered.

"Oh, it weren't just me," Annie added almost casually. "One of the guests that night saw you do it too, Mrs. Augustine. It was that widow woman. You know, the one with all the smiling dead husbands."

Beth sat very still. She dropped her big black eyes to her fingers, which were twisting nervously in her lap.

"Beth?" Meredith said as Annie fastened the dressing gown around her.

"I'll leave you alone now—" Annie started from the parlor.

"No! Stay here, Annie," Meredith boomed. Then, slightly embarrassed, she softened her voice. *"Please."* Beth was quick with her words and Meredith knew she might require Annie's proof in more detail.

Beth raised her gaze. "All right. I did it. I admit it. Are you pleased that you've finally pinned me?"

"No, I'm not." Meredith slowly lowered herself in her chair. "I only want to know why . . . why you feel a need to hurt me. I've never done anything to you. I—I only ever wanted to be your friend."

Tears suddenly glistened in Beth's eyes. "In school, you were always so pretty. People like pretty things. Poor, lovely Meredith never had to earn praise, attention or friendship—it was always just given to her. But I—I had to work hard for everything. Always had to. It was unfair."

"I never—" Meredith began, but Beth raised a silencing hand.

"You wanted to know." Beth reached out for her teacup and brought it to her lips as she leaned back in her chair. "And as we grew older, and left school, it never changed. I was in love with Lord Pomeroy, did you know that?"

Meredith shook her head.

"He loved me too—that is, until you showed him favor." She settled her teacup back on the table, then shrugged and gave a little laugh. "Why should a titled gentleman pay me any mind when a flaming-haired siren called to him?"

"I didn't know." Meredith rose and knelt before Beth. "He left me at the altar. He ruined me, Beth. And had it not been me, it would have been you. I am sure of it." She tenderly took Beth's hand into her own and squeezed it gently. "He never really wanted either of us. He only wanted money to refill his empty family coffers."

Beth looked into Meredith's eyes. "What do you mean?"

"When I could not break from my despair, my great-aunts shared some information that they had acquired from a runner they'd hired. It now seems, you and I were only two of several young ladies Pomeroy promised a ring of gold—all in his quest for money."

"But he was a viscount!"

"Yes, but a penniless lord on the run from the dun collectors. He eventually married an heiress some ten years his senior, who keeps him under lock and key in the wilds of Cornwall."

A hint of a smile twitched Beth's lips.

"So, you see, he never loved either of us. He cared naught except for himself. 'Tis the way with rakes."

Then Meredith saw something she'd never seen before—a tear trickling down Beth Augustine's freckled cheek.

"My heart breaks for what I have done to you, Meredith. It wasn't enough for me that Pomeroy left you standing at St. George's. You didn't seem to suffer, as I had. You held your head high and endured the shame."

"I did suffer, Beth. And what Pomeroy did to me haunts me, affects me to this very day."

"I didn't know that, though." Beth sniffled, then turned her dark eyes up to Meredith's. "When I saw what was written in your book of notes, I knew I held in my hands the means to destroy your relationship with Lord Lansing. Like me, you would lose the highborn love of your heart and be forced to settle for a man of mediocre means." Beth hugged Meredith to her. "I beg you to forgive me. Please say you will."

As they hugged, a tear ran from Meredith's upturned face and puddled in her ear. "I forgive you, Beth. For, indeed, we are the same, you and I."

When Mrs. Augustine closed the front door behind her—no longer an enemy but rather a sad kindred spirit left in the same rake's wake—Meredith's aunts rushed into the entry passage in a fury of cane taps.

Meredith only had words for Annie. "Why did you not tell me . . . or anyone that you'd seen Mrs. Augustine steal my book of notes? You knew we searched for it."

"Oh that!" Annie set her hands on her hips proudly. "I didn't see nothin'. Don't think that old widow did neither."

"You . . . lied?" Meredith gaped at her. "What if she hadn't taken it?"

"I was fair certain she did." Annie made a V with her index and middle finger and positioned it before her lashes. "It's all in the eyes. She was lyin', I knew that. I've had plenty of experience tellin' liars from those tellin' the truth—I can always tell when a footman's been cheatin' on me. I got the sense, I do."

"Dear, when you came in, you were crying." Aunt Viola focused two sad eyes at Meredith. "Things went badly with Lord Lansing then?"

Meredith exhaled. "No, we settled our differences. He still wants me to marry him."

"Wonderful!" Aunt Letitia bounced on her heels. She turned to her sister. "We should start penning cards right away. The guests should know we are replacing Mr. Chillton with the handsome Lord Lansing!"

Aunt Viola grimaced. "Sister, our Meredith was crying when she came home." She turned back to Meredith. "You are not going to marry Lord Lansing, dear, are you?"

"No, Auntie, I cannot. I will not leave anyone standing

alone at the altar. I know the pain of that too well and will not inflict it on dear Mr. Chillton." Meredith caught the newel post and sank down on the third step of the staircase. "So in three days time, so that I may accompany him to India, I shall become the esteemed Mrs. Arthur Chillton."

~

"He did it just yesterday. Paid the five pounds fer the special license," Three told Alexander, who sat in his library, leaning his forehead against his steepled fingers.

"Are you sure?" Alexander turned his weary eyes upward at his carriage driver. He hadn't slept since the afternoon he and Meredith had been caught in the rain, since she told him she could not marry him. And the thought of Meredith marrying that buffoon Chillton was killing him.

"Quite sure, my lord. I followed him right to Doctor's Commons. Stood behind him, just out of sight, mind ye, as he supplied the information they required and paid the clerk for the license."

Something flickered inside Alexander's head, propelling him to his feet.

Something clever. A little underhanded. Rakish.

Perfect.

Alexander started for the passage with a single-minded determination. "Three, ready the carriage and bring it round. One," he called ahead of him, "my hat!"

"Will ye be needing a flask?" Two prodded. "Or perhaps some sustenance fer the road? 'Tis a long way to Harford Fell."

"No, nothing . . . except five pounds." Alexander turned the key in his desk and withdrew a small document box.

He opened it and withdrew one of the small leather bags from inside. "I do not intend to make Harford Fell. I have urgent matters to attend to—at Doctor's Commons."

~~

Arthur Chillton did not have a valet of his own. For what was the need? He'd been dressing himself since he was a lad and found not the least difficulty in doing so. He wrapped his white neckcloth around his throat and tied it in the Horse Collar style. He'd heard once that dandies and fashion hounds, like that damnable Lord Lansing, considered the style vulgar and common. But it looked just fine to Arthur, and besides, he knew how to tie no other style.

He gazed into Hannah's cheval mirror and was pleased with the result. It was his wedding morn, after all, and Hannah had impressed upon him the importance of looking his very best. He turned around when he heard her footsteps in the passage just outside the door.

"Do I pass, sister?" he asked as she came to stand beside him. He did not really care what her reply would be, for he was turned out well enough and would not change one single article of clothing. Still, he thought he would do her the honor of asking her opinion.

Hannah looked him up and down, and wrinkled up her nose like she was about to sneeze. "Might have bought a new coat for the occasion, Arthur."

He glanced down at his blue coat, which he'd acquired only three years ago. "This is my finest coat for conducting business. It will do."

Hannah threw out her arms in frustration and, at once, he noticed something clutched in her right hand. "Arthur, this is not a business gathering," she complained "It *is* your wedding day."

Arthur tapped his temple with his left index finger. "Ah, but what you have failed to realize is that today marks my most important business acquisition ever—Miss Merriweather. With her aunts' connections, the doors and—dare I say—the pockets of London's most esteemed families will be opened wide to me."

"I-is that all Meredith is to you—a business opportunity?" Hannah sputtered.

Arthur could not understand how his sister failed to see the logic in his words. "What other use does a well-positioned wife serve . . . except to discharge an heir when the time comes?"

Hannah shrieked. "What of love?"

"Sister, my marriage today is a business arrangement. Nothing more." His gaze caught on the folded vellum in her hand again. "What have you got there? Is that for me?"

Hannah opened her palm and looked at the note as if she just realized she held it. "Oh . . . this was sent over from St. George's." She handed the note to Arthur; then with a disgusted grunt, she turned and started to stamp from the chamber. She paused when she reached the door. "Is everything all right with the wedding arrangements?"

Arthur opened the letter and read it quickly. "Fine, just fine. There's a new minister at the church," he said. He started to stuff the missive into his pocket, then pulled it back and held it before his eyes again.

"Reverend Herbert, that's his name. Wishes a brief interview with me before the ceremony—in private. Stands to reason, I suppose." He glanced up at Hannah. "I say, can you walk to the church? Since the nuptials commence in but an hour, I think I'll take the phaeton and meet with him now, if you don't mind."

Hannah growled again and he could hear her cursing him as she continued down the passage.

Arthur shook his head. Damned if he wasn't going to be the happiest man in the world when *she* walked down the aisle with some lucky gentleman—who would take her off his hands for good.

Beneath the columned portico outside of St. George's Church, Meredith stood, with her chin thrust proudly upward, waiting for Arthur so the ceremony could begin. Inside she was quivering. She'd been here before, two years past, and it had culminated in crippling pain and disgrace.

"Just let me have a chat with the minister," Aunt Letitia told her as she gave Meredith's back a comforting pat. "Never you fear, gel, I am sure Chillton was just delayed. Any number of mishaps could have caused him to arrive late. Why, I myself am late wherever I go, aren't I, dear?"

Meredith nodded dumbly, but she knew the truth of it.

It was happening all over again. As her eyes began to heat, she straightened her spine, determined to be strong.

Meredith had been standing outside for thirty agonizing minutes with her aunts, her sisters and their families, who'd all just arrived in Town, and a whispering crowd of London Society, mingling between the six Corinthian columns at her back. It was all fairly clear to everyone that she was being jilted.

Again.

Arthur looked at the kindly minister, already garbed in his vestments for the ceremony. He had been sitting in the closed vestry for over an hour, and had finally come to his conclusion.

The minister was right. There was no denying it.

He could not settle for a woman who was not everything he required in a wife. And, well, now that he thought it out, it was quite evident that Miss Merriweather, with her spirited ways and low-cut gowns, did not share all of his moral convictions. He'd known of her ruin, but Arthur considered this at the time to be a benefit—to him, anyway. Had she not been jilted, he never would have had a hope of winning over a woman of the ton.

But the minister spoke the truth. She was far too spirited, like the horses he glimpsed at Tattersalls. In truth, what he really needed was a more reliable, docile mate, more like . . . well, like his cart horse, Prunnie.

Arthur Chillton would not let it be said he had settled for second-best. No, he would much rather do without. Would be easier, anyway. English women tended to wilt in India's heat, and he planned to live there for at least three years—which is why he'd made arrangements for Hannah to be governed by the Featherton sisters. No, he should have never even considered taking a wife along to India.

Yes, Reverend Herbert was completely right.

His heart began to race. He could not do this. He could not marry Miss Merriweather!

"But . . . she will be ruined if I leave her now." He knew he should at least say this, though it was not quite the truth of the matter. She'd been left at St. George's once before and, like the phoenix, had risen from the ashes of her ruin quite nicely.

Reverend Herbert took his shoulders in his soft, godly hands and peered so deep into his eyes that Arthur could feel his presence in the depths of his soul.

"Ye must follow yer heart, dear sir. If ye do this, ye will always be on the path of righteousness."

So Arthur did just that. After looking into his heart, at last he knew what he must do.

Imperative Twenty-one

*No matter how charming the gentleman, a lady
should prize her own self-worth above a ring of gold.*

Suddenly the heavy door to the church swung open and
the crowd rushed inside. Meredith tried to peer into the
church from where she stood outside with her sisters and
their husbands, Aunt Viola and her former lady's maid,
Jenny, but her eyes were so full of tears that she could see
nothing.

"You do not have to do this, Meredith," her oldest sister Eliza reminded her, trying to be a comfort.

Her sister Grace reached down and squeezed Meredith's hand. "We can return to the house right now."

"No, Grace, I made a promise and I must keep it."
Meredith wiped her tears with the back of her glove. "I
will wait."

"Then for goodness' sake, stop crying. Your eyes are
going all scarlet," quipped Jenny. She dug down into her
reticule and withdrew a tiny silver case. "Here, just let me
dab a bit of cream around your eyes—"

"No!" Aunt Viola shrieked. "They are red enough. No need to . . . irritate them further."

"Jenny, let the lass be." Lord Argyll snatched the case from his wife's hand, then playfully pulled her back against him.

"No, no. I know exactly what to do." Jenny kissed her husband's cheek as she pulled away. Very quickly she separated the triple thickness of the gossamer veil that fell from Meredith's hat down her back, and drew the two shorter lengths over Meredith's face. "There, now no one shall know that you are not the happiest bride in London."

"Thank you, Jenny," Meredith said with a sniffle. "Though now I can barely see through the veil. 'Tis nearly opaque."

"Doesn't matter. You look extraordinary and that is what is most important. And you know, I quite like the effect, if I do say so myself," Jenny quipped, appreciating her own work. "Might even catch on."

Just then, Hannah came up the steps and took Meredith's hand. "Thank goodness you waited for me. Arthur wanted to arrive early to speak with the minister—so he made me walk!"

Meredith blinked. "Do you mean Mr. Chillton has been here all along?"

Hannah nodded, confused. "For more than an hour now. Must be meeting in the vestry."

Aunt Letitia rushed down the wide nave aisle and beckoned Meredith and the other ladies forward. "He's waiting for you at the altar. See there?" Her aunt gestured with a pudgy gloved hand to a barely visible figure in a blue coat who stood facing the altar.

Meredith expected to feel more relieved. Happy that she was not jilted again—but how could she be? For in the depths of her being, she knew she would prefer the pain and humiliation of being set aside than marrying anyone other than Alexander.

Tears came fast and heavy as she slowly proceeded down the nave aisle alone. As Meredith walked past the high boxed pews toward the altar, she was confused by the undignified and somewhat excited chatter bursting from members of London Society. She wondered darkly if there were bets being taken at White's as to whether she would actually emerge from the church a married woman. That certainly would account for the rude whispers and comments as she passed.

Swallowing deeply, Meredith came to stand beside her betrothed, as was her duty.

The minister opened a small book and began to read, but Meredith could not understand a word he uttered. Her heart was throbbing mercilessly in her ears, and one persistent thought pelted her mind—run. *Run!*

Meredith felt her new lace fichu, for Chillton had insisted she wear one for modesty's sake, slip from one shoulder. Instead of catching it, she let it fall onto the dusty floor. And it felt magnificent to be free of it.

Lifting her skirt in her hand, she prepared herself mentally for what she was about to do. What she *had* to do. Her heart would not allow her to marry anyone but her Alexander. Slowly she turned on the ball of her right foot.

Then a faint, slightly musky French scent sailed beneath her nose. She tilted her head up to breathe it in, feeling a calmness come over her as she did so.

He was there. Somewhere, Alexander was there. And, since she could smell it from her place before the altar, he was wearing quite a lot of scent.

Suddenly there was a clatter of hooves, shouts of

alarm from people on the street and a raucous orchestra of carriage wheels on gravel. The minister stopped speaking as the congregation turned, gasping and murmuring, as they strained to see out the church's open doors.

Meredith lifted the corner of her veil just enough so she could see a carriage pass by. But surely her eyes were deceived, for it appeared to be none other than Three, Lansing's driver, hollering and cracking a whip over his team. Even more stunning was whom she thought she saw looking out the window in the carriage door—*Arthur Chillton himself!* No, surely she was mistaken.

Her fingers trembled and the edge of the inner veil slipped down before her eyes. Meredith caught the edge and yanked it back over her hat, but it was too late—the carriage was gone.

Then a startled thought burst in her head. If Chillton was in the carriage, then who . . . ? She whirled around and stared at the man standing next to her.

"Alexander!" Her breath came faster and she felt herself begin to swoon. Was this a dream—a wonderful, perfect dream?

"Yes, my sweet," Alexander whispered back to her. "Your part is coming up. Best pay attention." He grinned at the man standing to his right.

Unable to think past that very moment, Meredith glanced at the gentleman as well.

Could it be? She rubbed her eyes and looked again. It could not be. The Earl of Harford stood proudly beside his son.

She looked at the earl, completely confused. "My lord?"

The earl smiled brightly at her. "Daughter . . . er . . . well, if you allow the ceremony to continue and marry my son, that is." There was a hint of laughter in his quiet words. He gestured to the minister and her eyes followed his lead.

Another gentleman, white-haired and quite familiar, nodded to her.

"One?" Her voice was as unsure as the sight her eyes beheld.

The minister looked up from his text and leaned close to her. "No, my child. Were I in Lord Lansing's employ, like my brothers, I suppose I would be 'Four.' But as it is, I am Reverend Herbert, the minister, trying very hard to marry the two of you." He smiled good-naturedly.

"Oh!" Meredith looked up at Alexander, who gave her a quick nod and glanced past Reverend Herbert.

"One is over there," he whispered. "I believe he was counseling young Mr. Chillton earlier."

Meredith gazed deep toward the sacristy and saw One standing in the shadows, dressed identically to Reverend Herbert. When he appeared to notice that he had the attention of his employer, he clapped his hand to his bicep and smiled broadly, a motion Alexander answered in kind.

⁓

As her family looked proudly on, Meredith dipped the nib into an inkwell and signed her name to the parish register.

She looked up at Alexander, her beloved husband. "So this is all quite legal?"

"Perfectly. Reverend Herbert has signed the license. You are mine now, Meredith, and there is nothing you can do about it."

"Except allow your father to kiss your bride." The earl

of Harford stepped past Alexander, meaning to press a kiss to Meredith's cheek, but she pulled back.

"I am sorry, my lord," she began, "but I do not understand. You forbade this marriage. Threatened to disown your son."

"Meredith—" Alexander tried to interrupt, but the earl raised his hand.

"I did not understand that he loved you." He bent his head and seemed to find particular interest in the joining of the floorboards. "After hearing of your past and your guidebook I was convinced that you sought only to make a mockery of him, of his past, something he was genuinely trying to put behind him." He breathed deeply, his eyes fixed on the wide oak floorboards, as if struggling to find the right words. Finally he lifted his round face to hers. "But when Alexander told me that he would rather live penniless than to live without you, I knew he truly loved you. And for Alexander to love anyone, more than himself"—the earl chuckled—"I knew that you must be an extraordinary woman to have so profoundly affected my son, *my heir*."

When a single tear trickled down Meredith's cheek, the earl dabbed it away with a handkerchief, then kissed the very spot it had fallen. "Forgive me . . . Lady Lansing?"

Meredith's throat was thick with emotion; so instead of speaking, she nodded, then hugged the earl to her.

Over the earl's shoulder, Meredith saw Alexander gazing at her through glistening eyes. She smiled across at him as she and the earl broke their embrace.

Hannah slipped forward and whispered rather loudly into Meredith's ear, "I am sorry about what Chillton did to you, Meredith. My brother is a complete fool. I suppose you and I were not to be sisters, after all."

Aunt Letitia caught Hannah's arm and drew back from the new couple. "No, gel, he is not. He knew that our Meredith belonged with Lord Lansing rather than with him. Can't fault him for that."

"Though I do wish he would not have waited so long to realize it, Sister." Aunt Viola sighed. "Would have made this day so much less complicated."

Meredith grinned at that. "And let me say, dear husband, that was a very risky scheme you and the Herbert brothers carried off this day. Your staff is very loyal, indeed."

The Herbert brothers, now joined by Three, stood in the back of the chamber, chuckling.

"What is so amusing?" Meredith asked, turning her head to look at them.

"They are not only my staff." Alexander exhaled a laugh, shrugged off his coat and rolled up his shirtsleeve. There, inked into his skin, was a Celtic ring. "They are my clansmen."

The Herbert brothers, including Reverend Herbert, bared identical marks on their own arms for her.

One separated from his brothers and came forward. "We're distant kin. All from the same village in the wilds of Scotland, I might add."

Alexander nodded, then dropped his coat on the signing table. In a very rakish manner, he swept Meredith into his arms and poised his lips above hers.

Meredith inched her mouth back and lifted a brow at him. "Might I add that your plan was also very *rakish,* indeed."

"Ah, that." Alexander snatched Meredith off her feet

and kissed her deeply, passionately, in a bone-melting way that only a very skilled rake could achieve. "Darling, I swear to you, it was my last rakish deed. I am now *completely* reformed."

"Are you now?" She smiled coquettishly at him. *"Pity."*

Epilogue

A reformed rake makes the very best husband.

Meredith squeezed her husband's arm tightly as Mr. Hurst, her publisher, placed a small red leather-bound book into her gloved right hand. Her guidebook had actually been published. Inhaling sharply, she flipped open the cover with her thumb and stared down at the title page.

A Lady's Guide to Rakes

BY LADY LANSING, NÉE MISS MEREDITH MERRIWEATHER

A Correct Guide to All Manner of Males, including, but not limited to, the Rakehell, Rogue, Corinthian, Dandy, Buck, Nonesuch, Blade, Scoundrel, Gallant and Coxcomb.

Printed for Longman, Hurst, Rees, Orme and Brown, Paternoster Row, London, and sold by all booksellers and at the bars of all principal Inns and Coffeehouses for the cost of 9 shillings, bound.

Alexander bent and kissed the top of her head. "You did it, Meredith."

"I did, didn't I?" When she was finally able to pry her gaze from the volume, Meredith summoned the courage to ask Mr. Hurst the very question that had been picking at her brain for a full week. The question that, until today—when Alexander had pitched her bodily into the carriage—had prevented her from even venturing down to Paternoster Row to retrieve her author's copy. "Dear sir," she managed, "has anyone . . . bought a guidebook?"

Mr. Hurst wedged his knuckles atop his hips, threw his balding head back and chortled his amusement, sending his large belly bouncing about like a carriage on a pocked road. "The booksellers have been clamoring for additional copies all week. Can't keep them in stock. I have already engaged every bookbinder in the city to keep up with the demand. Seems word has swept the matrons of London, and already we have sold nigh on seven hundred copies."

"So many?" Meredith felt the blood draining from her face and she felt just a little dizzy at the prospect. "But 'tis only a cautionary guidebook, not a great novel."

"*A Lady's Guide to Rakes* is filling a need, my good woman."

Alexander playfully nudged her. "I shall wonder what seven hundred readers will think once they learn the authoress married London's most notorious rake."

"My lord, I would venture to say that most of your wife's readers are already aware of that fact." Mr. Hurst nodded his head, sending both of his chins wobbling. "In fact, I am quite sure of it—hence the guidebook's popularity. A simple miss, scarred by her past, meets a rake and transforms him into an adoring husband, with nothing

more than her heart. It's a love story, pure and simple."
Mr. Hurst's gaze shifted suddenly to the guidebook in
Meredith's hand, as though something had just occurred
to him. He reached out and took it from her. "And then,
there is the last line."

Alexander took the guidebook Hurst handed him.

"Er . . . last page, my lord."

Meredith snatched the book. "Allow me, please." She
released Alexander's arm, turned to the final page of her
guidebook and cleared her throat.

*"Therefore, research has proved that a reformed rake
does indeed make the very best husband."*

Alexander's eyes twinkled as he pulled her back to
him. "Is that so?" His voice was low and smoldering.

Mr. Hurst grinned and turned away, pretending to have
business at the counter.

"'Tis." Meredith lifted her eyes to Alexander and
slowly moved as if to kiss him, but at the last moment she
turned her mouth to his ear. "And, *darling,*" she whispered into it, giving his earlobe just the tiniest bite, "I
ought to know."

About the Author

Kathryn Caskie has long been a devotee of history and of all things old. So it came as no surprise to her family when she took a career detour off the online superhighway and began writing historical romances full-time.

With a degree in communications and a background in marketing, advertising and journalism, she has written professionally for television, radio, magazines and newspapers in and around the Washington, DC, metropolitan area.

She lives in Virginia, in a two-hundred-year-old Quaker home nestled in the foothills of the Blue Ridge Mountains, with her greatest source of inspiration, her husband and two young daughters.

Kathryn is the author of *Lady in Waiting,* and *Rules of Engagement,* winner of Romance Writers of America's prestigious Golden Heart award for Best Long Historical Romance and Romantic Times Reviewer's Choice Award for Best First Historical Romance.

Readers may contact Kathryn Caskie through her Web site www.kathryncaskie.com.

More
Kathryn Caskie!

Please turn this page
for a preview of
Love Is in the Heir
available in mass market
Summer 2006.

Chapter 1

Kirkwell Abbey Churchyard
Devon, England

THE EARL OF DEVONSFIELD WAS HAVING A BAD HEIR DAY. And now his eternity looked equally as bleak.

He removed his beaver hat and lifted his freshly curled wig to scratch his bald head with ragged, chewed fingernails. "Well, what say you, Pinkerton, can it be done?"

His man of affairs was a lean, hawkish-looking gent, who at the moment was dangling precariously from a rowan branch high above the mausoleum. "I fear the reverend's man is correct, my lord, there is no way, at least none I can see, to add a second level to the crypt without compromising the existing structure."

This did not please the earl, who had hoped for an altogether more positive answer, but during his long life he'd learned that adaptation was necessary for one's own survival. "Then we have no other choice. We shall have to expand *outward*. Surely, with the right inducement—" the portly lord glanced at the name on the quartet of head-stones beside him—"the Anatoles could be persuaded to move their family plot across the way."

Pinkerton glanced down at the earl. The expression on his long face made it clear that he was dubious of a favorable outcome. Still, he was nothing if not loyal. "I shall contact the family to determine your plan's viability, my lord."

With hat and wig in hand, Lord Devonsfield walked through the spring grass that poked up through the crisp withered leaves alongside his family's crypt.

He sighed wistfully as he ran his pudgy fingers along its marble wall. This was just his sort of horrid luck—after two hundred years, the Devonsfield mausoleum was full up, just when his own time on earth was at an end.

It was his brother's fault, of course. Even after Lord Devonsfield's entire family was killed in a dreadful accident last month, there was still one space left and, damn it all, it had been meant for *him*. But then his brother, Thelonius, nearly ten years his junior, unexplainably expired while sitting atop his chamber pot, thereby claiming the last eternal resting place in the family crypt.

"My lord, may I descend from the tree now?" Pinkerton, habitually dressed from hat to boot in ebony, nervously straddled a thick branch.

"What? Oh, certainly. We're finished here." The earl flicked his wrist dismissively and waved his man down. "Though while we are on the subject of trees, will you explain your concern about my family tree—more specifically the branch where my *heir* might be found? It has been a month since the accident, and still you have not located the heir to the Devonsfield earldom."

Pinkerton cautiously stepped to a lower branch, bouncing a bit to test its soundness. "Oh, no sir, I know exactly where to find your heir—he resides in Cornwall. He is your late second cousin's son."

The earl's mouth fell open in disbelief and he scurried to the base of the rowan tree and rapped at its trunk with his cane. "Devil take you, Pinkerton. Why haven't you informed me until now?" Lord Devonsfield peered up through the branches. "I must speak with him at once. What is the gentleman's name?"

Pinkerton lowered himself to the ground, then brushed the bark shreds from his breeches. "I do not know . . . *exactly*. For I must inform you that your heir is—"

"What—a Whig? An invalid?" The earl sucked in a breath. "He's not . . . a wastrel?"

"No, my lord. He's a . . . twin."

"A twin? Is that all? What in blazes does that matter?" The earl huffed his frustration. "Determining which twin is heir is not half so difficult. It is simply a matter of knowing which child was born first."

"That's just it, my lord." Pinkerton peered down his hawkish nose at the earl, his eyes clouded with worry. "As preposterous as it might seem, no one knows which boy is firstborn. Even the parish baptismal records are unclear on this point."

"The hell you say." The earl slumped against the tree trunk.

"From what I've been able to learn, their's was a difficult birth, with a goodly amount of blood. Their mother did not survive, and since the boys had no hope of inheriting anything of consequence, their distraught father, your cousin, made no effort to name one twin or the other firstborn."

"Oh, good heavens." Lord Devonsfield wrung his pale hands. "Do you know what this means? Why, I dare not think what the House of Lords will do should I die without an heir—which of course I shall within the year, for you yourself heard the physician. I am not a well man."

"Actually, my lord, the physician only said that spending your days obsessing over death will see you to an early grave," Pinkerton muttered, but the earl paid his comment no heed. He knew the truth of it—what his physicians were *really* saying but sought to keep from him.

"One of the twins *must be* acknowledged as firstborn." The earl bit at his thumbnail as he paced back and forth between the tilted and crumbling gravestones. "We simply must find a way to see this oversight corrected."

"Indeed we must, my lord, for if no legal heir can be determined, upon your passing, the Devonsfield earldom will revert to the Crown."

The earl wished he could somehow stuff those blasphemous words back into Pinkerton's mouth and force him to recant ever saying them. But what he said was true, and there was no way that truth could be ignored. "I cannot allow the earldom to be lost. You know I cannot." The earl stood upright. His mission was clear. "We've not a moment to lose. Pinkerton, see that my portmanteau is packed. We must away to Cornwall—*tonight*!"

The Lizard
Cornwall, England

Griffin St. Alban adjusted the aperture on his telescope by the golden rays of the setting sun. The cliff above Kennymare Cove was the perfect spot for measuring the constellations on what promised to be the clearest night sky all month.

He bent and eased his eye to the lens, meaning to check his settings, when suddenly a falcon, riding a rise of warm air from the sea, swooped straight at him and clipped his shoulder. His feet rolled across the gravel, sending pebbles plunging over the cliff's edge. He slipped and fell hard to the ground, his back slamming down against the short, wind-shorn grass.

"Is someone up there?" A woman's faint voice came from over the cliff's lip.

Griffin sat up, startled. He rose and warily peered over the rocky ledge. There, clinging to the wall, was a young woman stretching out her arm to reach a beribboned hat caught on a protruding root. His foot accidentally sent another bit of gravel her way.

She glanced up with the sharpest look of annoyance in her eyes. "Do take care not to pummel me with pebbles, sir. As you can see, the wind is strong this day and my foothold is precarious enough as it is."

Good Lord, she could fall to her death at any moment! Griffin flattened himself onto his stomach and reached out a hand. "Take hold. I can pull you up."

"Are you mad? Without my bonnet? Not likely. My brother paid two guineas for it. *Two*. And you can be sure he'll not do that ever again." She stretched out her hand, straining for the hat, but it remained just beyond her fingertips. "Blast!"

"Let the gentleman help you, dear," called an old, twig-thin woman who was looking up at them from the lower cliff trail.

The rounder matron beside her cupped her hand to her

brow and looked up at the girl struggling to reach the hat. "Viola is right, dove. Take his hand. Perhaps your bonnet will be easier to reach from above."

The dark-haired young woman peered down at the two women, then turned her pale blue eyes up at Griffin, considering. "It seems I must trust you not to drop me into the sea."

"Take my hand, miss. You have naught to fear. My back is strong."

She glanced down at the waves crashing upon the jagged rocks far below. "That may be, sir, but 'tis not your *back* I worry about." Despite her biting comment, the woman lifted her left hand and clutched his wrist with a grasp so firm that a lesser man might have been put to shame.

Griffin wrapped his fingers tightly around her wrist. "I've got you. Let go of the rock."

"Only if you promise to retrieve my hat before it blows into the ocean." Her eyes conveyed her complete seriousness.

"I vow it," he huffed with frustration. "Now, please, let go!"

With one more cautious look at him, the girl released her hold on the wall. For a moment, she dangled like a limp rag doll from his arm, her momentum sending her swinging back and forth in a pendulum's motion.

All the blood in his body seemed to surge into Griffin's head and he struggled to raise her up to the cliff's lip. Finally, after two perilous minutes, her head appeared level with the ledge.

"We're almost there, Miss. Just a moment more and I'll have you by my side."

"Indeed." Then, with a level of agility Griffin could never have imagined, the woman slapped her free arm over the lip, kicked her right foot up and swung her body onto the ground beside him.

"Damn me!" While Griffin might have expected such an athletic feat from a performer at a fair, never in all his life would he guess it from a young lady such as the one who now sat beside him gathering her breath.

Griffin leaned back on his heels and stared with amazement at the fearless woman. Her hair was as dark as a starless night and her skin pale, save the pink flush that had risen into her cheeks. But it was her eyes that intrigued him most. Inside a ring of vibrant indigo was a burst of a pale silvery blue that made her eyes glimmer like a pair of stars.

"My bonnet, sir." Her voice was still thin and breathy from the exertion. "You did promise."

"That I did." Griffin couldn't help but grin at her stubbornness regarding a ridiculous hat. "I just need something to hook it." He glanced around for a stick.

The woman looked around as well, until her gaze fixed firmly on his telescope. A surge of worry shot through Griffin as she rose and started for his most prized possession in all the world.

"Perhaps we can lower part of this contraption over the edge and catch the brim of my hat." She reached out her hand for the brass instrument.

"No!" Griffin grabbed her wrist, perhaps a bit too roughly, for she whirled around, eyes widened with surprise.

"Not my telescope," he added, softening his voice. "'Tis very expensive, and I do not exaggerate when I tell you there is no other like it."

The woman lifted her chin and twisted her wrist from his grip. "I might claim the same about my hat, sir. Did you see the peacock feather on the band?" She nodded her head knowingly, as if this comment should make the great value of her hat plain to him.

Griffin knew what a ludicrous notion that was. There was no comparison. His reduced-sized Shuckburgh telescope had been custom made to his exact specifications by a protégé of Jesse Ramsden, London's all-time premier instrument maker. He doubted there was as fine an astronomical instrument in all of England.

The woman folded her arms across her sprigged gown. "I do not see anything else that might serve as a tool . . . so well as your telescope."

"I-I have a sheep hook at my cottage." Griffin smiled at the lovely woman, deciding that he'd like to know her a bit better if circumstances permitted. Still, finessing a woman had never come as easily to Griffin as it did his brother, and he knew he'd bungle it. But he would try. "Uh . . . if you like, you and your lady friends may take your ease in my home while I return for your bonnet. 'Tis just down the trail to the east. Not far, I assure you."

The young woman suspiciously raked him up and down with her gaze. "I thank you, but no. My bonnet might be caught by a gust of wind and whisked into the sea. I daren't leave it. Besides, I do not even know your name."

"St. Alban . . . Mr. St. Alban." He tipped his head to her. "And you are . . . ?"

Her pink lips formed a smirk. "Not so addled as to follow a man I do not know to his lair."

"*Lair*? My dear lady—" Griffin began.

"Oh, sir, please do forgive her. She meant nothing by it," said the heavier of the two old women, who now stood nearby huffing and puffing from the exertion of climbing the steep cliff-side path.

"She is Miss Hannah Chillton, our charge." The thinner old woman pinched the girl's arm, eliciting a clumsy curtsy from her.

Just then, the falcon that had struck him earlier spiraled low over the four of them. Griffin watched, with great astonishment, as Miss Chillton withdrew a leather glove from her sash, slipped it onto her hand and allowed the bird of prey to land on her forearm.

The thinner elderly lady laughed at Griffin's surprise. "And that would be Cupid . . . Hannah's kestrel."

"He is *your* bird?" Griffin stared at the young woman incredulously.

"Yes. Why is that so difficult to believe?" Miss Chillton said rather smugly.

Why, indeed? Griffin thought about it for several moments. Why should he be surprised that a woman he discovered fearlessly climbing a cliff wall, a woman with the strength to propel herself over the rock ledge, might have a hunting falcon as a pet?

"My dear lady, in the short time we've been acquainted, I have come to the conclusion that nothing about you should come as a surprise. For, indeed, you are the very definition of the word."

Miss Chillton looked uneasily toward the two old women, as if she had not the faintest notion how to respond to his assertion. Then, she turned her delicately featured face back to him and gestured to her guardians. "Mr. St. Alban, these are my duennas, the ladies Letitia and Viola Featherton, of London."

"And Bath, of late," the woman she'd referred to as Lady Letitia added. "We reside in the spa city for a few short months each year."

"In fact, our visit to The Lizard was to be the culmination of our grand Cornish excursion." The thinner woman, Lady Viola, smiled brightly up at him. "We are headed back to Bath this very eve."

"Not until we have my hat." Miss Chillton turned toward the sea, took a couple steps and peered over the edge of the cliff. She gasped. "Oh, *no*. It's gone!"

Lady Letitia joined her at the cliff's edge and wrapped her arm around the dark-haired beauty. "The wind must have taken it after all, child."

Miss Chillton turned her head and glared at Griffin. "You, sir, owe me a hat."

"*I?*" Griffin sputtered.

"Yes, for I would have managed to retrieve my bonnet *eventually* had you not interfered." She said something in a low tone to Lady Letitia, who upon hearing the words, reached into her miser bag and retrieved a card. Miss Chillton took it from her and shoved it at Griffin.

"The Oatland Village Hat is available from Mrs. Bell, 22 Upper King Street in London. Ask her to add a peacock feather please. Can you remember that? Good. When you have acquired it, you may deliver it to No. 1 Royal Crescent, Bath. The direction is listed on this card."

Her business with him concluded, Miss Chillton took each of the Featherton ladies by the arm and led them up the path to where, Griffin surmised, their carriage must await.

"Good day, Mr. St. Alban," she called back to him, a sentiment echoed by the two elderly women. "I do hope we shall see you soon . . . for the hat *was* my favorite."

She flashed him an amused smile, and then, if he was not mistaken, threw him a teasing wink as well.

When the three women disappeared over the rise, Griffin St. Alban absently strolled to the cliff's edge and peered down its steep wall for the missing bonnet. *Gone*.

He patted his head tentatively, wondering if perhaps he'd hit it when the falcon clipped him and he'd fallen— for surely he'd been dreaming.

That was the only possible explanation he could muster, for nothing so outlandish as what had occurred during the past quarter of an hour could have happened to *him*.

Life in lower Cornwall just didn't work that way.

~

Three days later

Lord Devonsfield and his man of affairs did not knock or even call out their arrival at the home of the St. Alban brothers. There wasn't time enough for that. The earl's hold on this earth was short and trifling with manners was merely a waste of what few moments he had left in life.

Through the tiny cottage's stone chimney, smoke trailed up into the cloudless azure sky. His heir was at home, or at least someone was, so the earl opened the flimsy plank door and he and his man stepped inside—to face the barrel end of a hunting rifle.

The earl stared at the two young men before him, who, at first glance, appeared identical in every way . . . save their mode of dressing perhaps. They both stood well over six feet and, unlike the earl, their heads were topped with an abundance of slightly curly sable hair. He supposed their eyes could be called hazel, but in truth they were more green than any other color, with a flickering of dark amber encircling the pupil. Their shoulders were broad and they had good, strong, square jaws, with a divot in the chin, the sort the ladies so seemed to fancy. Damned if they weren't a pair of the handsomest men he'd ever seen. This pleased the earl on more than one level.

He eyed the one who pressed the rifle, painfully he might add, to his forehead. Now *that* twin had courage, gumption. And, now that the earl had a moment to reflect (for there was no way he was going to make a move with a rifle to his head—he'd leave that to Pinkerton) this twin had a sportsman's build. He was quite strong, his arms well-muscled, as though he spent a goodly amount of time studying pugilism, as his own eldest son, God rest his soul, had.

The earl smiled broadly. Yes, his initial impression told him that this twin would make a brilliant heir.

"Sir, I would not be so quick with a grin when my brother has a rifle trained upon your head," said the strikingly handsome, but less muscular twin. "He can take down a bird in flight without effort, so I daresay he would have no difficulty bagging an intruder at such close range."

The earl lifted an eyebrow. Such a sassy mouth, this twin had. Denoted a clever mind. Unlike the other, this man's hands were smooth and his fingernails clean. His clothing was perfectly pressed and damned if there wasn't something the least bit aristocratic about his stance. Hmm. Not a bad option either.

Pinkerton, the bloody coward—for his hands shot into the air the minute he saw the rifle—finally spoke up. "My dear sirs, this gentleman means you no harm . . . nor do I."

Neither twin said a word, didn't move a muscle.

"Er . . . may I . . . lower my hands, young man?" he continued.

The twin with the rifle nodded his head slowly.

"And . . . uh . . . might you also deign to lower the weapon? We are unarmed, and as you can see, we are hardly in the first bloom of our youth . . . as the both of you are. Even if we wished to challenge you, you could easily subdue the both of us in mere seconds."

The twin paused a moment, then lifted the barrel of the rifle from the earl's forehead. Lord Devonsfield clapped his hand to his brow and felt the ringed indention left behind.

"Fine way to treat your father's cousin," he snapped.

"You are our father's cousin?"

The earl turned to see the more refined of the bookend pair of men studying his clothing.

"I am." The earl straightened his spine.

Pinkerton cleared his throat. "May I present the Earl of Devonsfield."

The twins exchanged confused glances, before returning their attention to the earl. Then, as if on cue, they honored him with a set of gracious bows.

"Of course we have heard of you, my lord," offered the twin with the soft-looking hands.

"Indeed," said the other. "We just never, in our lifetimes, expected to make your acquaintance. Our lives are so far removed. We work in iron, while your lordship—"

"His lordship does not labor at all."

The muscular twin raised an eyebrow. "Exactly."

The earl pivoted on the heel of his gleaming boot, strode across the small room and took his ease on a worn chair near the coal fire. "Well, my boys, your days toiling in the iron mines are at an end, as of this very day. Come, come. Be seated and let us talk."

"I beg your pardon, my lord, we have so few guests I fear our manners have become somewhat rusty." The aristocratic one snapped his feet together and gave the earl a nod. "I am Garnet St. Alban."

The earl nodded his head in greeting. "Garnet. Refined and polished like the gemstone itself. How very appropriate," the earl chuckled. He turned his head to the twin with the rifle. "So you must be Griffin. Part eagle, part lion." The earl smiled at him. "Yes, indeed you are. How splendid are your names. Perfectly splendid. I shall have no difficulty in discerning between you ever again."

An elderly woman entered through the front door just then, and was so startled to see visitors that she dropped her market basket on the floor, sending two apples rolling across the stone floor. "Oh, I beg your pardon. I had no notion you had guests."

Griffin crossed the room in two long strides and helped the woman gather her things. "You need not fret, Mrs. Hopshire. Lord Devonsfield is family. Though perhaps some tea might be in order."

The earl raised his hand. "Pinkerton, run out to the carriage, will you? Fetch us some brandy, for we must celebrate."

Garnet St. Alban caught Pinkerton's arm as he started for the door. "No need, sir. Mrs. Hopshire, some glasses please." Near the hearth was a box, a cellaret of sorts, from which Garnet withdrew a bottle of fine brandy. "We are deep in the country, but not without a few luxuries."

Mrs. Hopshire brought a tray laden with several thick, clinking glasses into which Garnet poured the amber liquid. He handed the first glass to Lord Devonsfield.

"Uh . . . you were saying, my lord, something about our days of toil being at an end."

"Indeed I did." The earl drained his glass and passed it to be refilled. "For one of you is to be my heir."

"Your . . . heir?" Griffin bent down and added a few more pieces of coal to the smoldering fire. He turned his head up to the earl. "Which of us?"

"My lord, what my brother means is that the law of primogeniture cannot be applied in our situation for we do not know which of us is firstborn. Never had any reason for it to matter . . . at least until now, it seems."

Griffin rose and came to stand beside his brother.

"I am well aware of our predicament." The earl studied both Griffin and Garnet in turn. Each had qualities to recommend him as heir, or at least so it appeared, and the earl had always placed great weight on the importance of first appearances. "Pinkerton, carry on please."

Pinkerton took a step forward. "The predicament, as the earl has put it, is far more dire than you could possibly imagine. Therefore, what I am about to impart to you must be kept in strictest confidence—for the future of the Earldom of Devonsfield depends upon your discretion." Pinkerton's eyebrows migrated toward the bridge of his nose. "Unless it can be agreed upon which of you is the eldest, which of you is the *legal* heir, the earldom will revert to the Crown upon the earl's passing."

"Obviously, I will not accept this eventuality." The earl came to his feet and clapped a hand to each twin's shoulder. "And so I have a proposition for you. My time is short. My physicians do not expect me to survive the year."

Pinkerton coughed, then looked up and caught the earl's stern gaze. "Forgive me, my lord. Go on, please."

"As I was saying, I will certainly not survive the year—but I do not intend to allow my family's legacy, the Earldom of Devonsfield, to dissolve."

He gave a nod to Pinkerton then, who withdrew two folded sheets of foolscap from inside his coat and gave one to each of the twins. "For this reason, I will make a secret pact with the two of you. And if you agree to my terms, one of you will become Earl of Devonsfield."

The earl gestured for the papers to be opened. "Read the terms."

Each of the twins opened his paper from its folds and for several minutes read and reread the terms the earl had written inside.

"Do you agree to the terms as set forth?"

Griffin and Garnet's eyes met, and for a clutch of moments, the earl had the notion that they might be silently conversing, as he'd heard some twins do. A slight feeling of distrust crept into his mind for a moment as the earl wondered if the two men would add some terms of their own. For it was clear they were aware of how desperately he needed their compliance. But, judging from the state of this ramshackle cottage, they needed him as well.

A moment later, he realized that his concerns were all for naught, for the twins agreed to every term, exactly as he'd written them.

"Brilliant, brilliant! Now, since you agree to the terms, cast the papers into the fire, for this discussion must remain a secret for all eternity."

Griffin and Garnet crumpled the papers in their large, capable hands, tossed the damning documents into the coal fire and watched foolscap ignite.

"We are agreed then. The continuation of the family is paramount. So, per the terms set forth and dually agreed upon, whichever of you marries a woman of quality first, will become?"

The twins, as one, intoned a single word.

"*Heir.*"

The earl, greatly relieved, smiled and signaled for another brandy. "Quite right."

For the first time in more than a month, the earl was having a good heir day.

Want to know more about romances at
Warner Books and Warner Forever?
Get the scoop online!

WARNER'S ROMANCE HOMEPAGE

Visit us at www.warnerforever.com for all the
latest news, reviews, and chapter excerpts!

NEW AND UPCOMING TITLES

Each month we feature our new titles
and reader favorites.

CONTESTS AND GIVEAWAYS

We give away galleys, autographed copies,
and all kinds of fun stuff.

AUTHOR INFO

You'll find bios, articles, and links to personal
Web sites for all your favorite authors—and
so much more!

THE BUZZ

Sign up for our monthly romance newsletter,
and be the first to read all about it!